FALLEN ROSE

AMELIA WILDE

CHAPTER ONE

Haley

THE DARK PRESSES in like a hand over my mouth, but I have to breathe.

Have to get out of this blood-soaked nightmare echoing with drowned breaths. With tortured gasps. With the sound of Leo trying to breathe while his lungs fill with blood.

The dream is fading fast. But everything feels wrong. I feel less like I fell asleep and more like I was put here against my will. *Wake up, wake up, wake up.*

My hand connects with something soft. Let it be Leo's shirt. Where is he, where is he?

There's nothing solid underneath. I push it away and it becomes a blanket thrown away from my body. A flutter of air as it flies away from me.

I'm on a bed, but it's not his bed.

Trapped by the sheets. My limbs are sluggish but not as useless as they were in the dream. I push my hair back from my face with numb hands. Both legs over the side of the bed. I could go back to sleep, which is screwed up, honestly. I've been sleeping for a long time. That's all I know. My eyes burn. Even my shins feel weird. There's a pounding in my head.

And this is not Leo's room.

It's lovely. Airy and pastel. Mint green and white. Accents in emerald. Every piece of furniture has been meticulously placed. An elegant chair by the window. A padded bench at the foot of the bed. A matching dresser with a round mirror. I can see myself in it.

I look rumpled. Confused. Terrified. Because I should be.

This is Caroline's house.

It has a scent to it I recognize. I can't name it but I know it. I've smelled it before. Something rich and luxurious and utterly fake. How the hell did I get here? My mind struggles against black emptiness. I shouldn't be here. She shouldn't want me here. Not when I've been with Leo. Not when she tried to have him killed. Not when I stayed. I stomp through my memories like I'm retracing my steps for a lost set of keys.

I can figure it out later. For now, I have to get out.

On unsteady legs, I rush for the door. The last

time I was here, I was at a party I didn't belong at in a borrowed dress. Now I'm twisted in Leo's shirt and my leggings. A tank top underneath. I don't have socks, and I don't have my shoes, but I don't care.

The doorknob turns under my hand. Solid wood swings toward me, forcing me back into the room.

Caroline breezes in.

If I didn't know what happened to her, I'd never have noticed the tense set to her shoulders. Everything else about her is polished. Perfect. Constantine. She's wearing a loungewear set with a blue cashmere wrap and an expression of pure concern.

I freeze in the middle of the floor. The scent was her perfume. It's light and expensive and everywhere.

It makes me sick.

The wrap whispers on her clothes as she reaches for me. I'm too frozen to stop her. Cool, small hands on the sides of my face.

"Haley, darling, we've been so worried." Bile surges to the back of my throat at the sound of *darling* in her mouth. And she's not done speaking. One of her thumbs idly strokes my cheekbone. "I heard what Leo Morelli forced you to do to save your father. I'm so sorry you didn't think you could come to me. Don't worry, sweetheart, you're safe now. He can't steal you away again. You're under my protection now."

Her hands slip down to my shoulders.

It's too much and I wrench myself away. There's nowhere to go, not really, but I can at least take a big step back. Caroline's eyes stay big and round and concerned. "He didn't force me to do anything. You brought me here. I didn't want to come."

The corners of her mouth turn down, and she shakes her head a little. "Sweetheart—"

"I'm not your sweetheart." My skin prickles, going cold with Caroline's presence. She'd be so pissed if I threw up on her nice carpet. "I want to go home. I want to see my father."

She clucks her tongue. "You will. Of course you will. And you won't have to worry anymore. I'm going to take care of everything. Aunt Caroline is here now."

Caroline steps forward, taking up the space I took back. I should run. I should shove her out of the way and run. But instead my muscles lock down tight, freezing one by one from my toes all the way up. Even my breath feels colder. Caroline isn't tall. She doesn't tower over me. I don't know what makes me so afraid I can't move. The glint in her eyes, maybe. Or the sickening scent of all her money and power. Her fingertips meet my cheek, and then she brushes a lock of hair away from my face. Her gaze traces my features like she's seeing me for the first time.

"I've neglected your little family for too long. It wasn't your fault."

The prison unlocks and I push her hand away. I'm too slow. Everything takes longer than it should. Breathing is harder. Thinking is harder. Leo, falling. The stretcher rails slipping out of my hands. Eva putting her hand to her eyes in the family waiting room. A long, silent ride home. Leo saying *run*. The black of his coat against the white of fresh snow. *I'm burning.* His fever. The half-conscious grip of his arms around my waist. He came back. He woke up.

And then.

The text messages. Why did I walk out into the snow without waiting for Gerard? If I'd waited, I wouldn't be here. I wouldn't have met Cash outside Leo's gate. I wouldn't have been standing there when—

"No, it's not my fault." I meet Caroline's eyes with fear and anger rough-and-tumble through my gut. "None of this is my fault. You are forcing me to be here. You're doing what you said Leo did. You *kidnapped* me. You had a man drug me."

Caroline gives a little laugh and it's so polite and incredulous that a pinprick of doubt digs in. Is it me? Am I the one who doesn't know what's going on? The last few days at Leo's house were a literal fever dream. A fever nightmare. Nothing existed except Leo and the endless stream of cool towels I put on his neck, on his back. Maybe we were both sick. Maybe I'm sick now. I test my own forehead. I don't feel feverish. I feel like I was drugged. Because I was.

"We're family, Haley," Caroline says. "It's my responsibility to take you out of a bad situation and bring you home. There's no telling what could have happened to you."

"You sent a man to bring me here against my will. You sent my brother—" I can't talk about Cash. Caroline has never sunk lower than sending her henchman to attack Cash, except for once. "He put his hand over my mouth. He drugged me." I get my hand up to my jawline and skim my fingers over the skin there. I don't have to look into the mirror to know there's a bruise—I can feel the sensitive spot where his fingers clamped over my face to hold the cloth over my mouth. "He did this to me." I lift my chin, angle my face toward the light.

She gives a fake, shallow gasp, and then she's reaching for me. I hold my breath. I can't stand it. Her touch is cool and featherlight. Caroline turns my face, peering at the bruise. It's not like how Leo touches me, it's nothing like it, and I don't know where he is. I've been here long enough for him to find me but he hasn't. The urge to hit Caroline, to attack her, dies a hasty death under my fear.

I know what she's capable of.

"It was probably Leo Morelli who did this to you," she says. "Everyone knows he's the Beast of Bishop's Landing. Violent. Unstable. Dangerous."

"You're the dangerous one."

She smiles, looking beautiful and cold. "You don't know what you're saying. It's probably Stockholm Syndrome. You've been kept captive for so long you actually sympathize with your kidnapper. I'll help you. I'll help you until you understand the truth."

This is not my home. I'm not this kind of Constantine. I never have been, and I never will be.

She strokes my cheek again, then takes my hand in hers. I pull mine back just as quickly, but she doesn't flinch, doesn't blink. "Let's talk about what you need. Something to eat, first. I'm sure you must be starving. And some new things to wear. What would you like? I've seen some lovely winter dresses that would be so gorgeous on you." Caroline waves her hand. "But don't limit yourself. You can have anything you want."

"I want to leave. I *need* to leave here. I need to be with Leo."

"No, darling." A sad, soft smile. "You only think you want Leo Morelli because he conditioned you to think so. He did so many terrible things, but they're over now. He probably had sex with you against your will. But he—what? He gave you an orgasm, perhaps. So you think you're not a victim, but you are. You were his victim, and now you're safe."

Except I'm not. Her touch lingers. A rush of goose bumps moves from my shoulders to my wrists.

I can still feel the five individual points where her fingertips rested against my cheek and her thumb turned my chin. Handprint-sized patches where she held my face. I have the horrified sense that I won't be able to scrub them away no matter how many times I drag a washcloth over my skin. I could cut all my hair off and still feel her brushing it back like she had any right to do it. I could wash my hands a hundred times and still feel her fingers on mine.

All of this is nothing, *nothing*, compared to what she did to Leo. I've lived with this for thirty seconds. He's had to live with so much worse.

Every day.

For so many years.

"I'm going to be sick."

I don't hear what Caroline says next because I'm heaving into a mint-green wastebasket next to the desk. She rubs my back the whole time in calm, slow circles.

CHAPTER TWO

Haley

I SURVIVE THE rest of the day by counting heartbeats. Counting breaths. Anything that means time is going by. I try to keep it simple in my thoughts. If Leo has enough time, he'll be able to get to me, and take me out of here.

Caroline comes in and out of the room. She makes a point of showing me to the en suite bathroom. A new toothbrush waits for me on the countertop along with a little clutch of products. Soon after she brings stacks of clothes. "They're brand new, but I've had them washed." I stare at the back of her head while she tucks them into the dresser. She would have had them washed and dried by someone else. Someone she pays. We washed our own clothes growing up, in a rickety washer and dryer that my dad kept around like a family pet. He chuckled while he fixed them over and over.

Leo has his clothes washed and dried, too.

Mrs. Page is in charge of all that. Caroline wants me to believe that his house isn't my home, but it is. It could be. I'll always be a little bit torn between his castle and my dad's house, but I can fix all that if I get back to Leo. If Leo comes for me. And he will. I know he will.

More expensive perfume wafts to the bed, followed closely by Caroline. "Are you feeling any better? I brought you a book. Sit up, darling. It's not good to lie in bed all day."

I sit up before she can touch me, and she puts the book into my lap.

It's a nonfiction book about the power of forgiveness. A watercolor leaf decorates the front cover. "Is this a joke?"

For a split second, her mask of concern slips and Caroline's eyes narrow. The blue there turns cold enough to freeze my spine. This is the woman who whipped Leo so badly he could have died from it. There's nothing to stop her from doing the same to me. She might do it anyway.

I was foolish to talk to her like that.

Caroline blinks and the mask is back up. The corners of her mouth turn into that sad smile. "Of course not. Just something that's helped me change my way of thinking."

I don't read the book, but I pretend to read it.

I put on the best show of my life, guessing how long it will take to read each page and then turning them at what I hope are accurate intervals.

It might as well be a book full of Leo's name, over and over again.

Caroline brings soup in a bowl and sits on the end of the bed while I eat it. It's a tasteless chicken noodle. She asks me if it's all right, and I tell her it's good.

When I tell her I'm tired in the early afternoon, it's not really a lie. Whatever her bulldog used to knock me out clings to my veins. My eyelids are heavy with missing Leo. With hoping he'll be here soon.

"Okay, sweetheart," Caroline says. "I'll check on you before dinner."

I count a hundred heartbeats after she leaves, then swing my legs over the side of the bed. She won't be back for an hour at least. If she thinks I'm sleeping, I could slip away. It doesn't matter that I don't have shoes. I might not be able to get to Leo's house barefoot but I can get to my dad's. I rub at my eyes on the way, willing them to stay open.

The doorknob doesn't turn.

I wrench it harder on the off chance my arms

are weak.

It doesn't move.

The back of the knob is completely flat, and my stomach turns over again. Caroline planned all this down to the last detail. I'm certain her guest bedrooms haven't always locked from the outside.

Or maybe they have. I don't know. Maybe she regularly keeps people in these rooms and no one knows about it. She's Caroline Constantine. She could do anything. She could keep me here forever, and no one would ever know. I pace back across the room and rush back to try the door again.

Locked.

But no. Caroline wouldn't keep my presence here a secret. She would tell people so they could praise her for rescuing me. Everyone would be on her side. No one suspects her of anything but being rich. Why would they? Leo's the villain in the story of Bishop's Landing. It doesn't matter that he doesn't live here anymore. That he hasn't for years. He'll always be the evil villain, and Caroline will always be a benevolent queen.

I'm driving myself crazy. I can't think like this. I have to keep it together until Leo arrives.

I drift into a dream about Leo's house. It's even bigger in the dream. Winter sunlight streams in through the windows on the second floor, illuminating the empty halls. Every room is empty. No Leo in his bedroom. No Leo waiting in the guest bedroom I slept in. No Leo disappearing around a corner. His office, maybe.

Where *is* his office? I pass the guest bedroom again and again. Finally I stumble over the big stairs at the front of the house and go down at a run.

Now that I'm closer, I can hear him.

I can hear him trying to breathe.

Failing to breathe.

My shoulder hits the doorframe with a thud and I get a glimpse of him on the floor, eyes wide, a pool of blood spreading around him.

"Leo—"

A door opens close by and I jolt upright in the bed. "Oh," Caroline says. "I didn't mean to startle you."

No. She meant to kidnap me, and then keep me here so we could "reconnect."

She doesn't leave again. Caroline never raises her voice but she is incessant.

The topic always comes back to Leo. *It's so wrong to lie to someone, don't you think? The way Leo lied to you. It's so unfortunate what happened to you, Haley. What he did to you. Criminal, really.*

I'm not sure when, exactly, it changes. But it does. Caroline stops saying things like *you must have missed your family so much* and starts saying things like *you were so scared.*

You were so afraid.

You were so terrified.

She says it while I run a brush through my hair. She says it while she watches me put on the makeup she's chosen in the mirror. She says it while I look mindlessly at a rack of clothes she's picked out and point at one.

You were so scared, Haley. He was so cruel to you. You had no choice but to give in to his demands.

Caroline repeats these things so many times they start to sound…

Reasonable.

It's close to the truth.

I *was* afraid of Leo. In the beginning I was so scared. Who wouldn't have been? Everything I'd heard about him painted him as vicious. Ruthless. Bloodthirsty.

The rumors were close to the truth. He can be vicious. He can be ruthless. But he is almost never bloodthirsty. He does what he has to do in order to stay alive and keep the people he loves alive. The Leo I met, the real Leo, thought guns were for cowards. He thought violence should be reckoned with. *If you're going to kill someone, do it with your eyes open.* He said that to me after he killed three men who tried to rape me in an alley.

There is real rage in him. Real pain. Real violence. But he struggles with it. He works so hard to keep it in check.

He does.

No matter how many times Caroline says *he was an awful, violent person to you.*

Which is close to the truth. Or only part of the truth. The other part is how much I wanted him. How much I want him now. Leo Morelli has never once touched me like I was fragile or breakable. He has always touched me like I belonged to him. Like he wants me more than anything in the world.

He does.

No matter how many times Caroline says *he hurt you for the fun of it. That's what he's like. That's what he does. He's heartless.*

It's not true. All my concentration goes to answering her silently. *You're lying. You're lying. You're lying.* I concentrate so hard that I go along with putting on the deep blue dress I chose without thinking. I sit at the bathroom counter and let Caroline curl my hair. I let her put a necklace around my neck and I slip my feet into the shoes she gives me and I only come to my senses when she leads me to the door.

"Where are we going?"

Caroline smiles. It's close to the truth. It looks real enough on her face, but I doubt she's happy because she thinks I'll enjoy this. "I set up a date for you. It's time to ease back into the world, don't you think?"

I don't. But I also don't have any choice. So I follow her down the hall. Caroline's house has a guest wing with everything you could possibly need, including, I guess, a dining room with a round table set with candles on one end of the room. There's a sofa on the other with a matching end table. It's dark outside. I can't see a thing past the reflection in the pane.

"Hello, Caroline. Hello, Haley."

Rick Joseph Jr., the man who wants nothing more than to be a Constantine, stands in the doorway in a turtleneck and slacks with a giant bouquet of red roses in his hands.

"Come in, come in." Caroline sweeps over to him and kisses him on both cheeks, then tugs him into the room. "These are beautiful. Look, Haley."

"Beautiful," I echo as she brings them to the

table and puts them into a vase. She had an empty vase here. Waiting for the roses. "Hi, Rick."

My temples throb with how awkward and strange this is. What is Caroline thinking? A date with Rick?

Rick comes over to me and bends to kiss my cheek. It's all I can do not to jerk backward. He's not a bad guy, but I don't want him, and I don't think he particularly wants me. It's obvious now more than ever. He'll do anything to get in with Caroline. Once upon a time, he even tried to get in with me. He gave me a ride to my car when I needed to go talk to Leo.

Maybe I could talk to him.

"How are you? Are you headed back to school after the holidays?" Rick directs the question at me, but his eyes slide to Caroline.

"Oh, Haley's taking a little break from school," Caroline answers while she ushers us to the table. I feel like a marionette on her strings. "It was all a bit much for her. She's here for a little rest. A little vacation." She laughs, and Rick laughs too. I manage the beginning of a smile.

Caroline pats my arm, and I take it for the prompt it is. "How is—" Oh, god, all I want is to get out of here. "How's your business?"

Rick's eyes light up. "Oh, it's great. It's great,

Haley. We're having the best quarter ever. I know you love books more than anything else, but if you wanted, I could bring you to the office and show you around."

He's so eager that it's almost sweet. A former version of me might have gone to his office to see—what? Computers? Spreadsheets?

"I'm so sorry," Caroline says from behind me. "I have to take this call." I didn't hear a phone, but Rick's eyes go above my head and he nods, the movement so subtle I could've imagined it. Maybe I do imagine it. She comes around beside my chair, takes my face in her hands, and kisses my forehead. "Have a good time, you two."

At that moment, one of the Constantine staff members comes in with our plates on a tray. More soup. I think of Leo, his face a picture of pain. *It's my fucking favorite soup.*

This is not his favorite soup.

Caroline slips out. The man in his uniform leaves us with the soup. And Rick looks across the table at me, his expression pleased but cautious.

I pick up the spoon. Put it back down again. I'm too impatient. But I need to get out. "Rick." The doorway's empty. I have to tell him now, and quietly. "You have to help me. I'm being held against my will."

CHAPTER THREE

Haley

RICK'S EYEBROWS GO up. His mouth drops open. He blinks in a triple flutter of his eyelashes, almost comically stunned, and oh, thank God. He believes me.

He finishes putting his napkin in his lap and glances down. Away from me. "Oh, Haley," he says. I'm ready to stand up and walk out of here with him. Run out of here, if he'll take me where I need to go. But then he looks back up at me with his green eyes, the eyes he can never change to Constantine blue, and they're filled with pity.

Not shock. Not determination.

Pity.

Rick takes a deep breath. "Caroline told me you were disturbed."

"What?" I don't know why it comes as a surprise, but it does.

"Yeah." He frowns, as if it was hard for him to hear. "She told me about your little delusions."

He makes air quotes with his fingers around *delusions*, and my stomach sinks again. Caroline's told her lies to Rick, just like I feared she would. Rick will only be the beginning. "Listen, Haley. Your family wants to help you get better. Caroline's trying to help you get better."

"No."

"She is."

"She's not. I want to go back to Leo's." This is too far to go with Rick. Too much to admit. "You could take me to my dad's. But I need to talk to Leo."

Rick shakes his head. "I've heard that before, and now look at you."

A shadow darkens the doorway and my whole heart leaps. Leo—it has to be Leo. Please, let it be him.

It's not. It's a guard in a dark uniform with a gun holstered on his hip. Rick nods to him and stands up.

"Are you leaving?" I want him to get the hell out of here, and I don't want him to go. Rick fell for Caroline's lies but he's better than Caroline. Anyone is better than Caroline. I'm already alone in this, alone in this place and trapped and helpless, and I will sit here and listen to him talk about his business if it means she's not in here.

"I'm not leaving." He's using a weird tone. I think it's supposed to be soothing, but it makes me feel even more cornered. "Let's sit together on the sofa."

"We're supposed to be having dinner."

Rick puts out his hand to me. I keep mine in my lap. "It doesn't have to be hard. Okay? It can be easy."

What is he talking about? None of this is easy. But now there's an armed guard at the door watching our every move, and I don't want to eat soup, so I put my hand in Rick's. I let him help me up and take me to the sofa on the other side of the room.

"Here. Sit right here, and I'll sit next to you."

He narrates this for me while he guides me down onto the cushions, his touch soft. I'd almost call it tentative if he didn't seem like he'd planned this. Rick settles into the next spot over just like he said he would.

And then he puts his arm around me.

My body freezes at the contact. I've been touched too much already, by Caroline and her bulldog, and I hate it. But Rick runs his hand over my arm. It's adjacent to the way Leo ran his hand up and down my arm when we got back to his house after the hospital, only it's wrong. Rick's rhythm is off. It doesn't match me the way Leo did.

"I know," Rick soothes. "She said you'd have a hard time with this. We can go slow. It'll be good, in the end. You won't regret it."

"Won't regret what?"

"We just have to spend some time together, Hales. It's part of your recovery."

What the hell? I want to scream the question at him, over and over until he answers. I wish I was the kind of person who screamed and fought. One of the many problems, though, is that he's not doing anything terrible. He's just touching my arm. His body is too close. I don't want him there. But he's not hurting me. Not really.

Rick draws me in and my breaths come shallower. It's not the first time we've been close. I've been on a few dates with him, and he plays the part of the gentleman. Once, when it rained, he tucked me to his side like this so we could both stay under his umbrella.

Now that I've been with Leo, I can't stand it.

We sit like this for long enough that the soup has to be cold.

No one comes back in.

The guard stands silently at the door.

"Okay," Rick says, and then he reaches for my

chin. His grip is even softer than Caroline's. Even more gentle. He turns my face to his and looks into my eyes. "There. See? Not so bad."

"What's not so bad?" I sound breathless and horrified because I am. My pulse bangs in my ears and it's not the pleasant high of Leo's restrained violence, it's my body trying to save me. From Rick. Who hasn't done—

He kisses me.

High on one cheek, then the other, and then his mouth meets mine.

It's such a soft kiss. Disgustingly soft. His lips are wrong. His face is wrong.

I can't move.

The air stops dead in my lungs. I don't want to breathe, to smell him, to kiss him back. I don't kiss him back, but that doesn't stop Rick. He darts his tongue out to brush against my lower lip and my arms lock to my sides. It's so unhelpful. God, I'm as useless as I was when Leo was shot. It's that bad.

I start counting heartbeats. If I can get through this kiss, he'll let me go back to dinner.

The kiss doesn't end. It keeps going, and going, Rick insisting. It's the most gentle insistence. A person could almost mistake it for being nice.

It's not nice.

Rick turns me to face him, angling me the way he wants, and I'm a puppet. I am actually a puppet. Something must tip him off that I don't want this, don't like it, that I hate it, because he stops kissing me. "It's fine," he says softly. "You're doing great."

"What are you talking about?" I get the words out just before his mouth closes on mine again. This time he's less gentle about it. Not by much. It's only a lapse of a few seconds and he's back to that horrible soft kiss.

Rick puts his hand on my leg, just above my knee. He slowly, steadily, opens my legs.

And I understand what's happening.

The sharp understanding pushes me out of my head. Shoves me out. I can't stay in my own mind anymore so I fly up to the ceiling and look down on us from a dizzying tilt. There's me, on Caroline's couch in a blue dress that's been pushed up almost to my hips. There's Rick, with one hand on my face and the other moving on my thigh. Even pressure. Even strokes. I feel it from far away.

And I watch as his hand moves up.

Rick kisses me while he inches his hand toward my waist. I feel that, too, but in a peripheral sort of way. I can't tolerate the sensation of it. Can't tolerate how wrong he is and how violating it is. Up here on the ceiling it doesn't seem so bad.

Maybe it's not so bad.

No.

It is very, very bad, and this is what Caroline's game has been all day. To put me off-balance. To put me in a state of mind where I might accept this. And I'm looking down the barrel of an endless string of days like this, where she'll repeat lies until they sound like the truth and bring Rick in for "dates" and put a guard at the door to—

Rick presses his thumb against my inner thigh, a soft brush of the curve just before my leg meets my hip, and leans in so I can't close my legs.

His hand drops to his belt buckle.

I fall straight down into myself. It's like plummeting through a frozen surface from a height. The ice cracks. It's frigid shock. And I snap like a dropped plate.

"What are you doing? Stop. Stop." It turns into a shout on the way out of my mouth at the same time my numb limbs come back to life. I wrench myself off the sofa and away from him, turning my ankle in one of my shoes in the process. I barely feel it.

He's on his feet right away, reaching for me. "Haley. Haley. I'm helping you. This is what we're supposed to do."

"What's the guard for, Rick?" I can't stop yelling at him. It borders on a scream, but I don't want to scream yet. I have to—I have to save the scream for when it's really bad, when it's all gone to hell. "What's the guard for? Is he going to shoot me if I don't have sex with you?"

"He's not going to shoot anyone. The guard's here to make sure—"

"To make sure that I go along with this? I'm not going along with this. I'm not going along with this. You can't do this to me." There's nowhere to go, and I'm so tired, and I need Leo to be here. I wasn't going to shout. I wasn't going to cry. But I burst into ugly sobs anyway.

Rick folds his arms around me before I can run. I push at him. He holds on tight. "Stop." Can't catch my breath. "Don't touch me. Get your hands off me."

"Haley." Caroline flies in past the guard. "Let her go," she says to Rick, and I catch the look between them and it's proof, it is *proof* of just how much they've orchestrated this. Rick releases me into Caroline's arms, and I could keep shouting, I could be sick, because they planned this. They planned for her to be the one to comfort me. I see what's coming. All the nights they've planned. Line them up. Knock them down.

He'll rape me, but he'll do it gently. Caroline will be there to pick up the pieces. Caroline gave him permission in the first place.

It makes me cry harder. That's the only solution I have, really. To cry so hard that Caroline takes me back to my room. I don't struggle against the tears. They feel like my only weapon, and they're not enough.

I don't want her hands on me, anywhere near me, but there's no way for me to get out of the dress with my hands shaking like this. She's the one who slips a nightshirt over my head and pulls back the covers. She's the one who pats my hair once my head is on the pillow. She's the one who turns out the light.

I hear her talking in a low voice outside the door as soon as it's shut. I bet there's a guard out there. I bet he'll stay all night.

"Please," I whisper to no one. To Leo. "Please come get me."

CHAPTER FOUR

Leo

THE DINING ROOM. It's the place where I watched Haley's face light up at the sight of her Jane Eyre. Now it's crowded with people who don't belong here.

Four representatives from the teams who were supposed to be guarding the grounds.

Six more people Gerard brought in.

All of them talk at once.

In the middle of this crowd from hell, I'm on fire. Worse than fire. The pain in my back has reached my ankles. The back of my skull. It's like being cut with a knife—long, thin stripes of agony that come over and over and over until I can't tell them apart. My head howls with it. My body has been screaming with it since Eva shook me awake in the night.

Eva told me the news. Gerard tells me she insisted on being the one. I'll never forget it. At the same moment I became aware of the cold sheet—I was just touching Haley's face—Eva said, "Haley's gone. Caroline's bulldog took her."

The next moment, I became a column of flame and rage.

I am that column now.

There is a fine line between the performance of fury and letting it sink into the bone, and I'm standing on it. One step and I could let go. I could stop holding it back. I could become the snarling creature who bared his teeth at my father until all his attention was on me.

Gerard won't shut up. "—move away from the house. I don't feel confident in—"

"Confident?" I snap at him. "I don't want your confidence. I'm not waiting for you to feel secure. We're getting her back. There's your certainty. It's happening."

"Leo." Eva's been at my side since she woke me up. She stood in the doorway to my closet and watched me yank a shirt over my head. All my muscles ache. I should be resting. That's what Carina said, and what Eva repeated, and I will be damned if I'm going to rest with Haley gone. "You need to calm down. Take a breath. We can go to your office."

"No," I thunder at her. "Fuck no. I'm not going to calm down."

My voice echoes in the room. Conversation comes to a startling halt. My temper is getting away from me. Just a little. Just enough to scare Eva. But I can't shut it off any more than I can shut off the shrieking pain all down my spine.

Someone from the household staff steps to my side, silent, keeping his eyes off mine. He has a case in his hands, the top held open so I can see the knives inside. I choose one and slip it into the Kevlar sheath on my belt.

Eva watches this with her bottom lip between her teeth. She bites down so hard the flesh is white. Nervous. She's nervous about what I'm going to do.

I take her face in my hands. It's too gentle a motion, too careful, and it's because we're so close to that line. I would love so much to let the beast take over, and I can't do it yet. So I take exquisite care with every movement.

I kiss my sister on the forehead, then put both hands on her shoulders to move her aside.

And then I'm going. Striding out of the room. There are more people outside the dining room. More guards. One steps into my path. "Mr. Morelli, it's not secure outside—"

I have his jacket in my fists before he's ready. No one is ever ready for me when I'm like this, when I'm on the verge of chaos. He's a strong man but I'm stronger. I am fucking furious.

It boils and burns, every muscle acidic with it. One step, two, and I have him slammed against the wall. The roar of rage is louder than his skull meeting plaster. My teeth grit together so hard they crack. "It's not secure anywhere, you fool. You let that bastard take her."

The rage settles inside me, deeper, deeper, until there's nothing left of me—of Leo Morelli. I'm the Beast of Bishop's Landing now.

He struggles against the wall. "Everyone who was on shift at that time has been removed from the property. They'll be sequestered until the investigation is over."

"Explain it to me some more." It's a taunt.

He looks confused, torn between his duty and his fear. "Sir—"

They're beginning to gather now. Closing in. I can see Gerard out of the corner of my eye.

"The only reason you remain alive is because I haven't yet reached for the knife at my belt." I keep my tone level, like we're having a conversation at a dinner party, but the dead silence in the foyer means they can all hear me. Good. "When I let go of your jacket, you'll have a choice. You can stay out of my way and live, or you can put your body in my path and die. It makes no difference to me."

A single nod.

I hold him another heartbeat because that's all I'm willing to spare, and then I let go.

It's not a guard who blocks the way when I turn back.

It's Eva, looking rumpled and exhausted and scared. She hasn't changed out of the clothes she was wearing when she woke me up. She's stayed in soft leggings and a sweater all day. "You don't have to do this," she says. "Let them help you. Don't leave when you're like this."

"I'll be back soon, sister mine."

She glances at someone behind me—Gerard, probably—and plants her feet.

I go around her. I'm already gone. I have to get out of here before I kill someone in the foyer, before I lose myself to that violence. I've reserved it for someone else.

In my garage I choose a nondescript SUV, black and featureless, and drive out into a winter night. Snow spirals in front of the headlights. A separate part of me, one not being consumed by blistering pain, is in control of the vehicle. The roads to Bishop's Landing are bathed in shadows.

It hurts so fucking much.

The pain is all-consuming and irrelevant at once.

It changes nothing. I'm done waiting.

I have waited for hours with Haley in the clutches of a monster, and it's over. I know she's at the Constantine compound. I've surveilled multiple Constantine properties for years, so I have video of a car arriving in the night. They bundled her inside with her jacket over her head like I wouldn't know what they were doing. I know she's there.

I just need confirmation she's still in the main house. Caroline's house. Confirmation they didn't take her somewhere else—a warehouse, a hospital. An unmarked grave. No. I can't think like that or I'll drive this vehicle through the front door.

I would do it, too. Except that Haley might get hurt.

Instead I have to sit in this SUV until I see someone leaving. It's hell to drive. I can't keep my back fully away from the seat but it wouldn't matter if I could. It's reaching around to my ribs now. The fronts of my legs. Everything hurts. There is a rumor in Bishop's Landing that I train to stay fit for killing people, but the truth is that when the pain gets this bad, it can cause a cascade of knots and cramps in my muscles that require movement to work out.

I try to stay ahead of them.

I'm not ahead of them now.

As I roll through the maintained, lighted street adjacent to the Constantine compound, a car pulls out of a side gate. The driver lifts a hand to shield his eyes against my headlights.

It's Rick Joseph Jr..

I suppress a brief urge to run him over with the SUV. It would win against his piece-of-shit car. But he has been useful to me in the past. He likes money, and he likes chances, and the fact that he wants to be a Constantine means he's worked to get as much access as he can.

He can be bought. I've done it many times before. I'll do it again.

It's painful to turn away from the Constantine compound when I think Haley's inside, but I force myself to do it. This is the only way I can be sure to get her out safely. Without a single scratch on her beautiful head. I have to trust that her family won't hurt her. At least not right away. She's one of them, after all.

I turn down a side street and race Rick to his apartment. It's the kind of bullshit place up-and-comers in Bishop's Landing scramble to rent, with fake columns on the ground floor and glass windows above. It takes nothing to get Rick's apartment number from the doorman, who doesn't care about his job. It takes a pathetic amount of money to buy his silence. The veneer of fanciness on this place doesn't prevent me from forcing the lock on Rick's door.

I have just enough time to stand in his shithole living room before he arrives.

He was at Caroline's house.

Caroline's focus is on fucking with me at this moment, which is why she's taken Haley.

Rick was there because he's working with Caroline. They'll have a mutual interest.

I'm waiting for him when he opens the door and steps in.

I must be a nightmare, coming at him out of the dark, but I'm merciful. I take his shirt in my fist and punch him before he has time to panic and run. His head snaps to the side.

Rick's an asshole, and an opportunist. "What the fuck—"

"What the fuck is right, Rick. What the fuck have you been doing at Caroline's? And here's the more important question. Are you ready to die for it? Because I'd love to kill you."

I back him up against the door in an adrenaline haze and punch him again. He was with

Haley. I know he was. He was with her, and he was with her because Caroline wanted him to be there, and I could kill him. I *will* kill him.

The second hit is too much for him, and when I release his shirt, he folds.

He gets his hands underneath him and starts to push up. I kick him before he can get to his feet, sending him back to the floor. One more kick to the rib. Every muscle tenses to deliver another one, and another, until he's dead, but I haul myself back from the edge with both hands.

I stalk into his living room, putting distance between me and that asshole, that motherfucker. There are tricks, there are strategies, to bring myself back when it's like this, when it's bad like this, when my fury swallows me whole. I remember the first lines of books. *Backward and forward.* Random bullshit from my library. It doesn't matter. *Count the words.* The pain has me in a tight grip. A crushing grip. But I have to calm down, if only slightly. Enough that I don't actually murder Rick Joseph Jr.. Because if I murder him, I can't use him.

He groans when he hears me coming back, and does it louder when I pick him up and pin him to the door by the throat. I want to drive the tip of my knife into his artery until he bleeds, but

I won't be able to stop. As it stands he'll have a black eye and maybe a cracked rib.

"You've seen her. Haley Constantine. At the compound."

Rick doesn't struggle. "Yeah." I've knocked the wind out of him. "Yeah. She's there." He blinks at me in the light coming from his microwave. "Why do you—why do you care?"

I drive a fist into his chest and he makes a sound like a wounded animal. My control is paper-thin. "Tell me how she is. Is she hurt? Is she afraid? Is she hungry?"

Rick's eyes slide to the left, and my heart implodes. "She's okay." He grunts again, and I discover I've moved a hand to a kicked rib and driven my knuckles into it. Good. I add more pressure and his teeth grind together. "She's okay, I swear to God. How could anyone not be okay in a goddamn mansion? Two-thousand-thread-count sheets, and all she can talk about is leaving. Talking shit about her family. Saying Caroline's holding her against her will."

The edges of my vision dim. This bastard. This son of a bitch. He talked to her, and he didn't believe her. My pulse races faster. I'm going to crush the life out of him. Now, now, now.

"She won't—" Rick sounds more pained by

the word. "She won't stop talking about you. Talked about you on our date. Did you hit it, man? I'm not mad about it."

An image of Haley springs into my mind. Sweet, soft Haley, who is filthy for me, who cries for me, couldn't keep my name out of her mouth even in Caroline's lair. I'm out of my mind, thinking of her trapped there. I'm out of my mind. But the last thing I want is for her to hear from Caroline that I've killed Rick. That I'm a murderer. She'll think I'm not coming to get her.

That's the only thing that pulls me back from the edge.

I yank him away from the door and throw him into his apartment. Rick crashes over a coffee table and crumples, clumsy and beaten. He puts one hand up to shield himself while I tower over him. "The next time Caroline invites you to her house, what are you going to do, Rick?"

He hesitates for only an instant. "Call you."

I crouch down next to him so he can see my face. "If you touch Haley, I'll kill you. No lock in the world can keep me out. No security firm can keep you protected. There's nowhere you can run. I'll find you, and I'll gut you where you stand."

One more kick. That's all I allow myself. I stand up and aim for his ribs.

Rick curls into a ball, heaving, and I leave him there.

Winter air snaps into my face as I step out into the cold, already dialing. I swore I wouldn't do this, not unless I had to, but we're here now. We're here. The time has come.

My brother answers on the first ring. "I thought you'd never call." There's noise in the background. He's at his club, or out somewhere.

"Hell must have frozen over." I wrench open the door to the SUV and climb into the driver's seat over the frantic protests of the pain.

"I'll be back in a minute," Lucian says to someone nearby, and the background chatter fades out. It sounds like he's walking fast. "What's going on?"

"War," I tell him, my throat tight.

"This is Caroline, isn't it?" He swears with creative aplomb. "I can't believe you whipped her. Of course she'll react like an injured dog. All for a goddamn business deal."

"It was more than that." The words emerge before I can stop them. If it weren't for the phone, I'd have both hands over my eyes.

He's quiet. "Leo."

There's so much unspoken between us. So much history and abuse in our family. I don't have time for any of it, not with Haley hanging in the balance. "Like I said, hell has frozen over. Because I'm reaching out to you, brother mine. I need your help."

CHAPTER FIVE

Leo

LUCIAN ARRIVES AFTER forty agonizing minutes. He must have driven a hundred all the way from the city, and by the time he throws his car in park next to the SUV, I'm standing outside in the cold. The snow is coming faster now.

I can no longer sit in the car.

My brother unfolds himself from the front seat. Lucian always looks like he came from the office, his dark hair neat, his wool overcoat flawless. What gives him away as a Morelli and not a normal businessman is the gleam of violence in his dark eyes. "What the hell is happening, Leo? If Caroline sent someone to your place—"

"There's another Constantine."

He comes to stand in front of me, his hands shoved into the pockets of his jacket. "No shit. They can't stop breeding. There are probably hundreds by now."

"This one's mine, asshole. Haley's mine. Haley—" I can't get a grip, but I have no choice. "Phillip Constantine's daughter. I made a deal with her."

Lucian's face doesn't change. "A deal."

"Her body for thirty days in exchange for her father's business deal."

"Then what did you whip Caroline for?"

"It doesn't matter." Lucian doesn't need to know about the revenge. "What matters is that she took Haley from my house. They have her at the compound. I have to get her out." Old habit and new rage propel me toward him, make me bury my hands in his jacket and shove him backward, into his car. I can't hurt him. Lucian doesn't knock my hands aside, only looks down at them, then back up at my face. "Do you have a way to get her out?"

"What happened to you?"

He's not asking about Haley, not really. I know he's not from his tone. He's asking what made me like this. "We don't have time for that discussion. Lucian—"

"Just—" He pushes my hands down and away from his jacket. "Christ. It's cold as balls out here. Can you get into the car? I'm trying to understand. So you're pissed she reneged on the contract? There are other ways to pursue this."

"I don't give a fuck about the contact. This is about Haley."

Realization dawns. "You care about her."

It's more than caring about her. It's survival. She's become the air I need to breathe. "Help me get her back or get out of here. I'm not getting in any car until I have a plan."

He arches one eyebrow. "Fine. Stand there, then, while I call Elaine."

There's only one Elaine I know of. "Elaine Constantine?" The fire and fury surges again. I've been on this breaking wheel all day, and there is no room between the low point and the high point. The peak is constant. It's killing me. "Why the hell would you call her?"

"Because we're together. I'm assuming by how unhinged you're acting that you have something like what I have with Elaine. And you think Haley's at the Constantine compound?"

He did not seem shocked enough when I announced Haley was mine. I see that now. But the thought of Lucian with a Constantine—I can't imagine it. Mortal enemies. Both of them the children of warring families. Yet there he is, pressing a number on speed dial like he's called it a thousand times. I'd ask him how long it's been going on, but I don't care. I can't care about anything else. Lucian and Elaine. What the fuck, what the fuck. "I know she's there."

"Sweetheart," he says, and I blink at him like a fool. I've never heard him say that to anyone without an acid tone, without it twisting into a cruel joke. "I need to get your mother out of her house for a while. Can you cause a bit of a scene?"

HALF AN HOUR later we're at the nearest corner to the compound. The first one that's not under their surveillance or ours. And I'm dying.

Sitting in the SUV is full-blown torture. Every muscle hurts and my back is a thousand fresh cuts. Phantom blood runs down to my waist. Soaks through my shirt. I don't know what to call it. It's not a hallucination. More of an echo. But it feels real.

"Just give her another couple of minutes, Leo. Jesus."

"She could be dead in another couple of minutes."

This is not my only fear. I can't name the deeper one, the one at my core, to Lucian. I won't. It's enough to know that there are worse things than death. Caroline has done them to me.

Lucian scoffs. "Caroline's not going to kill one of her own. Not even for being with you."

"Is she not?" I level him with a glare. "Or are you just saying that because you don't want her to kill Elaine? She's more fucked up than you realize."

The grin Lucian gives me is more bloodthirsty than any expression I've ever worn. I'm the Beast of Bishop's Landing, but that reputation has drawn attention away from Lucian, who is the real psychopath of the family. It's in his marrow. "Caroline won't do a thing to Elaine when she finds out. She'll attend our wedding with a smile on her face." Lucian insisted on sitting in the SUV with me after he followed me here in his car, and now he turns in his seat and cranes his neck. "Okay. She's leaving."

According to him, Elaine called her mother pretending to have a meltdown. Elaine is known for being dramatic, for being wild, and it must have been convincing. There's Caroline's security team, going out ahead of her. And another car behind. Lucian starts a timer on his phone. When they've been gone for three minutes, we get out of the SUV and stroll for the gate.

I want to run. Everything in me howls to run. But this pace won't set off any alarms for their security. We're just two people in dark coats walking down the street.

Lucian reaches the gate first and punches in a code. The gate retracts to let us in, and we're there.

The driveway is all that's between me and Haley. The driveway and God knows how many locked doors. I'll carve them open with my knife if I have to.

My brother knows where to go. This, at least, is not surprising. Lucian makes it his business to get information when he needs it, and he has what we need now. He leads us to a side door with another keypad. Another code. "Elaine wanted her to bring security. She'll have brought the men from the main house," Lucian says to me as we pull open the door and walk in.

The smell hits me like a punch to the gut. It turns my stomach. I swallow back being sick, my head pounding. I hate the scent of Caroline's perfume. I hate it, I fucking hate it, I need to be away from it.

But first.

I have to get to Haley.

A man in a staff uniform comes out of a door ahead of us and Lucian gets to him first, a big hand on his shoulder, twisting into the fabric of his shirt. "Hello," says my brother. "We're looking for a friend of ours. I could snap your neck, or you could tell me where Haley Constantine is."

The guy breaks and runs. Lucian and I both chase him. This time, when Lucian catches him, I don't stand back. I have the knife out before I know I'm doing it, I have it pressed to the side of his neck. The tip digs in. A bead of blood surfaces and runs down. He's trapped, Lucian shoving, me cutting him, and it would feel so good to carve into his neck. It would feel so good to let go.

"Easy, Leo. If you slit his throat, he can't help us," warns Lucian, his tone light. I let up on the knife. "No more theatrics," he says to the man. "Haley Constantine. Quickly."

We meet one other staff member on the way to the guest wing of Caroline's mansion. I have the first man's collar in my fist, my knife to his throat, so Lucian's free when the second one turns to run. My brother catches him on the shoulder, turns him around, and drives his fist into the center of his face. His nose crunches. He falls. Any more of them show up, and this is going to get complicated. The house is going to burn down with me if I don't get to her before then.

"Here," says the man I'm trying not to kill.

"Here. Let me."

There's a keypad on the outside of the door.

Caroline has locked her in a prison. She's made a prison for Haley, brought Rick here for whatever the fuck a "date" means, and kept her from me. I shake the man by his collar so hard his teeth rattle. "Do it before I carve you open."

With shaking hands, he punches in a code on the keypad and the lock clicks. Lucian reaches around and opens the door. The whole world draws down to this one moment. If there's anything on the other side but Haley, safe and sound and whole, I will lose my mind. I will never come back. New pain layers in over the inferno of my back.

But then.

A lamp turns on, the glow soft as she is, and there's Haley, blinking into the light. Her eyes fly open when she sees me and she scrambles out of the bed. She's wearing a nightgown I've never seen and I can't get to her because this fucking guy is in my hands. I shove him at Lucian, open my arms, and she's there, she's there, she's there.

Haley tumbles into me with a raw cry that's almost a sob and my heart bursts. I can't hear what she's saying, can't separate the words from the sound of her voice and the beat of her heart under my arms. I lift her face away from my shirt and smooth back her hair because I have to see if she's okay.

She's not.

"Leo. Come on. Let's go," Lucian says behind me.

Rick is a liar. Her eyes are red and swollen. She's been crying. They did something to her.

And then she turns her head.

A bruise.

On her jawline.

A *bruise*.

I pull her toward the bedroom door on pure instinct, pull her out into the hall so I can get enough air, and my vision goes red.

All the rage and pain and yes, terror—all of it erupts. I can't hold it back anymore. It's in my skin and bones and blood. My pulse. It's not always a show. It's not always pretend. Sometimes, if you play a role long enough, it becomes you, and that bruise on her face has stripped away everything but a searing thirst for retribution. Someone's going to pay for this. Someone. Now. I have her in my arms and the fury of my heartbeat is all I can hear.

Lucian's voice is a distant whisper. "This way," he's saying. "This way. We have to go."

"Leo," Haley says.

At the end of the hall, two more Constantines step into view.

Perry and Keaton. They're at home for the night, in comfortable clothes. "Jesus Christ," says Perry. "Are you invading our house? What the—"

He doesn't finish, because I've let go of Haley, and I'm on top of them.

You don't throw a punch the first time and expect it to do any damage. You practice. You throw hundreds of punches. Thousands. You train the motion of a kick until it can cause exactly the harm you intend. Fighting takes restraint, and it takes skill. It takes the most skill to subdue a person without hurting them. To use restraint.

I don't care about hurting Perry and Keaton. All of my skill has burned down into pure violence. There's nothing left but a killing rage. Perry first. A hit to the side of the head that rattles him. Keaton next when he tries to run for help. They're responsible for this. Haley has a bruise. They hurt her. The two of them try to work together but they weren't born into hell. Violence is not their first language.

It's mine.

Blow after blow. I don't feel it, don't bother

to feel the force of the hits. Don't bother to hold back. It doesn't matter that they land a few of their own. Every inch of me is already in agony. It changes nothing, nothing, nothing. All of them. I'll kill them all. Beat them to a bloody pulp and cremate them in their own house.

I haul Perry off the floor, where he's fallen, and I'm going to hit him so hard he never gets up again. I have my fist drawn back to do it.

The softest touch on my arm.

I look down at that gentleness and find Haley's hand there. Follow the path from her fingers all the way to her blue eyes. My pulse is outsized for my body. Every heartbeat hurts. But when I look at her, it eases enough to let me breathe. I've settled into the short, adrenaline-fueled breaths of a fight but now I take a full inhale.

And then, though I'm a monster, though I'm the most dangerous bastard ever to share space with her, she puts her hand on my cheek. Her thumb moves over my cheekbone. Slowly. Slowly. "Perry didn't do anything. He's my family, and he didn't know what was happening. Caroline told them I was sick. He and Keaton didn't do anything. Put him down, Leo."

"I can't." It's true. I can't. I can't open my hand. "They hurt you."

"No. They didn't touch me. I don't want you to be a murderer over this. It's okay, Leo. You can let go."

The red haze clears, washed away by her blue eyes. Unclenching my fist from Perry's shirt is another exercise in torture. My grip was already committed to what I was doing.

I hear him hit the floor and curse, but I don't care. I have my arms around Haley again.

CHAPTER SIX

Haley

LEO DROPS PERRY, who falls to the floor with a grunt and a soft *fuck*. Keaton, a hand pressed to his cheek, goes to his brother as Leo puts his arms around me. He lifts me into a carry and I focus on breathing. I could cry forever, but I won't. I have the sense that if I break down, it will be like when Leo was sick. He'll lose his mind. He won't know what's wrong.

There are lives at stake.

His brother is here. Lucian. The two of them look incongruous, standing in Caroline's house, but we don't wait for long. "This way," Lucian says again. I expected him to be cruel, to be…a Morelli. And he is. There's a set to his face that makes me think he might go back for Perry and Keaton if they say the wrong thing.

"Haley," says Perry. He looks like shit. Leo was going to kill him. There was murder in his eyes. It's there now, just beneath the surface. A translucent layer of civility is over the beast now.

"I'm okay," I tell him over Leo's shoulder. "Really. Just—"

Just don't do anything. Don't keep me here. The urge to beg him is strong, here in Caroline's house, but then Leo is moving with long, purposeful strides. Perry and Keaton don't follow. Perry sits down hard on the floor as we go, and Keaton kneels next to him, and I think the only reason they're not following is because Leo is such a menace.

Lucian is dragging a fourth person with us, all the way to the door, by the collar of his shirt. Leo's brother does this with such a casual stance that I have to think he's done it before. When we reach the door, he shoves the man into a corner and kicks him. Something cracks in the man's chest and he cries out. Lucian grins. I think Bishop's Landing has been wrong about Leo. They got the wrong brother. Lucian is the real killer. The real sociopath.

But—no. He's here, after all, to get me. To help Leo. I don't understand it and I can't find my voice to ask. I don't dare speak all the way out.

Leo bundles me close as we step out into the night. I'm in a nightgown, no shoes, no socks, and the wind cuts through the fabric. "It's not far," Leo says. His voice is different. A razor's edge. Sharper than I've ever heard before. Lucian walks by his side as we go down the block, away from Caroline's house. A click makes me lift my head from Leo's shoulder. Lucian's got a gun out, and he's taken the safety off.

Lucian meets my eyes. No trace of discomfort there, only an intense curiosity. "Did they hurt you?"

I shake my head. It's close to the truth.

"No more questions, Lucian," Leo says, and we're at his SUV. He opens the door, puts me into the passenger seat, and takes off his coat. He wraps it around me with efficient movements, his hands steady, and pulls the buckle over me. Clicks it into place.

His expression—

I don't recognize it. I've never seen it before.

"I'm following," Lucian says from over Leo's shoulder.

"Fine."

"I'm meeting with your security."

"Fine." Leo closes my door, and then he's in the car, and then we're driving away. A pair of headlights follows after us.

It's not the first time he's driven me like this.

A different route back to his house. Same heat turned up high in the car. Same full-body trembles that set in only after we've pulled away from the curb. Leo is silent in his dark clothes, his eyes on the road, his hands on the wheel.

I reach for him at the same instant he reaches for me. His grip on my hand is so tight it hurts, but I never want him to let go. He doesn't. He holds my hand all the way back to his castle of a house. All the way through the gate, and down the driveway. He only releases me for long enough to come around to my side and take me in his arms again. Up the steps. Into the foyer.

I'm expecting silence and space.

A crowd greets us instead. Men in dark suits are all over the foyer. Gerard. Eva, who gasps, and starts to come forward. Her face changes when she sees Leo's expression. "Come and sit with us," she says quickly. "Come and sit with us, and—"

"No," barks Leo. He goes for the stairs without looking at her.

"Let's have a meeting," Lucian says, his voice rising above all the chatter. The front door slams shut. None of it matters because Leo is taking me to his bedroom. My skin tingles with relief, and with delayed fear, and with everything I felt at Caroline's. With the shame of crying in front of

Rick. With the disgust of being touched by him. But it's over. It's over.

What's not over is Leo.

He kicks the door shut the moment we're past the threshold. Puts me on my feet. Pushes me back so I'm pinned against cool wood, slipping the coat off my shoulders as he does. His hands are so large on the sides of my face. They slip down to my neck. He's warm, and he's here.

Leo's grip tightens. He takes my air away. Makes it hard to breathe for long enough that my heart kicks up into a sprint. Even now, even when I can't breathe, he smells so good I could die. Like a clean winter forest. Like a dark night.

And then.

He leans down and bites me. His teeth sink into the place where my neck curves into my shoulder, the heat of his breath tracing the marks. I'm on fire, lit up with him, every nerve responding to the pain. He's never bitten me this hard before, never while he's choking me like this, and I suck in a gasp.

Leo shoves himself away from me. My spine knocks against hardwood as he backs away with a growl. "Get out of here," he says. "Go to the guest room."

"What?" I put my hand where he touched me,

press in like I can recreate the sensation. "No. I don't want to leave."

Leo looks me in the eye, and my heart thuds. Cracks. "I'll be too rough with you. I'll tear you apart."

A heartbeat of fear. Another one of recognition. The gold in his eyes blazes with fury he's not bothering to suppress.

Or that he can't suppress.

The truth arrives like a bullet.

I've only ever had sex with Leo Morelli. The man standing in front of me now is the Beast of Bishop's Landing.

This is the person Leo became to survive his father. This is the person he became to protect his siblings, and his secrets. I thought it was all an act. I thought he was only pretending to be angry. That it was skin-deep. A performance. And sometimes it is. Sometimes he allows people to think he is angry when he is really in pain. He allows people to think he's ruthless and bloodthirsty when he is considered and calculated.

But now?

Now it's real.

I'll tear you apart sounded so raw, so violent, that I know it's real. And it's too late to stop it. Too late to hide it.

He's trying anyway, though his anger is all in the open, it's crackling in the air around us. It's making the hairs on the backs of my arms stand up.

"Go," he orders.

"No." I separate myself from the door and take three steps toward him. Close enough for him to reach me. My body quakes with how lethal he is but I'll never run from him. Never. Never. Never. "I want all of you. Even the beast."

I look at him then. Really look. And I see everything. The agonized set of his shoulders. The way he stands up so tall as a way to keep himself in check. His hands shoved into his pockets to keep them off me.

The need in his eyes. A deep, animal need. He's practically vibrating with it. Leo's jaw works. "I promise, darling. I won't be gentle."

Leo's voice swears off softness. It's as clear a warning as I've ever heard. This is my only chance to back out of this. To run to the guest room and lock the door. He'll let me do it.

I lift one hand and pull down the neck of my nightgown to bare my throat to him.

I show him the marks he's already made.

"All of you," I tell him. "Please."

One second he's standing there, and the next

he's all furious motion. It's like the night he came after me. Watching him run into that alley was the most magnificent thing I've ever seen. He is equally stunning now. A graceful violence. His hands are all over me. Squeezing. Pinching. Bruising. He bites me again, layering more marks on top of the fresh one, and I cry out at how sharp the pain is. How little he's holding back.

Leo tears my nightgown off. Shreds the fabric. Splits it down the middle.

He tears through the panties I'm wearing underneath.

When I'm naked, when there's nothing left between us, he takes my face in his hands and kisses me in the ruins of my clothes. He kisses me so hard I taste blood. There is nothing gentle in his tongue, or his teeth, and I owe him everything, he is everything, because if he was soft with me now, I would be sick.

It's not cruelty, the way he hurts me now. We are beyond things like cruelty and kindness. This is claiming.

He takes his mouth off mine, fists his fingers in my hair, and drags me to the fireplace. Leo sweeps up the remains of my clothes as he goes. The fire springs to life when he hits a switch and he throws the clothes into it. The white turns to black curls in the flame as he forces me to my knees in front of the heat. One pull of his zipper and his cock is freed, thick and hard, and Leo doesn't hesitate. Not at all. He pushes the crown past my lips and I can't do anything but take it.

"Get it wet," he says. "You have ten seconds, darling."

What Leo means is that I have to survive the next ten seconds. I can't lick him, can't swirl my tongue around him, because he's shoving all the way to the back of my throat and down. Tears roll down my cheeks. It feels good to have them drawn out of me. It feels good to lose myself to this moment. My body tries to resist him but I don't want to resist, I want to take him, I want to. I need to. I'm hot between my legs. Wet for him already. I try to tell him but he's filled my throat so completely that all that comes out is a needy hum.

"Fuck," Leo says. He pulls out and strips off his clothes.

His hand goes to the back of my neck. Leo doesn't guide my head to the carpet. He shoves it there and pins me in place, one big hand in my hair. The other snaps my thighs apart and three fingers impale the soft part of me. Testing. He's testing me to see if I'm wet enough, and that's all, that's all. He fucks his fingers in and out, in and out, and then he pulls them away and wipes them on the small of my back.

Leo lines himself up and thrusts in so hard my face scrapes against the carpet. A vicious push. I'm not used to him, but he doesn't give me time to adjust. I scream at the stretch, at the pain, but he ignores me. Another thrust interrupts my breathing. Makes my heart skip a beat. My pussy clenches around him and I want him to stay, stay, stay, but he pulls out again so he can take me harder.

He's so strong above me. So unforgiving. His hand in my hair hurts, it hurts so badly, and it's a homecoming. He hurts me because I like it. Because I can take it. Tears slip down my cheeks. He takes his hand from my hair to swipe some of my tears from my skin. There's a *pop* as he sucks them off his fingertips, and then he laughs.

It's a dark, evil laugh, brimming with all the fury and violence he's been holding in, and it makes me tighten around him again. He groans. "I love it when you cry, darling. I love it. I love it. I love you."

Leo finds his rhythm now. Harsh. Unrelenting. He fucks me like he can bind us together through this act alone. Like he's trying to mate with me for life. Like a wolf. Like a beast.

"You're wet." Even his voice is rough. "That's the sound of your cunt getting wetter for me while I fuck you to tears. So loud. You love being fucked like this. Tell me how much you love it, darling."

I can barely move, he has me pinned so tight to the carpet. "I need it," I pant, and then I'm sobbing for real. "I need it." Terror washes over me. I'm not afraid of Leo. I'm afraid that this won't erase what happened. That the way Rick touched me won't ever go away. "Please," I beg, and I don't have the words to explain what I need.

Except.

Leo doesn't need an explanation. Five more strokes and then he turns me over, onto my back, and forces my thighs apart again. He fills me with another cruel thrust as his hand comes up around my neck. He angles my head up so my neck is exposed and pins my wrists to the carpet with his forearm. He kisses me brutally anywhere he can reach, his arm a steel cage across my wrists, and I sob and sob.

"It's over," he says into my ear, and his voice is half Leo, half beast, and it makes me cry harder. "I'm the only one who's ever touched you. I'm the only one who will ever fuck this pussy. It belongs to me. You belong to me, darling. Every last inch."

He punctuates *every last inch* with three thrusts that stretch me beyond what I thought I could take.

"Now come on my cock."

My orgasm tumbles free at the words. I'm spread wide, too wide, my thighs aching with staying apart for him. Trembling. It shakes me from head to toe, shakes me into the carpet. Shakes me into the center of the earth. Rips apart like an atom bomb. Washes everything clean. Leo pushes in deep deep deep and somehow, somehow, he gets bigger. I have a flash of fear—he won't be able to get back out, he's too big, he'll stay inside me forever—and then he makes a sound deep in his throat and shudders.

Leo squeezes harder as he spills himself into me. The world narrows to his hand around my neck and the hot rush of him inside me. Painting with cum. Deeper than he's ever gone before. He has absolute control over my breath, over my body, and he uses it while he comes. My vision dims. "Mine," I think he says. "Mine. Fuck."

Both of us are slick with sweat.

When he's finished, I come back to the sounds in the room. The crackle of the fire.

Someone is crying. It's me.

Leo kisses my temple. Kisses the bruise. Kisses the bite marks he made.

"Are you—" I want to ask if he's himself, but that wouldn't be a fair question. He's himself when he's angry and hurting, too. When he's the beast.

"No," he answers, and the honesty in his voice hurts. "I'm not. But I will be."

Leo eases out of me and takes me in his arms. Takes me to his bed. He lies on his side and pulls me close. I put a hand on his chest to feel his heartbeat. He's not out of breath, but it's pounding. He strokes my hair, putting it back into place, for a long time. Then he moves his hand to my arm. Back and forth. Back and forth. Down to my forearm. He repeats this process on my fingers, and it's only then that I feel how tense I am. How ready to fight.

"Tell me what happened."

"Nothing happened." The lie crushes in like a jagged stone. "It was nothing to complain about."

His hand stills, and then he slips it beneath my arm and runs his palm over my waist. "I know Rick saw you."

The convulsion that moves through me is so strong it makes my stomach clench. There's no hiding it from Leo. He sits up in the bed, his body away from the pillows, and pulls me up with him. Curls me into his lap, into his arms. Like he knows I don't want to look at him while I say this. "It was Caroline. At first, it was Caroline. She kept touching me. I—" An embarrassed cry works its way out of me. "Leo, I can't. This is nothing—"

"If you say it's nothing compared to what happened to me, I swear to Christ, darling, I'll punish that idea out of you." His tone is matter-of-fact but there's an undercurrent of blistering rage.

I believe him. I believe he'll do it. So I steady myself to keep going.

"She kept touching me. And she kept saying things that sounded true. Things that were—that were close to the truth."

"Like what?" He's rubbing slow circles on my back like he can stop my heart and lungs from freaking out, even if he can't stop the tremble in my voice. It's working.

"She said I was afraid of you. That I was so afraid of you."

"You were afraid of me. You were right to be."

Hot tears leak out from under my lashes. "I like to be afraid of you."

"I know. Your body tells me so." He leans down and kisses the tears away. Leo's whole body is alive with fury. I can feel it running under his skin like electricity. The sex didn't make it go away. "Where did she touch you?"

"My hair." Leo brushes it away from my face, deliberate. Forceful. Not like Caroline did. In the way that only Leo would.

"Where else?"

"My face."

He takes my face in a tight grip and brings it to his. Delivers a hard kiss. Harder. To the point of pain. To the point I gasp.

It erases Caroline's fingerprints.

"Where else?"

"She held my hand."

He threads his fingers through mine and lifts them to his lips. Then Leo presses his teeth into every one of my knuckles.

"Where else?"

"Nowhere else."

"Where did Rick touch you?"

"He kissed me," I admit, and it feels urgent now, it feels awful. It feels like a confession. My voice breaks. Crumbles. "I hated it. He made me sit on the couch with him. He leaned over me—"

Leo tenses, his arms pulling me in closer.

Locking me in. I'm safe here. "Did he—" He's not the kind of man who hesitates, but he does it now. The heartbeat of silence is an open wound, papered over with pain and violence. "Did he rape you?"

"He tried. And the worst part—the worst part was how gentle they were. I know it doesn't make any sense. It shouldn't have been so bad, since they didn't actually hurt me. They were soft about it." My stomach recoils from the memory.

He feels my involuntary, disgusted shudder and crushes me to his chest, squeezing so hard I can't breathe. And I don't want to. Because on the next inhale—

All the horror and fear of that moment comes back in a series of choking sobs that threaten to drown me. Leo turns me, arranges me, so that my head falls onto his shoulder, and my arms can go around his neck, and he can hold me there while I wring myself out. His hands splay out on my back, warm and solid. "I should have killed him when his neck was in my hands."

I swallow my next sob so I can hear, so I can think. "What?"

"He's a dead man."

I bury my face in Leo's neck. "Please, don't. Don't, Leo. Please. Just don't go anywhere tonight." I'm a mess. Falling apart.

Leo holds me tighter. To him, I'm not fragile, even now. He shushes me with his hand on the back of my neck, with his arms cradling me. "Not tonight," he promises. "Not tonight."

But there's tomorrow, and the next day, and the next. How are we ever supposed to have peace?

CHAPTER SEVEN

Leo

HALEY CRIES HERSELF to sleep on my shoulder.

She tried to minimize what Caroline did to her, and it is a fool's errand. Touch like that is a violation, and Caroline did it on purpose. She gave Rick permission to do what he did. There's no doubt in my mind. It was all planned by Caroline, all ordered by Caroline. The way her body shakes when she talks about it, even in the safety of my home, is a testament to how much she hated it. How much it repulsed her. How much shame it forced into her.

I know.

It takes her such a long time to relax that by the time her head is heavy, by the time she's given up all her weight to me, I'm on fire again.

I brush her hair away from her face and murmur in her ear. She doesn't stir. She stays asleep when I put her on the pillow and tug the covers over her. I'd planned to take her to the shower with me. It'll have to wait until morning. Probably better. That way, she won't see what a wreck I am.

Getting out of bed means gritting my teeth to stop myself from making any noise. My back is a mess of pain. All my muscles react to it. The only time it felt better was when I was fucking her, and I want more. The urge prowls under my skin. If she could handle it, I would bend her over the bed. I would fuck her all night. I would fuck her until a solution presented itself. I would fuck her until the end of time.

Instead, I go into the shower and turn it to cold. It's a pure chill, like a mountain spring, and it makes my lungs contract to stand in it. This is something to try when the pain has gone so haywire, when it's run so rampant, so out of control. I force myself through a full shower. Shampoo. Soap. And then I add several minutes of tolerating the freeze.

The pain lessens a little. It relocates itself in my back instead of all the way down my legs and over my head. The intensity remains the same.

I'm going to have to keep Haley with me. For her safety. For my sanity. I need a break. A minute.

The slicing sting relents a bit more when I get into bed with her and pull her warmth against me. She breathes faster at my touch but doesn't wake up. I drift next to her the rest of the night. No dreams come. Her skin under my hand is the only dream, and it batters my heart. Makes it ache. "I thought I'd lost you," I whisper to her at some point before dawn.

"I'm here," she says, her voice sleepy and warm, and after that I really do sleep.

Eva is waiting in the dining room in the morning. She's showered and changed and looks far less panicked than she did yesterday, though she scrutinizes us both shamelessly as we sit down at the table. I have Haley's hand in a tight grip. She didn't say she needed this from me, but she's coming down from the terror of being taken. She hesitated at the door to my bedroom before we came down. Swallowed hard. Put her hand in mine.

"How are you?" Eva asks Haley, who puts on a smile.

"I'm good," she says. "I'm good now."

Eva clearly doesn't believe her, but she nods, glancing down at her mostly untouched plate. "I think I should go home. Now that you're all right."

"I think not," I tell her. My back throbs this morning. Too dull to be excruciating, too painful to ignore. "You're staying until I've gone over your security teams. You need another layer until Caroline's under control."

My sister makes a show of looking around the dining room, but her shoulders have let down. "I don't see Lucian here. Why didn't you make him stay?"

"I'm not worried about Lucian. But if you're worrying about a lack of company, don't. Daphne is on her way."

If she's not in the car now, she will be as soon as she's up. I don't know what kind of hours she keeps with her art, and I don't particularly care. What I want is to have her where I can see her. Not in some studio apartment that's more difficult to defend than my home.

I ignore the thought that Haley was taken from this place and not Daphne's studio apartment.

"Good," Eva says. I didn't expect an argument from her, but I did expect protesting. My sister likes to think she's outgrown a need to be protected. She is mistaken. The enemy is not our father anymore. It's many more people who are enough like our father that they present a threat on the level of the Constantines.

I don't tell her about the worry that dogs me when it comes to security, that follows me now. Especially now that Lucian and I have gone into Caroline's house to retrieve Haley. Especially now that I've left evidence of my visit on her sons' faces.

We've moved to the den by the time Daphne arrives. Eva has gone upstairs to rest. I tried to make Haley rest too, but she wanted the den. Now she's under a blanket on the sofa and I'm at the window, looking out on the snow-covered courtyard. The alert that Daphne's here comes through on my phone, and a few minutes later, Daphne follows it.

She comes in like a wave moving quickly over sand. A beeline to where I'm standing, and I bend to angle her arms around my neck. It's never been more imperative that everything stays away from my back. Even with Haley in sight, I'm a human tripwire.

"Oh my god, Leo, you can't just summon me here," Daphne says as she releases me. "I'm fine. You could have texted me to ask if I was fine."

I steer her to the couch by her shoulders. Daphne sits, and watches me as I take the opposite seat. Haley closes her book and sits up.

"Hey, Daphne."

Daphne searches Haley's face, her artist's eyes taking everything in. "Something happened."

"Caroline sent one of her people here."

My sister's mouth drops open. "Did they come inside?"

"No. They didn't have to. Caroline's people put together a plan to cause a diversion and distract my security while Haley went out to meet her brother." It's a true effort to speak about this without snarling. Without standing up, finding the nearest guard, and beating the shit out of him. "They took her when she stepped outside the gates."

Daphne pales. Her head swivels to Haley. "Took you where?"

"Caroline's house."

Her brow furrows, and Daphne twists her fingers together in her lap. "I don't understand." This is why I brought her here. Now. This morning. Because she doesn't understand. I've worked so fucking hard to let her have her innocence that it's made her an easy target. "Caroline's your family. She sent someone to kidnap you?"

"Yes."

It sinks in for her then, what kind of family

the Constantines are. Daphne's expression turns utterly serious. "Did they hurt you?"

"No," Haley says.

"Don't lie," I tell her. Her blue eyes meet mine with a silent plea.

"I'm not lying."

"Don't. Lie."

The tension draws tight between us. I want to kneel down at her place on the sofa but I don't trust myself not to drag her upstairs by her hair and push her over the bed. I need it.

Haley takes a deep breath, then looks back at Daphne. "It's complicated," she says, and understanding passes over Daphne's face like she's heard Haley say this before. She probably has. They've had more than one conversation without me. "Nobody hit me. But it was still—" She shakes her head.

"I'm sorry." Daphne reaches for her hand. Squeezes it. Her eyes shine with unshed tears. "I'm sorry, Haley. I don't—I'm sorry."

"It's okay." This, from Haley, on a breath. Practically soundless.

"It's not," I say. "That's why you're here." Daphne's eyes snap to mine. "It's not safe for you. For any of us."

"I'm perfectly safe." Spots of color bloom high

on Daphne's cheeks. "Nobody's messing with me. Nobody even really knows I'm a Morelli, because I'm not—" She's about to say *not like you*. "I'm not open about it. Nobody's even been in my apartment at all, except—"

Except.

All my cells are on alert. Every muscle. It's the way I used to feel when I saw my father's car pull into the driveway at the end of the day. "Except?" I demand.

Daphne sighs. "Except for one person."

"Except for one man."

The deepening red of her face tells me all I need to know.

"Nothing happened," Daphne insists, letting go of Haley's hand.

"Bullshit. Explain."

Daphne bites her lip and lifts a hand to pull her hair back over her shoulder. A sidelong glance at Haley. "I wasn't even there. He just left something for me. A gift."

The words tick down like the timer on a bomb, and unadulterated rage bursts heavy onto my skin. It feels made of glass, made of molten glass, and every breath I take becomes an excruciating exercise in control.

I have never let Daphne see me at my worst.

Never. I've carried her in my arms to get her away from the sight, to keep her away from the knowledge. She can't know how close this animal is to the surface. How, if Haley wasn't here, I would get up from my seat and go hunting.

Haley is not Daphne. She and my sister might have had a similar innocence to begin with, but for one key difference—*I* happened to Haley. So Haley knows what she's looking at now. She feels it. Daphne is wide-eyed and red-faced. She doesn't know what I am.

"You have," I begin, and it takes everything I have to keep my voice even. "A fucking stalker."

Daphne's hand goes to her collar. "No! No. He just—he likes my paintings. He buys a lot of them. You know. Like a collector."

"He wants to collect your body in his basement, Daphne. He doesn't want your paintings. Men don't want your art. They're all sick fucks who want to use you for their own purposes. They'll discard you when they're finished, if they haven't murdered you first."

She lifts her chin, jaw tightening. "Oh? Like you're going to do to Haley?"

My entire soul recoils, hissing, feral, disgusted. "No," I snap at her, and Daphne flinches. I barely manage to get a handle on my tone even through the pang of regret. "Not like me with Haley."

Haley lets out a breath, and I can tell how badly she wants to come over to me, but she's torn. She's sweet, and she's a good friend, and she's torn, because to come over here would mean leaving Daphne by herself. And she won't do it.

"He's not dangerous," Daphne says.

"That's. Fucking. It." I go to the door and open it. Gerard's waiting outside. "Send a team to Daphne's apartment. Clear it out."

He nods and goes, and when I turn back, Daphne is staring at me. "What did you tell him to do?"

"I'm sending a team to get your things. You're moving in with me."

"Leo, no!" She stands up too and squares off with me, but it's useless. She's petite, like Haley. She's no match for the things I know, for the things I've lived. "I'm fine in my apartment. You have security there, too."

"I'm firing all of them. It will take some time to find replacements."

"Why? Why? I like them."

"Because they let a stalker into your apartment to leave a gift. What's next? Are they going to let him in to watch you sleep? Shower?"

"How is it better if you're the one watching

me sleep?"

"I'm not going to watch you sleep. I don't care if you sleep. Stay up all night, if you want."

"I want to stay in my apartment." Her eyes flash. "I belong in my apartment. I'm fine in my apartment."

"Will you be fine when you wake up to him standing over your bed one night?"

"Leo—"

"Will you be fine if you wake up gagged and bound? Tell me."

"That's not going to happen."

I step closer, look down at her, make her look up at me. It's an asshole move, and I know it. "And will you be fine if I have to come identify your body after he's murdered you? I'm the one who would get that call, by the way. Would that be all right, Daphne?"

Tears have gathered at the corners of Daphne's eyes. She doesn't let them fall. "He's not going to kill me." Her hands ball into fists at her sides. "He's not like that."

"Tell me his name, and I'll tell you if he's like that."

Daphne looks away. "I'm not telling you his name."

"Do you even know what it is?"

"Yes. I'm just not telling *you*. You'd go after him."

"He probably deserves it."

A ringing silence. Haley smooths her blanket over her legs, her eyes on mine. Does she wish I was softer, in this moment? I hope not. I can't be softer. Not with this rage eating through skin and bone.

"You are ridiculous," Daphne says, but I can feel her giving in.

I can also feel her resentment towards me, but that's all right. It doesn't matter if she hates me. As long as she's safe. I've always protected my sisters, from the time we were little, when our father hit us, but it feels sharper now, more acute since I almost lost Haley. "Good."

"How long am I supposed to stay here?"

"Until he forgets about you." I try to sound soothing. Even though I'd like to keep her here forever, locked up in some tower like a fairy tale princess.

"Like you're going to forget about Haley when she's gone?"

My dear sister says the question sweetly, because she knows, she *knows* I'll never forget about Haley. I will never get over her. "It's different," I say, which is a lie. It's not different.

She rolls her eyes. "It's different because you love her."

The word *love* makes my skin turn hot and then cold and clammy. I'm careful not to look at Haley. I don't want to see her reaction—either her hope or disappointment. "This isn't about me," I say, my teeth gritted.

"Isn't it?" she asks, her tone gentle, her expression knowing.

I'm reminded that even though she's innocent, she's a woman now. A woman who sees through my bluster. Who knows I'm exactly as bad as the man I'm guarding her from. I didn't get my reputation for nothing. The beast is too close to the surface. "This is about you being in over your head. I always knew you were naive, but I never thought you were a fool."

She gasps. Hurt simmers in her dark eyes. Anger, too.

"You want to end up on a true crime podcast? Not on my watch. I'm sorry if I ever gave you the impression you had a choice in the matter. You're staying here. End of story."

CHAPTER EIGHT

Haley

LEO'S HOUSE IS laden with silence. The quiet bleeds into every room, thickening the air. Making it hard to breathe. Hard to walk. My feet feel like I'm dragging them through water. I've woken up late. Late in the day, I mean. The sun angles dimly through the second-floor windows. How did that happen? A person doesn't just sleep all day and wake up to emptiness.

"Leo?"

My voice doesn't reach as far as it should. I clear my throat and try again. The house is quiet. I'm quiet. We're all quiet, like we've been tucked under blankets of insulation, like we've been buried in snow. Except I can see through the windows. Snow's not falling today.

No Eva in the guest bedroom.

No Gerard at the top of the stairs.

No Mrs. Page in the dining room.

It takes forever to walk from one room to the

next. I keep getting turned around. I think I'm near the den, but then I go in the door and it's Leo's bedroom. He's not in here. I trace a careful path back to the stairs and go down.

I reach his office door an eternity later. The door is shut tight. Jiggling the doorknob does absolutely nothing. Did he seriously lock me out of his office?

If he's in there now…

I press my ear to the hardwood, a dull indignation at the center of my chest.

And then I hear it.

A wet, choked rasp.

No. No, no, no. Leo's in there, and he's dying. I jerk my head away from the door but the sound only gets louder. I can hear him so clearly, but it won't open. Smooth metal denies my scratches. "Please," I beg the doorknob. It doesn't turn. My hands slip on the surface. I pound at the wood with a fist but it's solid, not like the flimsy doors in my house, it's solid enough to keep me from him. An agonized wheeze fills the hall, echoes in my ears. I can't find my phone. Where is my phone? There's no time to call anyone. I just have to get inside.

The doorknob rejects me. My hands slip off. I'm useless. So useless. I can't even put pressure on the wound. Silence rings around my scrabbling at the doorknob. No sirens. No one is coming.

I turn to look down the hall—Gerard has to have heard me—and when I turn back there's no doorknob. "No." It comes out on a whisper, my voice gone. All I have is my hands. I beat both fists against the door, again and again and again. It does nothing. Nothing. I beat harder. I'll tear through the damn thing. I'll tear it down. I clear my throat and try to shout for help again. A whisper. A pathetic whisper. Jesus.

"Help," I scream.

I try to scream. And fail. I am so useless that I can't even scream. My throat feels pinched tight. A hoarse whisper isn't going to get anyone's attention but I try again. "Help. Please, help."

Pain splinters through the side of my hand. My heart crashes in my throat. Pain has to be a good sign. It has to. The door shimmers in front of me. I'll let my hands break, I'll let the bones shatter, before I'll stop.

"Haley."

I don't turn toward the sound of my name. It's too easy to get turned around. Too easy to lose the door. I won't lose him, I won't, I won't. "Help." I get a whisper, but I need a scream. I need him.

"Darling. Wake up."

I bring my hand down hard, the pain bruising now. Someone catches my hand. "Stop. No. Stop." Arms now. Strong ones, wrapping around me from behind. Adrenaline surges, cold and silver through my veins. "I have to get to the door. Let go, let go—"

"I need you to wake up. You'll hurt yourself."

A big hand comes around to my face and shakes. It breaks my focus on the door. No, damn it, I can't lose it. I don't know where to kick, where to aim my punches, and there's nowhere, because he's behind me.

"You're dreaming." Leo's voice is pure, dark command, and it shatters the door, the dream, everything. "It's not real. You're safe. Wake up."

My body throws itself against his arms, struggling. Fighting to get free. The dream has shadows on me. Tendrils. The panic. It won't let go. "Stop," I gasp.

"No. You were beating the shit out of the headboard." He drags me back. Holds me to his chest. "Stop fighting or I'll hold you down."

"I can't stop." Taking a normal breath is beyond me, too. They're coming faster than I can control. I'm kicking at nothing. Meeting blankets and pillows. I dig one heel in and throw all my weight against him. It's so close. The blood. The drowning gasps. They could pull me back under, and I wouldn't resurface. "You have to make me."

Leo's arms tense, his body braced behind mine. I'm a whirlwind. Everything is disjointed. He's the only thing in the room that doesn't spin. I can see the outline of his office door. I get one fist up, but he gathers it in and pins both my arms to my chest.

"You were having a nightmare," he says into my ear. There's no power in shouting, I see now. I know now. He could own me without ever raising his voice. I need him to own me now. "You're not with Caroline anymore. She can't touch you. Rick can't touch you. This is my house."

A lightning flash of memory, of fear. "It wasn't about Caroline." My lungs contract. Not enough air to breathe. Not enough to scream. "It was about you."

He goes absolutely still, the only movement of him a counterpressure against me. Against my struggling self. Shock vibrates through his body. "About me."

"You were shot." I can feel a wave of sobs about to crest, and I don't want it, I don't want to cry about Ronan shooting Leo, I don't want to cry about a nightmare. "You were dying. I could hear you breathing but I couldn't get into your office. I couldn't do anything. I was useless. Useless to protect you, to save you. You were dying behind that door, and I couldn't do anything."

"Jesus," he says on an exhale, and then we're moving. It's out of my hands. He's too strong, and I'm in his arms, and I can't stop him. Leo stands us both up and bends me over the bed.

"I can't stop." It's true. I'm resisting him, pushing up against his hands. It's not enough.

A low laugh. "Do you think for a moment I can't stop you?"

"You got hurt." I hear the sound again. "Maybe—"

He wrestles my arms behind my back. A drawer opens. His bedside table, I think, and then he's binding my wrists together. So practiced. So measured. So mean. But not like he was. He's different now, different since I told him about the dream, but I can't place how. Leo keeps me down with one broad hand on my upper back. My cheek presses into soft covers that smell like him.

The drawer snaps closed. Leo's hand is at my waist, doing away with my panties, and when he's finished he kicks my legs apart. "Wider," he demands. Rough. Impatient. I inch my feet out.

"Until your thighs burn, darling. Don't make me wait."

A whimper escapes me. They're burning now, and I'm at the edge of a precipice. Right on the threshold of another nightmare. The pressure on my upper back increases.

And then, between my legs—

Cool leather.

I can't stop my frantic inhale, or hide it. My knees buckle at the kiss of the strap.

"You remembered," Leo says.

Yes. Yes, I remember. I remember being bent over the bed in the guest bedroom. I remember how the leather felt like fire against my ass. I remember *I like it when you cry.* I remember everything.

Leo slides the whole length of the strap over my pussy. "You're out of control, darling." He tests the theory by lifting his hand off my back. My whole body bucks. He pushes me back down with a disapproving sound. "Three should bring you back."

The strap meets my wet center again, and with a shock I see what he's going to do. "Not there," I beg.

"Keep your thighs open, or it'll be six."

"No—"

The word is broken in two by the first blow. I turn my head and howl into the covers. My legs shake. My toes dig in. Leo doesn't relent. He presses the strap against my pussy again—to warn me, I guess, of where it's going to land—and draws it back.

The worst part isn't the pain. The worst part is how good it feels to scream. This hurt is one I recognize. It's sharp, oh, god, it's sharp, it hurts, but I know where it ends. It's not the depthless panic of hearing him drown in his own blood. It's just pain that Leo's causing. Because he can. Because he lived. He didn't die. I was there with him.

Something unwinds, and tears run down my cheeks. Leo's hand gentles on my back but doesn't let up. "Hurts like a motherfucker," he says softly.

I get in a hitching breath. "Give me. The third one."

He does, and when it lands, I can't tell if I'm moaning or sobbing. Both, I think. Both, and it's humiliating, and it's perfect. Because Leo's alive. He drops to his knees behind me and then his mouth is hot on my aching, punished flesh. He spreads me wider with both hands, leaving me slumped over the bed. The softness of his tongue is intensified by the hard slap of the belt and my hips don't know what to do. They rock back and forth. His tongue. The edge of the bed. His tongue. He licks higher, over even more sensitive, secret parts of me. The trembling is all pleasure now. All freedom.

It doesn't matter that my hands are tied. The nightmare is gone.

Leo pushes his tongue into me.

"Oh, I want, I want—"

A slap to my ass stops my pointless begging. I don't have to ask. He'll give me what he wants to give me, and it'll be just what I need. I lose myself in the pressure and glide of his tongue. He won't stop. He just keeps pushing and pushing until I'm at the peak. Until I'm over it, coming on his tongue, and even then he keeps up his relentless assault on my clit. A soft, torturing thing that gives me aftershocks of orgasm. He makes a sound like he's just eaten something unbearably sweet and stands up.

Pushes my legs together. Makes me arch. He's making me tighter for him. I realize it in a delirious haze just before he shoves the head of his cock into the place he's just prepared.

I'm still new at this. I have to stretch, even though we've fucked, even though I've been fucked by him. Leo shivers behind me. He has to let go for that to happen, I know now, he has to consciously decide to be that way. To be that revealing. It's so hot. His fingers digging into my hips. His thickness filling me. He's in control of himself. That's what it is. He's not the beast, not now. Something brought him back from the electric, boiling tension of the last few days.

He's in control of himself, and he's in control of me.

"I wasn't your nightmare," he says, tone almost conversational, but I can hear the raw need in his voice. "You weren't dreaming about me. About me hurting you."

"No." It's hard to say anything else with him stroking into me, harder with every thrust, my hips hitting the edge of the bed with thud after thud. "Not you."

Leo does something at my wrists and my hands come free, but he doesn't let them stay that way for long. He curls his fingers around both wrists and pins them to the bed so he's over me. So he's everywhere in the dark. In the moonlight. The head of him meets some inner place he hasn't touched before and I spread my legs on instinct. Give him more room. He's so big, he needs more room. He drops a kiss to my shoulder. A bite.

He releases my wrists. One of his hands goes

to my throat. The other between my legs. I whimper when his fingers meet the soreness from being strapped there. A pinch to the clit makes my legs give out for real. I'm held in place by his hands, and his cock, and if it weren't for those things, I'd be a puddle on the floor.

"Your pussy loves that," he growls into my ear. "You like when I hurt you."

"Just you," I breathe as his fingers play at my clit, gentler now but no less insistent. He's going to make me come again. "It loves you. Anything you do to me."

"The next time you try to hurt yourself for me, I'll fuck your ass until you scream. I won't stop for tears. I'm the only one who hurts you. Do you understand?"

I can't speak. I'm too close to a violent orgasm, one brought on by his words and his relentless fingers. Too close to coming apart. The nightmare carried me to the edge. Leo Morelli's pushing me over. He's the only one who can hurt me, and he does it so well.

His grip tightens around my throat. He thrusts his cock home. "Please," I choke out. "Yes."

"I'll be your nightmare," he says, and I come so hard I drag him over with me.

CHAPTER NINE

Leo

THE VOICEMAIL COMES in too early to be a polite call. Just after seven. I didn't notice the call itself. I've been sitting in the only way I can at this moment, with my head in my hands, watching the corners of the room take on the hue of the dawn. At various intervals I look out the front windows of my house, down onto the driveway. From this smaller library and sitting room I have a clear view of anyone approaching the house from the road.

Sleeping is becoming impossible. Fucking Haley last night, feeling her cunt ripple and clench around me, bought me three hours. Then came the pain. Then came the guilt. She was terrified when I found her in the bed. Cracking her fists against the headboard like it was a door to a prison cell. What she imagined was worse. My office. Not being able to get to me.

A better man would have whispered sweet

nothings to her and stroked her face until she fell back asleep.

I'm not a better man.

And Haley, for all her innocence, for all her sweetness, can't stand gentleness. Not right now.

So I have been awake. My back is killing me. Razors down my spine and across my ribs. And a restless, unsettled pit that can only be soothed in a way that's not available to me in the daylight. That will have to wait.

My phone buzzes again and I swipe it off the table by my chair.

A voicemail from Lucian.

Lucky me.

I lean on the arm of the chair, prop my forehead in my hand, and hold the phone to my ear. I don't particularly want to hear what Lucian has to say on his way home from his sex club. His recent involvement with my security team means I have to listen. I don't trust how much he's become involved. I don't like how much he knows. My eldest brother is coming dangerously close to the real secret of what happened with Caroline, and I hate that.

I hate it so much I miss the beginning of the message and have to start over.

"Learn to answer your phone when people

call, Leo. Voicemail is for hired help and women you want to avoid. Elaine has had an interesting conversation with her mother." He takes a barely noticeable breath. Elaine. That's right. Has he been at the sex club with her? Without her? Why the hell is he up so early? I don't care. "Caroline has been bribing Rick Joseph Jr. with a place in the Constantine family in exchange for doing her a favor."

The favor will be to kill me.

"She wants him to kill you. Kill the Beast of Bishop's Landing, and Caroline will make him a hero. She'll make Haley his wife."

My spine goes up in flames at the suggestion. At this fucked-up promise that Caroline can't make, but that she has made to Rick Joseph Jr.. That's why he kept his mouth shut while I beat the hell out of him. He thought he had something on me. He thought if he could survive me, he'd have a chance to get what he wants.

An insidious voice hisses like a snake in the back of my mind. *She would be better off with him. Hand-picked by the Constantines. He'd give her family back to her.*

It's bullshit.

What's not bullshit is the thought underneath.

97

She would be better off without me.

Lucian's voicemail continues.

"—come to dinner—"

What the fuck?

I start the damn thing over and listen again.

"I'm so pleased to accept your invitation, Leo. Of course we'll come to dinner tonight. Happy to accept your thanks for helping to rescue the love of your life and then ensuring your safety while you shut yourself up in your room with her. Elaine can't wait."

That's where it ends.

I let the phone fall onto the bedside table. "Christ."

"What is it?"

Haley's at the door, cheeks pink with sleep, her hair so adorably rumpled and gold in the morning light that I could believe it had some healing quality to it. Like running my fingers through it could be a kind of blessing. She wore one of my shirts to bed last night. I almost order her to take it off, but she needs an answer first. This surprise dinner party will take up the rest of the day.

I beckon her over to me and pull her into my lap. She's as warm as she is pink, and the scent of her skin calms some part of me that's been knotted and tense while I waited for the night to be over. Haley kisses the side of my neck, waiting.

"Lucian called," I tell her. "He and Elaine are coming for dinner tonight. Now lift up your shirt. I need to see you."

✧　✧　✧

HALEY STANDS IN the middle of my bedroom in an Armani dinner gown in black, looking down at its shimmer, which reminds me of starlight. She bites at her lip. "Are you sure about this?"

"It's the perfect dress for you."

"I meant—"

I finish buttoning my jacket and cut off her question with a kiss. A forceful grip on her chin, her lips soft against mine. "I know what you meant. And you're coming to dinner."

Haley has been fretting about the dinner since I told her about it. I've been pretending to be completely at ease with a dinner party that my brother has demanded. Let him in the house once, and he'll keep coming back. Of course, I am not at ease. Of course, pain has spidered out along my ribs from the added stress.

Nothing to be done about it now.

"Do you always dress up when your brother comes to dinner?" She's peeking at us in the mirror.

"Lucian's never been here for dinners. But for other family gatherings, we dress."

A slow nod. "Have you been to one? Since I came to stay with you?"

"No." Haley doesn't ask why, but the answer is obvious. She was here, and then Ronan paid his visit, and so far I have missed one family dinner. I've missed other commitments as well. Commitments I've never told her about. Important ones. "Let's go, darling. They'll be here any minute."

I usher Haley out of the bedroom and down the stairs to the foyer. We arrive at our place by the doors just as the doorbell rings. I didn't give a shit what Lucian did the night I brought Haley home, but now I feel unsettled to have him here. It's less tightly controlled than I'd prefer. My life is less tightly controlled, now that Haley's in it.

Gerard opens the door to let in Lucian and Elaine. Haley steps closer to my side. She saw him at Caroline's, but this is different. He's sharp as a knife in his suit, a stark contrast to Elaine's red dress. She's a ruby come to life, her eyes as bright as his. A match.

Like Haley is a match for me now. She's the one who chose black, and she draws herself up next to me, her chin lifting. If I didn't know her, if I didn't spend every available second drinking in her expressions, I wouldn't know she was nervous. It's not just Lucian, either. It's Elaine.

Elaine, who might be Caroline's wildest daughter, but who is still Caroline's daughter. I can tell from Haley's shallow breaths that she doesn't think she measures up. But even without her hair shining in its twist the way it is, even without the dramatic makeup, she surpasses every other woman on the planet.

Lucian brushes a stray lock of hair back from Elaine's cheek, the two of them making a portrait. Morellis are always putting on a show. He is no exception. He's created a dark frame for Elaine's red dress.

"Hello, little brother," he says, glancing between Haley and me. "Haley."

"Haley," Elaine echoes, her pointed, perfect smile broadening. "I didn't think I'd ever find another Constantine in this family." She leaves Lucian's side and links her arm through Haley's. I hold my breath. "How are you?"

Haley allows herself to be led away, glancing back at me only once. I don't hear her murmured answer. The touch was a risk on Elaine's part, but Haley doesn't pull away. This is perhaps the first time in history that Lucian's presence has made a situation more tolerable. Less tense. Elaine can't be with Lucian and be in league with Caroline.

When they've disappeared into the dining room, Lucian scans the foyer. The visible security. The lack of our sisters. "Where are the girls?"

Eva and Daphne. "Upstairs. They should be down soon." A sigh escapes before I can stop it. "Daphne isn't speaking to me."

Lucian arches an eyebrow, watching my face with that pointed stare of his.

"The security in her loft is shit, so I made her move in here for the time being. And she has a stalker."

He blinks. "What the hell?"

"I'm taking care of it."

Lucian slides his hands into his pockets, his posture casual. "You always did that. Take care of the family." A pause. "It should have been my job."

I look away, toward the dining room. Toward anywhere that isn't him. I don't want to get into the past, though it's true. Lucian was always a cold motherfucker. Some of it came from living under our father's influence, and his fucked-up behavior driving a wedge between us. Some of it was his inability to feel pain. And some of it was just Lucian Morelli.

"You're back now. Aren't you?" I will never expect for him to take over from me in any meaningful way, but with my back on fire and Caroline making unhinged promises to anyone who will listen, a part of me wishes he would.

Pointlessly. Foolishly.

"Yeah," he says, eyes meeting mine. "I'm here to stay."

"Were you waiting for us? How nice." Eva descends the stairs with Daphne by her side. Daphne's worn a gown of emerald green, her hair in loose waves, and Eva's in sleek black with her hair in a twist that matches Haley's. Eva is the only one to look at me on the way down.

"Of course we were," says Lucian. "We have manners."

Eva rolls her eyes. "Debatable." But she leads the way into the dining room anyway, where Elaine and Haley are by the window. The six of us take our seats around the table. My staff spent the day rearranging the room, taking furniture out, and redecorating for this dinner. It's understated, black and gold, and Lucian takes it in with an appraising glance. Eva waves the staff in as soon as we're seated.

"You have enough room to fit all of us," Lucian comments. "Do you plan on it?"

"Not today." Not ever. I have never planned to have all my siblings to dinner at my house.

"I can't believe you left Lizzy out," my brother needles. "You couldn't have flown her here?"

"You put Leo in charge of the guest list?" Eva asks the question with faux shock on her face. "You're lucky he let you in." True. "Which one of you forgot Sophia?"

"No one forgot Sophia," I sigh. "No one forgot Carter. No one forgot Tiernan. If you missed me this much, Lucian, all you had to do was call. You didn't have to insist on a dinner party." I invited Sophia but she declined to come. She's probably in some unsavory part of the city stirring up trouble. Carter is the quietest of all the Morellis. Serious. And a genius. He went to Oxford for college and stayed overseas, preferring it to the drama of home. And Tiernan—Tiernan is my father's hired hand. He's always been so determined to get our father's approval that he's let himself be used to hurt, to maim, to kill.

"You invited me," Lucian says, a glint in his eyes.

"You mean he didn't throw you out," answers Eva.

"Not yet," says Haley. Eva snorts. The tension

breaks. And it's dinner, and not some high-stakes negotiation like it is at the Morelli mansion.

It's different, without my parents here to mangle it. Daphne won't look at me, but Eva is a good host. She asks Haley about a book she's read and Elaine about a new restaurant that opened in the city.

"You should try it," I tell Eva, when Elaine finishes describing the place. I've hardly heard her, but Eva looks interested. "I finished the security review yesterday."

What I mean is that she's free to go back to her apartment, if she wants. "Thank you," she says, and reaches over Haley to pat my hand. Elaine watches this with interest. I can see her Constantine mind working, replacing what she's always known about us with what's happening in front of her.

"You're welcome."

Everyone loves the first course, smoked trout crostini with grilled fennel that Eva chose. She didn't mind planning the party, just like she didn't mind redecorating my guest bedrooms. She's smiling with pleasure by the second course. My sister thrives in last-minute situations. In the hurry and the adrenaline and all the many, many details. It gives her a slice of happiness to do this, but I wish there was more.

More happiness than a damned dinner party. I despise Lane Constantine. May his soul rot in hell forever.

One of the waiters is refilling Lucian's wineglass when my brother turns his attention to Daphne. "So," he says to her. "I hear you have a stalker."

Daphne glares at me, forgetting to keep her eyes carefully away. Haley puts her head in her hands. And Elaine coos, "Oh, sweetheart, the obsessed ones are the best ones."

As she says it, Lucian traces a single fingertip over the curve of her neck, his eyes drinking in his touch on her flesh like he can taste it.

"He's not a stalker," Daphne insists.

"He is." I address Lucian and Elaine, because Daphne and I have had this argument. "He came into her apartment when she wasn't there and left a gift. I had to fire a whole security team for the lapse."

"A charming stalker?" Elaine's eyes light up. "How'd he get past them?"

"Just because he likes my art doesn't make him a stalker, Leo," Daphne says pointedly.

"No. His having your address, going inside your apartment, and leaving things for you when you're not there makes him a stalker, Daphne."

"Anyway," she says. "I don't understand why I'm so interesting. Are we not even going to talk about how there are two Constantines at the table? Our mortal enemies?" Daphne says this with a Morelli gleam to her narrowed eyes. She's paying us back. Causing a bit of trouble. It's for show. She likes Haley, and given time, she'll probably like Elaine too.

"Constantines can be convinced," Lucian says, toying with the strap on Elaine's dress. "It's hard to stay mortal enemies if you put enough sweat and tears into the project. They are stubborn, however. I plan to keep convincing Elaine forever."

I swallow hard around a knot of jealousy in my throat. Haley leans into me. It's subtle, but I feel her heat now. I want more of it.

I want forever with her, but I can't even promise her tomorrow.

CHAPTER TEN

Leo

EVA LEAVES THREE days later. Daphne doesn't come down from the suite in one of the towers. I don't know what she's doing. Painting, maybe. Doesn't matter. She can be pissed at me all she wants.

Better that than dead.

Haley is restless after Eva leaves. It's a bitter day, and she looks longingly out the window in my bedroom. "I wish it wasn't so cold."

I wish I could heat the earth for her. Make it summer. I would love to see her in a sundress. The dress she wears now is alluring for how much skin it covers in its comfortable fabric. I want her in it. But I want her in warmth, too.

"We can walk inside. You haven't spent much time in the rest of the house."

Her eyes light up. "Yes, yes, yes. Show me somewhere I've never been."

Haley's seen the den, my office, the kitchen,

and the courtyard. Once we're past the kitchen I let her open doors at random. "Leo, this ballroom is *huge*."

I look in over her shoulder. It's a dark room, the windows covered with curtains, the furniture covered in white cloth, gathering dust. "I've never used it. I don't throw parties."

"Dinner parties count, don't they?"

"I don't throw parties like this. With that many guests."

She purses her lips, but doesn't ask why.

I'm hardly thinking of the shelf, pushing the thought away, when she opens a door and draws in a breath. "What's this room? Another living room?"

It's flooded with light. The furniture is recently dusted. Everything perfect. It's not like the den, where Haley might leave a book out. Where a blanket might slip down off the couch and have to be straightened. "It's a study. I don't use it either."

"No? It's gorgeous in here." Haley steps inside, and I follow her, ignoring the unease at the pit of my gut. She does a slow turn in the middle of the floor.

"What do you think about building a library?"

She stops, a delighted laugh on her lips.

"What about your den? It's so nice."

"What about you liking libraries?" I follow her farther into the room, my pulse ticking up. "This space could use more books."

Haley's traveling around in it now, skimming her fingers over the back of an elegant sofa and opening a drawer on the desk to see what's inside. A mirror behind her gives me a perfect view as she pulls the antique handle. The drawer is empty. When her eyes lift from the drawer, they brighten with curiosity. It sparkles in her blue eyes. For an unused room, there's plenty to see. Haley drops her gaze again and continues around the room. She stops at a painting on the wall. Skims her fingertips over a miniature statue of a rose, perched in an alcove on the wall. Touches a piece of stained glass hung up on a stretch of white.

I follow her toward the desk, but it's too difficult to watch. I've become used to her looking through the shelves in the den and pulling out my books. I'm not used to this. My stomach tightens with nerves. I could stop her. It would be easy to stop her, to hold her down, to kiss her and fuck her and demand every scrap of her attention.

The first time she discovered one of my secrets, I let the beast loose on her. Fucked her throat. Scared her so badly she ran from me.

This time, I turn away and reassess the room. No library I built would be complete without one or two reading nooks. It would take some relatively involved renovation, but it wouldn't be impossible. I could do it. Leave the light intact, but make it comfortable. I try to picture it.

I end up envisioning Haley. Innocent, perfect, depraved Haley, curled up by all these windows with a book. Only in this vision I'm reading with her. In this vision, I'm reclining on the couch, Haley nestled next to me, and nothing hurts at all. It's as vivid as any daydream I've ever had. Meanwhile, she's behind me, rustling through the space.

There's a chance she overlooks that bookcase, that shelf. What's on it.

I go back to picturing her naked, bent over an armchair. Waiting for punishment or pleasure or just me.

"Leo." I turn at the sound of her soft voice, turn to her blue eyes, filled with worry and hope. A memory, too. Me storming out of my shower. Her with nowhere to run. "This is you. Isn't it?"

She has the photo in her hand. The photo, in its plain black frame. It's been sitting on that arched bookcase since the day I moved in here. At least once a year I think about throwing it out.

I've never been able to.

I take the frame out of her hands and look down at my fourteen-year-old self. In the photo, I'm sitting on a dock somewhere in the Bahamas in a pair of blue swim trunks. Nothing about them was custom-made or special. They didn't have to be. Something happens to my heart. A punishing squeeze. A tear. I don't look at that shelf, or that photo, because this feeling is hard to name and harder to feel.

In the photo, my entire back is visible. There's not a mark on it. My head is turned, and I'm grinning at the camera, as carefree as I ever would be again. Laughter in my eyes. My father was a prick. An asshole. But the bruises he left always faded. They were tempered by a righteous cause. Any mark he made on me was one less he made on my siblings, so what did I care?

Haley presses her side against mine so we're both looking at it together. Now that she's here, now that she's close, I would call this feeling grief. I'm looking at a person who's been dead for eighteen years. Who never had a chance to become anything. The person in this photo died at Caroline's hands. My death began before the whipping. With touches that didn't cause the kind of pain my father did. That they were gentle in comparison to my father changed almost nothing.

I feel flayed by this moment. By Haley, standing next to me, looking down at this person I haven't been and never will be. I look happy. There's light in my eyes. An ease to my body I can't remember having at all. Caroline took that from me.

Haley loops her arm through mine and rests her head on my arm. "How old are you in this?"

I clear my throat. "Fourteen. This is—" Fuck. I haven't spoken these words to anyone. Ever. "This is the last photo of me before Caroline." It's the last photo taken of me when I had a chance to be different. I only kept it because my sisters are in the background in matching bathing suits, getting ready to jump into the water. Laughing and laughing.

"You're grinning," Haley says, her voice soft as a rose petal.

"I was a different person then. A person you've never met."

She studies my face, then looks back down at the photo. I hope she can ignore the subtle shake in my hands. Emotion bristles and cuts, magnified by the pain in my back, intensified by her presence. My siblings sat around the table in my dining room last night. Haley sat with them. Elaine. It felt almost normal. That normalcy is unsettling. It makes me think there's a life that doesn't involve constant battles, constant pain.

But that can't be right. I'm the source. I'm the one who fights. I have to. Always, always.

"You're not so different. You still care about your family. You still protect them."

By being the villain. Pain flares over my scars, and I grip the frame tighter. I am not the person in this photo. I will never be that person, no matter how many times I wish or hope or pray.

"No. I'm the beast now. The nightmare." Looking at myself as I was before offers a wrenching contrast to now, to this emptiness, to the hurt that fills every breath. "I'm different. Ruined. Violent."

Haley slides her hand around my bicep, stroking like I'm on the verge of losing control. I'm not. It's just old anger coming to the surface. It's just old habits, as if being confronted with this person is a threat. He is not. I'm the threat. "I see you for what you are. You're a prince. My prince."

I can't be. I can't do this to her. Haley is like the person laughing in the photo. She is still relatively clean. She is still undamaged, if I can keep her that way. The biggest danger to her has always been me. Ever since the moment I saw her in that alley. Ever since the moment her eyes met mine.

"I'm not a fucking prince." I drop the frame and it clatters onto the rug, turning facedown. And then I undo the buttons on my shirt. Strip my undershirt over my head. My heart pounds at the exposure. At the shame. Haley backs up a step, her lips parted, her blue eyes wide, and I can't bear it, the look in her eyes. I turn away from it. Plant both hands on the desk. The sun breaks free from a cloud and golden light pours into the room. It shows everything. "Look at me. *Look.*"

I demanded that she look at me, but I'm the one who can't stop looking at her. In the mirror Haley is a creature of sunlight. All sweet, gold softness. And I'm myself. I wait for horror to overcome her features. Or worse, pity. I wait for the expression on her face to match the hurt that roils through me.

Her eyes meet mine in the mirror. They're crystalline blue in this light. The color of the water in that photo. "I've seen you, Leo. Lots of times. When you were sick. When you brought me home."

"Not like this. Not in daylight. You can't deny it to yourself here, darling. I'm a monster."

Haley takes a deep breath and steps closer. Closer again. She's doing what I told her to do. She's looking. Outside of a parade of anonymous doctors, outside of Eva, I've never allowed anyone to look at me like this. It hurts like a motherfucker to hold still and let it happen. Haley studies the scars without flinching. Without recoiling. Without disgust twisting her lips.

"It's just scars. It's just your skin."

A bitter laugh slices out of my throat. "It's proof of how weak I am. What kind of fucked-up soul I have."

Haley shakes her head, and I didn't know how much I needed for her to deny this until she does. "It's not." She carefully, deliberately touches the top of my shoulder, where there are no marks. "Does it hurt right now?"

"All the time. Since you were taken. Every moment."

"Is there anything you can take? Like when you were in the hospital. Is there anything you can have that would help?"

"I can't take them. The only ones that touch the pain are so powerful that I can't avoid unconsciousness. And I can't be unconscious, darling. I can't protect anyone that way. I can't keep myself alive."

I expect tears. I expect to have to console her in this, but Haley nods. Her eyes catch mine again in the mirror. "Will it hurt more if I touch them?"

"Do it anyway."

She has always been so careful, since that day at the shower, never to cause me more pain. Haley. The innocent I'm in the process of ruining. And she is careful now. Her hands are soft, like they were when she cleaned my stab wound, like they were when she held me after I was shot. Her breathing is even, as if she's not looking at a horror show. She strokes her fingertips over my unmarked flesh, down toward the scars, and my body braces itself for searing pain.

But there's only a featherlight touch. Soft as one of my shirts. I discover I've closed my eyes when I open them to seek her out in the mirror. Haley's looking at her fingertips on my destroyed skin. My heart is a raw, convulsing thing. Hope and pain are both jagged in my veins, in my muscles. She ignores the barely controlled trembling. Haley traces one scar, then the next, and the next. The anticipation of pain bleeds out of me. My skin has gone hot with the shame of having to be touched like this, like I'm made of glass, but that dissipates, too.

It leaves something else in its wake.

She reaches the last scar, the last wound, the last inch, and lets out a breath. "You," she says, and then she leans in and kisses the first scar, the one across my shoulder blades.

It hauls a gasp out of me. Haley might as well have my whole bloody heart in her palms.

She kisses me again.

It's too much, and I'm too desperate for it. It's absolution I don't deserve. That I never thought was possible. I turn around and kiss her mouth and she flings her arms around my neck, holding on tight while I bite her. Claim her. Let her see.

CHAPTER ELEVEN

Haley

LEO CRUSHES HIS mouth to mine with so much force that I can feel him breaking underneath it. I can feel how far this has pushed him. He's right. I've never seen his skin in daylight before. Only the murky half-light of his bedroom when he burned with fever, and I didn't really see it then. I was too focused on keeping him alive.

But now he is alive, now he is warm and alive and holding me to him with all his strength. His kisses are echoes of the way he looked at me in the mirror, echoes of the blaze in his dark eyes. The fire there. The storm.

The sun gets brighter as he lets me up for air, catching in his dark hair like a halo. Sun, no sun, it doesn't matter. I'm lit up with him. Panting with the kiss and this fresh intimacy. We've never been this close. Never, never, and my heart bruises and breaks.

Leo's eyes rake down over me. They stop at the hollow of my throat. At my chest, rising and falling. He's thick and hard between us. His hand comes up to circle my throat.

"I'm a monster," he says again, squeezing.

I use the last of my breath to deny him. "No."

He hauls me up onto the wide desk with him, making me straddle him. My thighs spread wide over his hips while he pulls me down for another kiss. The fact that I'm on top changes nothing about his control or his dominance. I might as well be bound with my wrists above my head for all the power I have now.

His hand remains wrapped around my throat. Dark eyes hot and wounded on mine. He's waiting for me to admit that he's monstrous, that he's terrifying, that he's a ruined soul.

If Leo Morelli is ruined, so am I.

He watches me pant in his grip. Looks down at my dress flowing over us both. "Take it off."

I shove it over my head, more aware of it now. I know by the feel of it that it was made from the same fabric as his shirts. He's started dressing me in it, too. He makes a low noise at the sight of my bra and panties. "Show me your tits. I know how much you love that."

He accused me of it before. Of liking to show

myself off for him. I tried to tell myself I hated it, but I don't. I love it. Heat flashes across my face, but I keep my eyes on his when I take off my bra and arch my back.

Leo squeezes my neck to make me arch it more and curses under his breath. It seems impossible for him to maintain such perfect balance without bracing himself, but then he has to be strong like this. He's had no choice. His abs have been carved out by necessity.

He uses his free hand to brush a thumb over one nipple, then the other, until both of them stand out. "Have you ruined your panties yet? Touch them and tell me."

I slip my hand down to the delicate fabric. "They're wet," I whisper. He pushes his thumb into my throat to feel the words. "Does that make them ruined?"

"It makes you filthy, darling. Your cunt loves a sadistic bastard. Your cunt loves a monster."

A squeeze cuts off my ability to say that it's him I love. It wouldn't be the first time. I've told him twice, but he was sick or sleeping and didn't hear.

He hooks a finger through the waistband and pulls them against my hip until the threads fray. One swift yank finishes them. A breath of a moan works past his hand and he makes an answering sound. A pleased one. I want him to be pleased. I want him to not be in pain. I would trade anything for that, I think. Anything.

"Look in the mirror."

I'm busy melting into his touch, melting into his control, but I open my eyes and look. I can see him. His hair, his arms. See his grip on my neck. See every one of his scars. He's giving me permission to see them. Leo could order me to close my eyes and I would, but he doesn't. A frisson touches down. It tightens my nipples. Sends a chill racing up my spine. In the mirror, Leo bows his head and sinks his teeth into my collarbone.

It pulls a cry out of me that he soothes with a kiss, with his tongue. Thick fingers make contact with my pussy, stroking there, dragging through a wetness that humiliates me. Or maybe I just like being humiliated by him. His thumb circles my clit. Leo kisses the side of my neck. "Your thighs are shaking," he murmurs into my ear. "You're a slut for my hand around your throat."

He works his fingers inside me and everything clenches. Leo won't let me move down, won't let me fuck his fingers. He holds me up by the neck. I'm flushed in the mirror, my eyes wide and desperate. My lips parted. Wanting him. He's angled us so I can see everything he's been trying to hide. His back. His pain. Me. He's tried to hide me, too. To protect me? To protect him? It's too hard to think with his thumb on my clit. He's mean that way, not letting me take any more of him. This is the only time it's good to be useless. It doesn't make me feel bitterly ashamed. Because he loves it so much.

I chase more contact with his thumb, chase more contact with his fingers. My orgasm stays just out of reach. I don't know why. I'm so wet, so hot, and—

"You need to come."

"Yes," I gasp. "I can't. And I don't—"

"Is it the mirror?"

"No." I could look at his body forever. I don't care if he has scars. I meant what I said. It's his skin. It's him. I'm not afraid of it, not disgusted by it, or him. I reach over his shoulder and brush my fingertips against one of his scars. The act of doing it, the act of being this close to him, makes my pussy pulse around the invasion of his fingers.

The sound he makes then is closer to the beast than to Leo, and then his hand is gone from my throat. It's fisted in my hair, pulling my head back, letting me sink all the way down to his fingers. "It hurts," I breathe, pain arcing over my scalp.

Leo hooks his fingers and my orgasm implodes. I keep my eyes open. I know he wants me to. So I see his eyes burn. I see them flare with possession and pain and a deep relief. "Fuck, darling," he says. "I want your cunt squeezing my cock. You're going to give it to me."

I haven't stopped coming, my breaths coming too fast and hard, when he pulls his fingers out. Shoves down his zipper, and his pants. Then his palms are on my hips, guiding me to his cock, and thrusting in.

He groans, and for the first time he has to adjust. Leo plants one big palm on the desk behind him and puts the other on the back of my neck. He's already made me come once and it still takes time to get used to him. To get used to the presence of him inside me. He's so big. So hard. He's the only man who's ever fucked me. He's the only man I want. I hook my chin over his shoulder. Let my arms drape around him. Work my hips. Leo's letting me have the illusion of control. He could take it back any time, but it's a test—that's what it is, a test. He can't help it. He needs it.

My thighs burn with the effort of fucking

him. Of staying as close as I possibly can. I push myself down another inch and groan at the stretch. Under his skin, his heart pounds. The only gentle touch is his hand in my hair, keeping my head in place. Holding me. It doesn't seem as gentle against the hard thrust of his cock. All of this in one person. Gentleness and pain. Anger and love. He's a complicated person. He'll always be complicated.

I trace one of his scars and grind down harder on him. With Leo inside me I can feel the whole-body response he has, feel how it travels through him head to toe. "Christ," he says. "I never thought." He doesn't finish the sentence. One hand on my hip takes over the rhythm. "You're so tight. You can't hide anything from me."

It's a double-edged sword. He's also saying he can't hide anything from me. A tear slips down my cheek at the admission. I watch myself fucking him in the mirror, watch myself straddling him, but my own face isn't what keeps me looking. It's him. His movements. His strength. His searing honesty.

"Fuck me like you want it, darling." My thighs protest but I move my hips with more purpose. It hurts more, to take more of him, but I need it. "That photo," he says. "I should punish you for looking."

"You. Didn't." Hard to catch my breath. "You let me see. And I saw." With my chin on his shoulder like this, I can't see his face in the mirror. I can only see him turn his head toward me. Only feel it, his cheek against mine. The subtle hitch in his chest. I touch his scars again, mind struggling to fuck him hard and touch him softly. I feel him brace. Not real fear, not with Leo, but a habit. He knows that pain is coming. And when it doesn't, his body settles. No—I need to be honest. He feels it. I'm just not causing more. His pain is here with us, even now, but I'm not making it worse.

He presses his lips to the pulse at the side of my neck as sweat beads on my skin. I'm running out of breath but my heart feels so huge. It aches so much for him. It wants so much from him. I want so much from him.

I take as much of him inside me as possible, until it hurts. Until I cry out. He pulls me closer, stroking my hair, and nips the flesh at my shoulder. I have that shimmering feeling, like the whole world turns on this moment, and I touch him again. Another scar. There are so many.

"I wouldn't wish this on you," I tell him, and he buries his face in my neck. Bites me there. "I'm so—I'm so sorry it happened to you." Another tear falls. Lands on his skin. "I grieve for you. For anything you lost or you thought—you thought you lost." Leo's breathing hard, my skin heating with it. My heart on fire. "But I love this version of you."

He pushes me off his shoulder, puts his hand around my neck, forces me to look into his eyes. Black and gold. Fire and darkness. He takes away some of my air. Not too much. It makes my hips move faster. "I hate that photo." Leo's jaw works. "It's mortifying for you to see it. To see me when I was weak like that. I was a fool who let—" I'm so frantic against him that it breaks his sentences apart. "Darling."

"You weren't weak." I lean into his hand. "You were strong enough to survive. And you became—" His cock. His hand. All of me liquid pleasure and liquid pain. "You became this man, you became this beast, so you could live." He lets out a shuddering breath. "So I could find you. I had to find you. I needed you like this. I need you. Like this. Exactly how you are."

He turns us with a feral growl, shoving me down to the desk. A rough hand under my leg angles it up, opens me for him, and Leo takes me in one stroke. I touch him and touch him, my hands on his face, his shoulders. He kisses me while his hand works between us. He's rough on my clit. Pinching. Making me writhe underneath him. He pulls away just long enough to slide down, to bury his face between my legs. "Look," he orders, and I turn my head and see myself splayed on the desk, his hands wrapped around my thighs, his back partially hidden by his position. By the way he's eating me like he'll never eat again. He teases my clit with his teeth, holding me open. Five fingerprints on each thigh. Ten bruises forming.

"Oh, no," I gasp. "Oh, no."

Leo hauls me right to the edge of orgasm and throws me over. It's a mean one. It makes my toes curl and my nerves spark and my body goes wild. As wild as he is.

He takes his mouth away. No. Not fair, not fair. But he's using his hands and his body to lever me into the position he wants for fucking. He takes me with a bite and a growl and a vicious thrust. One hand on my head so that I have to watch myself come on his cock as he fucks me. So that I watch him come too, every muscle working. He's terrifying in the daylight.

Beautiful. Terrifying. And mine.

I never want to look away.

CHAPTER TWELVE

Leo

I'VE NEVER BEEN so shaken in my life, except for the moment when Haley entered the room before Ronan shot me. She had no reason to return for me. No reason to think I was worth risking her own life for. All I'd given her was punishment, rough sex, and a visit to the library.

I'd given her the equivalent of a cracked-open door. Practically none of me. And she'd rushed back into the middle of an execution. For that. For me. I can't sort any of my thoughts. They refuse to line up and make sense. So I place the call after dinner. Send the advance team. Sit with Haley while she reads that fantasy book her brother packed for her when she first came to me—a new copy, to replace the one I tore apart. When she falls asleep over the book, I put her in bed and leave her sleeping.

A frigid shower tempers the pain enough for the trip, but I can feel it waiting there. Crouched and clawed. It can't be separated from the wreckage of my feelings. They've become too real. Too strong to bear.

Gerard waits outside the bedroom door. "It's all clear. They'll do a second check before you arrive."

"If Haley wakes up, I need to know."

A nod. "I'll take the post until you get back."

I don't have to explain myself to him, but I feel compelled by the tide of the day. By everything that Haley said, and everything we did. "It can't wait. Otherwise I wouldn't leave her. Is there any indication—"

"None. All quiet."

I listen outside the door for another minute, then tear myself away. It hurts to leave. The agony in my back relented while I was fucking Haley, but it's come back full force now. Top of the wheel. Sitting in the car is misery.

It's nearly midnight when I arrive at church. Thomas, my most trusted driver, drops me off behind the building. Stained glass glows against the dark. It's never fully lit when I come. Bright enough to find my way and no more. The door at the back is open. The lock clicks closed as soon as I'm inside.

I've entered at the far end of the sanctuary,

near an archway that opens onto an aisle. I pass rows of shadowed pews on the way to the narthex. My own confusion, my own unrest, doesn't begin to calm until I've reached the baptismal font and made the sign of the cross. It should burn me. I'm going to hell. But it doesn't. I shrug off my overcoat and hang it on one of the hooks off to the side. There are no others here. There are never any others here when I come to Mass. This is how I have to arrange it.

I know how fucked up it is that I'm here. Most of my siblings have dropped out of the church entirely. I don't blame them for that. Some unholy shit has gone on behind the doors of most churches. Crimes. Of all of them, I'm the least likely to do this at all, ever. The Beast of Bishop's Landing doesn't believe in God. He definitely does not attend church.

It's remained as big a secret as the wounds on my back. If anyone were to find out, they'd use this place against me. They would hurt the people inside it. And I won't have that. I've worked too hard to make it what it is. A real sanctuary.

Father Simon moves behind the altar as I reenter, lighting candles near the crucifix. It hurts to bend my knee at the side of the last pew. My chest aches where I was shot. My muscles are all overtired. But following the ritual feels better than not following it. When I've finished I drop into the closest seat, fold my arms over the back of the next pew, and put my head down.

It's against church etiquette. It's not the worst I've done. Fortunately for me, Father Simon is a forgiving priest. He's also the only priest who knows about Caroline. He is the only one who knows about the wounds, and the pain. Another reason I arrange private midnight Mass. Sometimes I need to be here. And sometimes I can't stand up. Sometimes I need a minute in what he calls my personal attitude of prayer.

He moves unhurriedly down the nave a minute or two later, making no comment as he goes. He'll be waiting for me in the confessional.

I spend another few minutes breathing in incense and polished wood, then follow him. The confessional itself is large, wooden, and meant to look like an antique. It's not. I had it built for the church eight years ago. The one at the church where I was baptized, the one where I was an altar server—that confessional was too narrow. After Caroline, I couldn't stand to be in a space that small. I made this one easier to breathe in. There's a narrow shelf near the grate where I can lean, which is good, because I'm so out of sorts that sitting up straight would be the last straw.

In the dark of the confessional, I can only see Father Simon's outline through the wooden grate. I make the sign of the cross. "In the name of the Father, and of the Son, and of the Holy Spirit. Amen." He murmurs this along with me, and I hear him settle in afterward.

"Good evening, child of God."

"You always say that to me. Child of God. But it's not the usual greeting."

"Some penitents cannot help but close their hearts if I say *my child.* I say it to remind you that I am standing in for Christ, not for your father."

Well.

"Bless me, Father, for I have sinned. It has been…" Jesus. How long? An eternity, and not long enough. "Five weeks since my last confession."

"May God help you to know your sins and trust in his mercy."

"Amen."

"For the steadfast love of the Lord will never cease. His mercies are never ending. They are new every morning."

So is His judgment, but that's not why I'm here. Not all of why I'm here.

"Tell me," says Father Simon.

"I've been busy." From the moment I got Phillip Constantine to sign that contract to now feels like a hundred lifetimes.

"It's been a long time. I thought you had forgotten me."

"No, Father. I've broken every commandment at least twice, but I never forget."

He pauses. The first time Father Simon did this, I wanted to tear the confessional down around me and light it on fire. I was sure he'd turn me out. Confirm what I already knew. "I sense a struggle in you. Something's changed since you were last here."

Something. Someone. Haley walked into my life, and now I'm another person. Or now she's seen the heart of me. I don't know which, but a heavy despair pulls at me with grasping hands. This is the only place I don't have to hide it. It's too late, and I'm too wrecked, to hide it. "What do you do when you've sinned, you've committed crimes, you've hurt an innocent and—" Fuck. Hard to breathe. "And you don't regret it?"

"God's mercies are never ending," he answers. "As is love."

My sharp laugh is answered by fresh pain where the bullet wound has mostly healed. "Is that what this is?"

"That is not for me to say. But I think you have much to tell me."

I let out a breath. Will the agony to ease up a little. "I confess to Almighty God that I forced a woman. Not the way people would think it happened. Not in an alley with a knife in my hand. I used a pen instead. I forced her to sign an agreement. She had no choice. I used her love of her family against her so she had no choice, and then I used her body for my own pleasure. Again. And again."

"Hmm. Go on."

Father Simon has never been shocked by what I tell him. He has never broken the seal of the confessional. We had a frank discussion about that once. He's bound to go to his grave with these secrets. But in this church, in *my* church, there's a line. As far as I know, no one has ever confessed to hurting a child, and I would know about it.

"I killed three men. I almost killed a fourth. For putting their hands on her. I wanted to." Rick's throat in my hands. His eyes widening. "I don't regret any of that, which must be another sin. And there's something else."

"Confess."

"I confess that I took revenge on a woman.

On Caroline." Thank God he already knows about Caroline. "I hurt her. With a whip. I thought—" I swallow around an ache in my throat. "I thought it would free me, but I just felt hollow afterward."

"Paul gave us guidance on this, child of God. Do not take revenge, dear friends, but leave room for God's wrath."

"Yes, yes. Vengeance is mine, I will repay."

"Yet you took matters into your own hands."

"We're supposed to be messengers of God."

"And God told you to seek vengeance?"

I lean my head on my hand. "I swore I'd return the favor for what she did to me. And then I survived to do it, which seems like encouragement, if not endorsement. Whatsoever a man soweth, that he shall also reap."

Father Simon waits. I haven't made a convincing argument. There isn't one. I'm here to confess, not to argue about Caroline.

"Her name is Haley," I tell him, and my heart punches at my rib cage. "And I want to keep her. It would be—it is a sin to keep her."

"I disagree."

The sound I make isn't appropriate for a confessional. "I'm sorry, Father. I'm fucking—I'm shocked you would say that. I have to let her go.

How can I let her go?"

"If God has given her to you, then would it not be a sin to send her away?"

"God didn't send her to me. I went after her family. Her father. And then I found her, and I took her."

"The Lord moves in a mysterious way, His wonders to perform."

"That's a poem, Father, though I appreciate your sense of humor."

He sighs. "You are a good man. If Haley needs your protection, then you will find a way."

A flicker of anger. Of grief. "Your faith is clouding your vision. I'm not a good man."

"The children who study at the after-school program you fund would disagree."

My face goes hot with suspicion. A sensation of being seen when I didn't want to be witnessed. It's true that I have made good here. Anyone who works with children has been background-checked to within an inch of their lives. There are rules in place to protect them. Protocols. I am heavily involved with the teachings at the after-school program. I've forbidden the staff from using guilt as a cudgel. It's different here. I have anonymously pissed off the diocese and the Vatican on more than one occasion because of it.

"That's not—"

"You remain anonymous to our church and to the world," Father Simon says, his tone soothing. He's completely unafraid of my temper. Completely unthreatened. "But you are known to the Lord. He knows what you give."

This doesn't settle me. It doesn't give me the calm I came here to find. It's not true, but when he says it, I want to believe it. Just like when Haley says I'm a fucking prince. Princes don't have to confess to being nightmares made flesh. And I am a nightmare in more ways than one. "I confess that I came near to death."

"Dying is not a sin, child of God."

"I got shot in the chest. The bullet collapsed one of my lungs and almost killed me. I bled out all over Haley's lap. I didn't make an act of perfect contrition. I spoke to her, not God, and the whole thing terrified her. It's given her nightmares."

"Bear ye one another's burdens, and so fulfill the law of Christ."

"I'm the burden, Father Simon. Are you even listening?"

"To your every word. And the words you are not saying."

I cover my face with both hands. Make the darkness more absolute. Breathe.

"I can't burden her with me. With the—with the magnitude of my sins. I need penance." I take my hands down. "I'm sorry for these and all the sins of my past life."

"To satisfy your penance, you will pray three Hail Marys and one Our Father."

"That's bull—"

"And you will open your heart to this woman. To Haley."

It takes several moments for his words to filter through my rage. My hurt. The grief that Haley stirred up and named when we looked at that photo. She's seen it now. She's seen *me* now. The things we did today, in that room—

"I can't get much more open."

"Tell me. Does she know you are here with me now?"

I stare at the outline of him through the grate. "No."

"You hide yourself, but that is not the way."

"Hide me under the shadow of your wings," I say to him.

"From the wicked that oppress you," Father Simon answers. "From your deadly enemies. Not from Haley."

I don't know where he gets the nerve. I can hardly speak. "Lord Jesus, Son of God, have mercy on me. A sinner." The biggest sinner there ever was. The worst nightmare ever to walk the earth. But I'll repent forever if it means keeping Haley. Forgive me.

"I absolve you from your sins in the name of the Father," begins Father Simon, and something behind my heart releases. "And of the Son. And of the Holy Spirit."

"Amen."

Another pause. I catch my breath.

"The Lord has freed you from your sins. Come out into the church, child of God, and celebrate Mass."

CHAPTER THIRTEEN

Haley

M Y PHONE RINGS early, but it doesn't come early enough. I'm dreaming of Leo again. Leo bleeding. Leo gasping. The buzzing on the bedside table pulls me out of it before it can drag me down completely.

I've slept late. My heart beat hard all day yesterday after we came out of Leo's study. Before we left, he picked up the photo in its frame and put it in my hands. He waited while I put it back on the shelf. And then I couldn't stand to be apart from him. It felt like fighting against a tide. Or gravity. We talked about dinner and books and nothing at all. What do you do, after a moment like that? I felt torn open by it. Exposed by it. Like all the soft parts of me had been turned inside out and put on display for him. I can only imagine how he felt.

The sun streams through his bedroom window. Bed's empty. I push my hair out of my face and grab for the phone, fumbling it at the name on the screen. I get it to my ear just in time.

"Petra?"

"Hey, Hales." My older sister sounds fresh and awake, unlike me. But concern has made her voice higher. And something else—surprise? "Did I wake you up?"

"It's fine. Are you okay?" I ask, pushing away sleep. Her husband doesn't like her to have much contact with us. She visits the house once a month, but we barely talk otherwise.

She sounds uncertain. "Of course. I was just calling to say congratulations."

I run my hand through my hair again. Without Leo in the bed, without him in the room, I feel unprepared. For phone calls. For everything. I want him here.

"Congratulations—for what?"

"For your upcoming nuptials?"

Petra's the one who did things right. She was in love with this boy who did underground boxing, but of course the family would never approve. Caroline Constantine would never approve. So she picked someone out for her to marry. They were introduced at a party. It was essentially a modern-day arranged marriage, and Petra went along with it.

She was the steady older sister who took care of things. Who got good grades. Who unburdened our dad as soon as she could so he could focus on his work. She's a good sister. I miss living with her. And now I hear the hurt underpinning her polite question. I know she was torn between leaving and staying. Between making a life for herself and making one for us. She would be devastated if I got engaged without telling her.

A pang of guilt. I haven't told her a thing about Leo. There hasn't been a good moment. "Petra, I'm not getting married. I don't know who told you that, but—"

"The Tribune," she says. She means the Bishop's Landing Tribune. "There's an announcement in the paper today for your engagement. And your wedding."

Oh, Jesus. Oh, shit.

"It's right here in the society section." A page turns. She's flipping back to it. I can see her standing at the kitchen island of her house, keeping her neutral expression on while she leans an arm on the table and reads. "The Constantine family is pleased to announce the engagement of Haley Constantine, daughter of Phillip Constantine, to Rick Joseph Jr., son of Darla and Richard Joseph of Bishop's Landing. Invited guests will gather at the Sweetwater Country Club on the second of February—"

I put a hand to my chest. It does nothing to calm down my terrified heart. "No. Petra. Stop. No. This isn't real. This is—this must have been Caroline."

"Caroline?"

"She's been really out of control lately." Regret wraps itself up in a ball and sits heavy in the pit of my stomach. I should have told Petra everything to begin with. Then it wouldn't sound like this. It wouldn't sound like some random accusation.

"What does that mean—out of control?" More confusion has clouded her voice. "Why would she think you were getting married if you're not? Are you—" She lowers her voice. It makes me wonder if her husband is there. No, he has an office. Maybe there's a maid or something. "Are you okay? Like, are you leading Rick on?"

Acid scorches the back of my throat and I swallow it. I'm not going to be sick. Not here. Not because of Rick. He was willing to do anything to me for Caroline, up to and including rape. It's not Petra's fault she doesn't know. "I am *not* leading him on."

"Hales, I'm not trying to upset you. I just

don't understand how this happened. Have you been clear with Caroline? I know she has strong opinions, but she gave me the choice. When I got engaged, we talked about it beforehand. I agreed to it."

It wasn't a real choice. I long to tell her that. If she didn't marry who Caroline wanted, we would have been ostracized from the family. "I was as clear as I could possibly be."

She had me in her house. She's capable of hurting people. Of damaging them for life. So Petra's suggestion feels like a condemnation of what I did, even though it can't possibly be. She doesn't know. Petra is assuming that Caroline is the woman we've always known. Cold and demanding and judgmental, but not a psychopath. Petra is assuming that Caroline is a garden-variety Constantine. And Caroline, for all she's done to me, has never done anything to Petra beyond choosing her husband.

"Well, maybe you should give her a call. Set things straight. It'll be a little awkward, but you don't want people wondering if they're invited to a wedding that doesn't exist." My sister laughs a little. It's an attempt to smooth things over, but I'm all jagged edges. I breathe deep, trying to clear that knot from my stomach. Trying not to be sick. A notice in the paper—Jesus.

"I can't call Caroline." I don't know what else to tell Petra. Where to start the story. How to tell it in a way that she would understand. "That's not really an option for me right now."

"About that." She makes a clicking sound with her tongue. Petra always used to do that when she was thinking. She would lean against the countertop and look out the window. "Is that because Leo Morelli won't let you call her? Is he controlling your actions?"

All of my emotions tumble free. Guilt that I didn't tell her earlier. Shame that I believed what the Constantines thought about Leo. Hurt that she's come to such a wrong conclusion. Such a terribly wrong conclusion. "Why would you think—Petra, why would you think he wouldn't let me call Caroline?"

"Cash told me you were with him. At his house."

I put my hand over my eyes to cover the burn of my tears. I haven't heard from Cash, or talked to Cash, since he lured me outside to get kidnapped by Caroline's henchman. And now he's telling Petra things about me. It's more than the rug coming out from under my feet. It's the whole floor.

"Are you okay, Hales? Should I—" Her voice drops again. "Should I call the police?"

"Jesus, Petra, no. I'm fine. I promise."

"How did you end up with him, though? That's not like you. Cash said something bizarre about some papers Dad signed, and I can't—" This time, when she laughs, the sound is all hurt confusion. "You're not like that. You don't date guys like that. Stay at their houses."

"Guys like that," I snap, and then I bite it back, I shut it down. Petra doesn't know Leo, and I haven't done a damn thing about it. I haven't told her the truth. I haven't stood up for him, the way I should have. Not that it'll ever convince her, or any of the Constantines. It just hurts. Because Rick actually is a guy like that. Rick was the one who told me that I was doing great while he had his hands on me. I didn't want his hands on me. I detested his hands on me. Thinking about it now makes me sick. Because I know what it is to want someone. I have always wanted Leo. From the first moment I saw him, I wanted him.

"Haley," she says, and I realize how silent I've gone, how cold.

"I'm really, really okay." It's a lie. I'm not okay, but it's not because of Leo. The only reason I'm sleeping at night at all is because of Leo. A tear leaks out from under my palm. Petra can never hear that I'm crying. She would assume it was because of him, when really it's Caroline. When really I'm tired from being woken by nightmares. When I want Leo to be here.

When I'm not sure if I'll ever be fine. If we'll ever be fine. If Caroline won't leave us alone, then how can we be fine? How can we be happy?

The door to the bedroom opens and closes. A pause. And then swift footsteps over to my side of the bed. Leo tugs my hand away from my eyes, and when I open them he's on one knee in front of me, dark eyes taking everything in. He runs a steadying hand down one of my legs with enough pressure to keep from setting me off.

"I don't know if I believe you," says Petra. "You sound like you're crying."

I look into Leo's eyes. At his viciously beautiful face. The curve of his lips. The mouth that's been everywhere on me. That I want everywhere on me now. "I promise, I'm not. And I'm also not getting married. I want to be here with Leo."

Leo narrows his eyes.

"Okay." Petra sighs. "Will you call me if you need anything? I'm always here, you know. We're sisters no matter what."

"No matter what," I echo. "I love you."

"Love you too, Hales. Text me soon."

She hangs up before I can answer, and I let the phone fall to the bed. "Tell me," says Leo.

"Caroline put an announcement in the paper. For my engagement to Rick." My chin trembles. "I just—I just don't think—" The tears come, and damn it, I wasn't going to do this. I wasn't going to cry first thing in the morning. "I don't think she's ever going to stop."

Leo pulls me off the bed, down into his arms. He lets me cry until I'm done, running his fingers through my hair, tugging at it when he's removed all the knots. Little bits of pain and pressure to remind me that it's him.

What irony, to need pain like this. Or maybe it's not irony. Maybe it's meant to be.

He has enough pain to spare.

Even after the tears and shudders have left me, he holds my body. He cradles me, his touch at once soothing and inflaming me. But he doesn't make me promises he can't keep. He doesn't promise to stop Caroline, because she can't be stopped. It's like hoping that an earthquake won't shake the earth. He's strong, but even stone can shatter.

CHAPTER FOURTEEN

Leo

I'M DRIFTING INTO hard-won sleep under a blanket of pain when Haley screams.

I hear her breath first. An enormous gasp, like something's come to the side of the bed in the night. The gasp dumps adrenaline into my veins but the scream is a baseball bat to my heart. It sends it flying. She's sitting up, her hands frantic at the covers. Pushing down. Searching, searching, searching. "No." She breaks into a panicked sob and screams again.

It's not like her screams when I'm fucking her. Those are all hot pleasure and pleas for more pain. These sound like she's dying.

Or someone else is dying.

Over the last several days her nightmares have been getting more frequent, but this is the worst I've seen.

I take her by the shoulders and she startles, all of her resisting. "Stop," she screams at me, her eyes wide. Cold dread bleeds down my spine. Her eyes are open but unseeing. This is worse than a nightmare. It's become something else. She claws at the covers. Tears them back. "Help me."

The door to my bedroom bursts open. "Mr. Morelli—"

"You have to get out." Gerard has rushed to the side of the bed, closely followed by two agents from the security team. "All of you." He's already reaching for his phone. "What the hell are you doing? Don't call anyone. Just get out. Take them and get out."

A protective instinct snaps and howls. I don't want them seeing her like this. I don't want this to be happening at all. Haley's sobbing, tears streaking down her cheeks, her body shaking. "Darling." I get closer. Stroke her hair away from her face. Her expression contorts and she jerks her head away. Christ. No one can be here for this. No one will understand. They won't understand what she needs. God help me if I don't know what she needs.

I can only start where she's at.

"Get out," I tell Gerard. "Wait in the hall if you want. I don't care. But if she wakes up and you're in here, I'll have your job."

The door closes a moment later, and I reach

for Haley's hands. Pull her toward me. She falls, her balance deserting her, her palms landing on my chest. One connects with the bullet wound. "Fuck. Darling. It's me. Wake up. You're dreaming. Wake up."

"Leo," she says, and her voice is so broken, so terrified, that my throat constricts. Her love for me follows her everywhere, even to her nightmares. "You're bleeding. You're burning up."

"I'm not." I take her hand and press it harder into the wound. It hurts. "Feel my shirt. It's dry. There's nothing there. I'm not bleeding."

"I have to stop it," she says. Haley scrambles up onto her knees and brings her other hand up to my chest. "I have to stop it."

I have to get her out of this. This dream, this night terror, whatever it is—it's hurting her. I put both my hands over both of hers and hold them there.

"Good girl," I tell her, because I don't know what else to do. I don't know how else to be with her, other than to step into the nightmare too. "It's already less. It's stopping. It's—" My god, this is painful. Her touch on sensitive, damaged flesh, yes. But seeing this happen to her with clear eyes—"It's not so hard to breathe."

She blinks, then blinks again, staring at my

hands over hers. "I—" Another sob. This one softer. "I'm having a terrible dream."

"I know."

Her eyes come up to mine. "It won't let go," she whispers. "I have to stop it."

I take her chin in my hand. She's not falling into whatever this is, not for another second. "You're awake now."

"I don't feel awake." Worry is creeping into her tone. "I can't take my hands away."

"Look at me." Her eyes have slipped down to her hands again, but they come back now. Tears drip from her lashes. It makes me furious. At Caroline, at Ronan, at myself. One long blink, and her eyes go wide again. Her hands push in. Sitting here in the dark isn't going to do it. We need a clean break. And I need to fuck her.

I take Haley off the bed in my arms. She fights to press her hands to my chest again and I let her. She doesn't seem to notice when I stop at my closet. Her focus is back in the nightmare. The dreamworld. Whatever the hell is happening. I'm getting her out. I'm bringing her back to me.

I'm keeping a promise.

"Stand here." I put her on her feet on the rug by the armchair.

"No. Why?" Haley's crying. Reaching for me.

"Because, darling, you're half-asleep, and I want you awake when I fuck your ass."

The windows here look like solid panes of glass, and they are. But they open on an angle. I wouldn't live in a house where I couldn't open the windows. I press the switch at the bottom of the one nearest and open it halfway.

Winter air rushes in and Haley lets out a soft gasp. She crosses her arms over her chest. Her expression is the picture of relief. I'm not going to let it stay that way for long. She scared me, with all that screaming. My heart pounds with fresh anger. How dare Caroline. How fucking dare Ronan.

I go to her, thread my fingers through her hair, and kiss her until she whines. Until I know it's verging on too rough. And then I take her clothes. My shirt. Her panties. Gone in a heartbeat. Her nipples are hard from the frosty air. I push her hands out of the way and pinch them. Haley tips her head back, her eyes closed. "You pinch so hard."

I pinch harder. She makes a hot, wounded sound at the back of her throat. "I'm awake now," she gasps. "I'm awake. I promise."

"Awake isn't enough." I pull her in and bite. Another, just below her ear. On her neck. On her shoulder. I back her up while I do it. When she's in the right place, I shove her over the arm of the chair, the beast snapping at the end of his leash.

Shove her face right into the cushion. "You're going to stay where you are." I allow her to turn her head so she can breathe. That's it. "And you're going to cry for me. Not for some fucking dream. Not for that coward with his gun. Me."

I undo my pants and test her with my fingers. She's wet. Nothing gets her wetter than being bent over and ordered around, the filthy thing. It's like she was made for me. I push into her, filling her pussy, stretching her, and she grips the cushion. "Leo—"

"Let go with one hand and play with your clit." Haley obeys me, pushing back against me to give herself enough room. "You have thirty seconds to come."

I make her spend the first ten seconds in silence. She's panting by the end. On the verge of begging. I can tell. Her muscles ripple around my cock but she doesn't come. Haley rises on tiptoe, trying harder, trying her damned best, and it's all I can do not to destroy her now. Her screaming. Her terror. I'm barely hanging on to my humanity.

"You can tell me, darling." I slide my hand up

her spine to the back of her neck. Her pussy clenches when I add pressure to her head.

"Tell you what?" Haley's cheeks are a deep, lovely pink.

"That your fingers aren't enough. That you're stretched too far to come without help."

New tears shine in her eyes. "No. I can do it."

"But you're not doing it. I don't feel your cunt getting tighter and tighter until your body can't take it anymore. I don't feel you getting wet enough to drip down your thighs. I promise you, darling, you'll want my cock to be dripping."

"You're not really—" Another squeeze to my cock, and I groan. "You're not really going to fuck—"

"I keep my word. You only have ten seconds left. I've brought the strap in case you don't make it. How many would it take? Ten? Twenty? How many until you're out of tears? How many until you never scream for anyone but me again?"

I bring my hand down hard on her ass and Haley comes with fluttering muscles and a trembling body and a gorgeous moan. A gust of cold air sweeps in from the window. I'm so hot for her, already on fire. It doesn't touch me. But Haley shivers. I let her feel the chill. Her whole body tightens with it. Good.

"Hold on."

She grabs the sides of the seat as I gather lube and press two fingers against her hole. It's tighter because of the cold. More resistance.

I push past it, and Haley turns her face into the cushion. "Oh—oh, oh." She's so tiny, and so tight, and her muscles tremble and tense. "Wait. What if I can't—what if I can't—"

"Wait? You want me to wait? Fuck no, darling. You woke me up with your screaming." I fuck my fingers into her while she tries to push me out, her face buried in the cushioned, pained moans vibrating through her body. "I'm the only one who hurts you." I push my fingers in deep and she cries out. With my free hand, I stroke between her legs. Dripping. "I'd give you more fingers to get you ready, but you deserve what's coming."

Haley's wound so tight she won't let my fingers go. "Please. Help me."

"No." I pull my fingers out and replace them with the head of my cock, and now all her fear is mine. I have it in my grip. I can feel her shaking around me, feel her trying to angle her hips to get away. I pin her with a hand to the small of her back and laugh at her. "Are you going to run?"

"I'm not—I'm not—"

"Do you think I wouldn't catch you? I'm taking this hole, darling."

Haley takes a shuddering breath and stops resisting. She turns her face to the side so I can see her. "I'm sorry. For waking you up."

"I'll make you sorry. You scared the fuck out of me." Animal anger, animal need, claws through the rest of my patience. I force the head of me inside her and Haley whimpers. Fuck, fuck, fuck she's tight. "I thought you were hurt." If anyone else ever touches her, if anyone else hurts her— thinking of it turns the edges of my vision red. "Are you hurt now?"

"Yes." She offers herself to me, calves straining, body struggling. "It always hurts. And I—" I take another inch of her, pushing past her barriers, forcing them down. I'm an asshole. I'm a nightmare. She'd be writhing if I gave her any room to move. "And I feel so helpless."

"And who's allowed to do that, darling? Who is allowed to make you feel helpless and stretched and hurt?"

"You." Her voice is choked with tears.

"Anyone else?" I thrust into her, my control fraying at the seams. Haley howls into the cushion, the sound twisting into a moan.

"No, no, no."

"It felt like hell to hear you scream like that." Gritted teeth. I'm going to lose myself in her soon. "How does it feel to pay for it with this tight little hole?"

Her thighs become small earthquakes now. She's trying so hard to give herself to me. "It hurts. And it's—it's so embarrassing. I can't stop having the dreams." Haley bursts into tears, and I run my hands over the small of her back. Over her ass. Spread her wider. "I don't know how to stop having them."

"I'll fuck them out of you. Stop worrying about the dreams. Worry about taking this cock. Relax, or I'll hurt you."

She's shivering. "It's hard—harder in the cold."

"You don't feel cold. You feel hot." Haley clenches, and it drags a groan out of me. "Soft and tight. Like a vise. But you're not listening. I told you to *relax.*" She reaches for it, struggles for it, her breaths coming fast. She's letting me in. She's doing her best. Her resistance fades. They hurt her. These dreams hurt her. I'm going to destroy them. A growl works past my teeth. "I have to fuck you, darling, and I can't be gentle."

One violent thrust, and I'm home. Haley sobs as her body grips me, her body electric with how hard I've taken her. She moans as she cries, her body quaking, but she doesn't let go of the cushion. "Jesus. You're being so good for me. Every time you sob, you get tighter."

I reach around in front of her and work my fingers over her clit. Her hips rock helplessly against the arm of the chair. I fuck her with deep, relentless strokes, driving the breath out of her. I shrug off some of the pain. I'm on the edge of giving her too much. I'm on the edge. How am I ever supposed to live without her?

Haley gasps with every movement of my hips and I push in deep, deeper than I have before, so deep she lets out a low cry. I stay, and stay. Her hands grip the cushion so tight her knuckles have paled. She is completely at my mercy. Completely in my power. She will only be powerless for me.

With my own body still I can feel all the tiny tremors in her muscles. Feel the caged tilt of her hips. I circle her clit with my fingertips. It's swollen, sensitive, and she begs me wordlessly for more.

"You're helpless," I tell her. "Because you belong to me. I hurt you. I make you come. Nobody else. Nobody. Fucking. Else. Who's the nightmare, darling? Who is it?"

"You."

"And your pussy loves it." She squeezes my cock again, and I make my touch rough, I make it ruthless. I drag her own slickness up to her oversensitive clit and circle it again and again and again until she screams.

Screams, and comes, every muscle working over my cock. It was so hard for her to take me. I love it. As much as I love feeling her come apart under the pain and the pleasure and the cage I've made of my own body.

My own orgasm starts in my toes and explodes upward until it grabs me by the hips and turns me into a monster. I fuck her with such hard strokes that she comes again. "You're so big," she cries. "Oh my god. Oh my god. Please."

"Please?"

Haley reaches back and grabs for my hand. Holds on tight, though I'm the one hurting her and enjoying the hell out of it. "Please don't stop."

CHAPTER FIFTEEN

Leo

I TAKE HALEY into the shower and make her stand in the water while I wash her. Father Simon doesn't know what he's talking about. I'm not a good man. My darling is awake now, bright-eyed and needy, but I'm teasing her. Torturing her. I won't touch her clit or finger-fuck her.

I *will* angle her toward the water.

It's too soft for her now.

I don't say a thing about how the sound of her screaming is burned into my memory. How the sight of her in the clutches of that nightmare made my stomach turn cold. Or how fear is spreading like cancer, multiplying by the second. I love the way she cries for me. But now that the beast has settled, I want more. I want everything.

I'm not giving up gentleness to Caroline. And fucking Rick.

So we'll start here, with the water. I hold her close with one arm slung across her chest, her delicate shoulder blades pinned against me, and hook my other hand under her knee. She shivers when I lift it up and open her wide. Haley grabs for my arm. I don't think she's aware of trying to scratch me. Her breathing quickens. I won't show her a second of my fear that she'll spiral away from me again. "It's soft. It's too gentle."

I won't let her turn away. I keep her open to it. "It's just water." I nip her earlobe and she gasps. "It's only touching you because I want it there. I've opened your cunt to it for that purpose."

Haley lets her head fall back against my shoulder. Her chest heaves. "Why are you doing this?"

"Because I'm a monster. I'm a cruel bastard." Her hips push back. Haley can insist that I'm a prince all she wants, but this turns her on. "And I want to touch you however I want. I don't want a single door closed to me." I don't want any doors closed to her, either. I don't want her to grow more and more sensitive until there's no touch she can tolerate. It's not for a person like Haley. I know.

"You like—you like to hurt me. I want you to hurt me."

I laugh at her. "It's more complicated than

that, darling. I can't always start with pain for you. It'll only end up—" Well, fuck. I didn't intend for my throat to get tight. I didn't intend to get this close to the truth. That it's too late for me, but it's not too late for her. "There's a limit to what you can take."

"There's not."

I put my hand over her throat and press. "There is. If you want me to find it for you, I'll find it. But right now you're going to come from the water running over your pussy."

"I can't."

"You can. I'm making you do this. I'm ordering you to do this. It's soft, and it's warm, but it's fucking relentless. It won't stop until you come for me. I want this. I want you to feel this, just like I wanted you to feel me stretching your hole until your little ring was white and you were crying." Haley trembles now, her hips rocking. "And if you're very good, I'll fuck you again. But your cunt needs to be wet. You need to come before I'll touch you. Because once I start, darling, there's no stopping me."

She makes a sound of despair. Of hope.

"I'll tear you apart." I keep these words soft. Low. "I'll be too much for you, and you'll take me. You'll take this. It's making you come. You're filthy, and all it takes to make you come is the water."

Haley takes in three quick breaths and then her orgasm arrives. It's a hard victory, and her thigh quakes in my hand. She rocks up onto the ball of her foot and tries to fuck the air. Jesus, she's sweet. And crying. A relieved cry. I'm going to reward her for it. I'm perfunctory with the towels because I don't care. All I care about is getting her to the bed and pulling her to the edge so I can kneel between her legs and tongue the evidence of her pleasure off heated flesh.

"Please, Leo," she begs. "Please, please. I need you."

One last lick of her, and then I'm on the bed, pushing into her warmth. She's soaked. I was cruel, with the shower. I knew it would be difficult for her. But I have to erase what they did. And if I have to hide gentleness in a show of cruelty to get her through, I will. I have to hope and pray it works. I have to hope there's a way to at least replace the sensation. To overwrite the past horror.

For now I fuck her with one hand braced on the headboard. "Hold yourself open for me. Like I just did to you."

Haley's breathless as one of her hands goes

under her knee. "Oh—it's deeper like that. I can feel—"

She's swollen. Sensitive. Tight. The fluttering of her muscles cascades through her body and into mine. "Fuck, darling. I'm going to come. Your cunt is mine. Mine." Harder. Deeper. Pleasure unhitches itself from my hips and surges into her. Haley puts her hand on the back of my neck. It pushes me over the edge. I can't stop fucking her. Can't stop rutting against her. Into more heat now. My heat.

The bedroom door opens.

"Leo?"

Daphne.

Haley freezes underneath me, but I don't freeze. I can't. Every muscle is wrapped up in filling her with cum. There is no stopping it.

My sister makes a strangled sound. Like she's crying. Or about to scream. And I am so sick of screaming. I am so irritated. I push up from Haley as the last shudder fades. "What the hell, Daphne? You throw a tantrum for days and now you want to talk in the middle of the night? Get out."

Then I see it. The slant of light through the door. Illuminating our bodies. Mine, mainly.

Haley buries her face in my neck.

My bare neck.

I don't have a shirt on.

This is what it must be like to step on a landmine. My heart stops. I have enough time to realize what I've done before the explosion of heat and shame and rage. Daphne wasn't supposed to see this. No one was ever supposed to see this. Showing Haley in broad daylight was like excising my soul and laying it out for her.

"Jesus. Daphne—"

She runs out, leaving the door open behind her, and I drop my head onto Haley's shoulder and breathe her in. With one gentle hand, she rubs the back of my neck. "Are you okay?"

I kiss her collarbone and get out of bed, which is the last thing I want. "I'm fine." Lie. "I'm going to go talk to her."

Once I'm fully clothed, I pad across the house. Daphne's staying in a tower suite overlooking the woods. The floor above the bedroom is a small studio where she can paint.

Light from Daphne's room cuts across the floor. She's left the door partway open. It swings open under my hand. This is not the first time I've come to Daphne's room to talk to her. It's a different room now. She's older. But some things are the same.

She sits at her desk, head down, face buried in

her arms. My chest caves in. I've done everything in my power to let Daphne be whoever she wants to be. Sweetness and innocence don't last long for Morellis. I've given her as much time as I could. Shielded her from as much pain as I could. I didn't want her to be like me.

And yet.

This pose is so familiar. She could be me, sitting in that pew at church, waiting for the pain to pass and knowing it never will.

I step into the light. "Daphne."

She lifts her head from her arms. In the soft lamplight her eyes are red. Cheeks splotchy. "Who did that to you?" A pause. Her chin dimples, the way it does when she's going to cry. "Was it Dad?"

HALEY'S IN MY personal library when I get back, curled up under a blanket with Jane Eyre in her lap. Every one of my scars is on fire. I can feel the individual wounds. My head swims with exhaustion. With the agonizing stress of having to have this conversation with Daphne. So when Haley opens her arms, I go. It infuriates me that we're limited in the ways I can hold her, that I can be with her, because of me.

But fuck it. I get to my knees by her chair. Rest my head on her lap. Let her fold her arms over me.

It feels familiar here. Haley reaches for the lamp and turns it off. Starshine feels better than naked light.

"You did this once when you were sick," she says, running her fingers through my hair.

"Did I?"

"Yeah. You were having a nightmare."

"I was dreaming of hell." I remember that part. I remember Eva, and Haley. I don't remember doing this. It feels like a last resort. It feels like having my chest cut open and my heart exposed. "I was dreaming of—other things."

If Haley asks me, I'll tell her. I told her after my fever stopped boiling my brain that we would talk about what happened, and we haven't.

She takes a deep breath. "How is Daphne?"

"She's pissed at me. Even more now. For not telling her earlier."

"You couldn't tell her."

"No, I couldn't. She was five years old when Caroline happened." Regret taps at my ribs. "She's hurt, and she's angry that I'm keeping her here, and it's—" I let out a breath. Haley curves her hand over the back of my neck. "I'm not happy about it. She used to tell me everything. Even shit I didn't want to know. Not anymore. And now she thinks I kept a secret from her because I thought she couldn't handle it." There. Is that enough penance? Everything above my waist aches. "Do you miss your family?"

Haley considers this. "I miss my dad. I want to talk to Cash. Whatever happened must have been bad if it convinced him to do that to me. He has to feel like shit. I miss Petra, too, but she has her own life now. And I—" Another heavy breath. "I don't know if I can fix all of this. Not just for now, but forever. I don't know if I can keep them in my life."

She doesn't say the rest. She doesn't say *if I'm with you.*

I hear it anyway.

"What do you miss?" I miss very little about my childhood. I have no desire to spend more time with my father, or my mother. The photo Haley found was a rare moment of happiness on my part. We had money, yes. We lived in a mansion. Attended an expensive school. And suffered a private hell. The best times were undoubtedly the vacations, like the one in the photo. My father wore his public persona when we were on vacation. He didn't beat the shit out of me in the Bahamas.

"You've met my dad," Haley begins, "so you know how he is. He's so excited about his work. And he's absentminded. He's always been like that. His mind is always in his own world, with his inventions and his projects, so sometimes he missed things. Sometimes it was Petra who came to my after-school things and not him. But we spent time together." I can't see her face, but I can hear the smile in her voice. "On the weekends he would take us to the public library. Petra would go to the romances. Cash and I would go to the youth section. My dad would go to the science section, and we would spend hours there. We would go and find him when our stomachs started growling."

It sounds so normal. So un-fucked up. "And then you would go home?"

"We would stop at this hot dog stand outside. I would get mustard, and he would get ketchup with relish." Haley laughs. "I can't stand relish. Sometimes the hot dog guy would get mine wrong, and Cash would always make him fix it." A sad sigh. "He would defend me. He was younger, but he would always stand up for me."

"At the library?"

"At the parties." Haley outlines the shell of

my ear with a fingertip. "We had to go to the Constantine parties, and I would get teased."

I pick my head up, take one look at her face in the pale light of the stars, and switch with her. Gather her into my lap. It's times like this I wish I could just sit in the chair like a normal person. But I'll be damned if it stops me from holding her like this and looking out into the night. "What could anyone have to tease you about?"

Haley snorts. "You ripped up all my Target clothes the first night I was here. Which was kind of hot, honestly. But that's what they would tease me about. My dresses wouldn't be designer. They would be secondhand or borrowed, and I always brought a book with me. Cash would get into arguments about it. Fights. Even though he wanted to fit in. He was the best at fitting in."

"I didn't know Constantines would use such terrible manners at parties."

A sad laugh. "I felt bad when it got that far. When he could get hurt. And then Caroline's henchman hurt him again. It's my fault. I left him out there on his own, and they had to break his ribs to get him to do what he did. More than that, probably. He must have thought—" She shakes her head. "I feel bad that it came to that. I hate that it came to that."

"Don't." Haley turns her face to mine, her eyes luminous. "He defended you because he wanted to."

She runs her fingertip along the collar of my shirt. "Like you defended your siblings?"

I turn my face away. Pure instinct. I don't want to talk about that. Don't want to go back to that time. Except this is what that bastard Father Simon meant. Damn him and his penance.

God's penance.

Fuck.

When Haley puts her hand on my cheek and turns me back to her, I let her. "You don't have to talk about this," she says softly.

"My father was a real bastard." It feels like new whip wounds, to say these things. "He would get into a mood. Something would set him off. He hated to see us being human. Being weak. But that was always a moving target. He liked it best if you were a ruthless prick like him, but always with flawless manners. That's why he liked Lucian best."

"Manners?"

"Yes. The Constantines think we're uncultured fucks, but they've never sat for a formal dinner with my parents. None of them would have survived." Haley leans her head against my shoulder. She's too soft to hear this. "I couldn't stand the waiting. He'd take it out on one of us eventually. Someone would use the wrong tone at dinner or say the wrong thing, and then what are you supposed to do? The last time I—" Jesus. This is way too far. It's like being burned alive. "He thought he was doing us a favor. He would say that. *I'm doing you a favor.* It would only ever be one of us at a time, because he would get tired, or he would get bored. Only Tiernan ever escaped the abuse, because he was a bastard. My father never saw him as a child, more like a tool he could use. The rest of us, though, we were his. His to raise. His to beat. It was his version of parenting."

"So you—" She's crying. "You put yourself in the way?"

"I'll never forgive myself for this time I let him get to Eva. She insists it wasn't my fault. It was one night at dinner, and he was in one of his moods, and she made some comment. At first I thought she'd get away with it. That motherfucker waited until after everyone was done eating to call her to his office. And her face afterward—" I can't let myself think of it now. "Anyway. I decided then I would be the target. Whatever I had to do."

"How old were you?"

"Eleven." I kiss her because I can't say anything else. I can't drive the knife in any deeper. The taste of her, sweet mint and Haley, soothes the wretched fear that telling her is itself a weakness. Even if I've been compelled to do it. "This has to be enough penance," I grumble against her mouth.

She pulls back, stroking the sides of my face. "What?"

I was wrong. There's a deeper cut to make. I'm going to make an enormous donation to that church. Maybe then Father Simon won't try to kill me on a regular basis. "You know that my family is Catholic."

"Everyone knows that, I think."

"We never missed a Sunday Mass. We never missed anything at the church. We had to be a credit to our parents. That was—" It hurts to laugh. "That was the great irony of life. That he could be such a piece of shit at home and an icon at church. Most of my siblings stopped going after they moved out." I hate this. I hate this. "But I couldn't let it go."

Haley stares, her blue eyes wide. "Really?"

"I know. I should burst into flame when I step past the threshold."

"No." She puts her hands on my chest. Gentle, gentle. Puts one over my heart. "I never guessed. I never knew."

"Yes, well. I don't advertise it. And it's very different now. I obviously can't go to a regular Mass, and no amount of money would convince me to go back to the one we attended. It was too corrupt."

"So…what do you do? Where do you go?"

"St. Thomas's. In the city. The priest there holds midnight Mass for me. He hears my confession first."

Haley's eyes shine. "Confession?"

"I'm a sinner, darling."

"I have a confession."

I lift her face to mine. "It's not a sin to love the way I fuck you."

She laughs, a tear slipping down her cheek. "When we were fighting before. When we weren't talking? I went to the kitchen at night. Gerard was there. And I met Timothy."

"I know. Gerard told me."

A huff. "I thought he might. But that's not the confession."

"Tell me."

"Timothy told me about your dad. He told me about the maids, and about being your half brother. And he told me—" A deep breath. "He told me that you think you're going to hell. Is that what it means—is that why—"

I kiss her into silence. Jesus. There's always more she wants from me. She's down to the bone already. "Timothy's wrong. For a long time, I thought I was already burning."

"What changed?"

"You." Haley pulls me close by the neck. Kisses me. Her tongue darts out to meet mine, and goddamn, I want her. "You're too innocent for hell, so this can't be it. Even if it hurts like a motherfucker."

"You're corrupting me, though. What then?" That she can play with me, at a time like this—I'll never be worthy of it.

"Then I'll go to church and ask for absolution. I'll do the penance, if that's the cost." I lean down and brush my lips over the downy skin at her neck. "I confess to you, darling, that I go because sometimes it eases the pain."

"Like a miracle?"

"No. Not like a miracle." I could breathe her in forever. "When I was growing up, it was a safe place, which I know is another ridiculous irony."

She makes a sound of sorrow, but I shake my head.

"For that hour, my father had to be on his

best behavior. He couldn't beat anyone in the pews. So I looked forward to it. I looked forward to church, and vacations, and birthday parties, even though they were always strict, formal affairs usually attended by the bishop. My destroyed nerves recognize that, on some level. It can be less painful when I walk in the door."

"Leo." She can't keep the sympathy from her voice.

"It wasn't all a nightmare, darling. Don't get that into your head."

She runs her lips down the line of my jaw. "The birthdays. Were they big parties?"

"Yes. My mother has always been good at throwing elegant events."

"We have them, too," she says, sounding almost wistful. "The Constantines, I mean. Elaborate parties with ball gowns and tuxedos, with cakes that are as tall as a person. With fireworks and pop stars and every other kind of thing you can imagine."

There's a pressure in my chest as I imagine her with her family. Will she miss them if she's with me? Of course she would. "Pop stars, huh? Who was at your birthday party? Ariana Grande?" Jealousy makes my voice come out gravelly. I don't want her having a crush on anyone, even a famous pop star. "Or maybe Harry Styles?"

She gives a nervous laugh. "I never had a birthday party."

I pull back so I can see her face. "What?"

I can't see the pink of her cheeks, but I know it's there. "We had family parties. Before my mom died. I don't mean to say—" Haley swallows. "She was working, and my dad was so busy. She would make a cake from a box and we would sing, just the five of us. There wasn't always a lot of extra money, so…" An embarrassed breath. "After she died, Petra would make the cake. But we didn't have guests. I'm not complaining," she says in a rush. "I would never complain. They loved me. It just wasn't—we didn't have parties like that."

Outrage tightens my throat. "What about the huge Constantine parties?"

Her lips twist. "We're not really Constantines. At least, not the real ones. The favorite ones. The rich ones. And I don't think I would need a huge gala anyway. It's ridiculous. I know that. It's just something fun to daydream about around my birthday. A small party just for me."

I'm a fucking fool. "When is your birthday, darling?"

"Does it matter?" She bites her lip. Blushes.

Damn her family. They made her feel like she

wasn't important. The Morelli children were strapped like animals, and even we got birthday cakes. "Of course it matters."

"It's...it's on Saturday."

"This Saturday."

"It's not a big deal," she whispers, though it sounds less like she's trying to convince me. More like she's been trying to convince herself of that for her entire life.

"How old?" I'm pissed about her treatment, so it comes out gruff.

She shivers in my arms, but she answers me— my obedient girl even when she's afraid. I pull her against my chest, comforting her even while I order her around. "I'm turning twenty-two," she says, trying to sound nonchalant. And failing. It's important, this milestone. She's turning twenty-two, and she'll have a damned party if it's the last thing I do.

CHAPTER SIXTEEN

Leo

'M IN MY office planning a party for a Constantine when the text arrives. The last of the daylight is fading in the courtyard. A bird from the trees taps at my window. "There's new birdseed," I tell it, though it can't hear me. "Go away."

It flutters off the sill as I pick up my phone.

A message from Eva.

Turn on the TV—channel 9

I loathe the sound of live TV and rarely require background noise to work, so I don't have one in my office. There's one in the den. It spends most of its time hidden by a panel above the fireplace. "Gerard," I say as I open it. I know he's nearby. I heard him in the hall.

"Sir?"

"Is Haley upstairs?"

"She is."

She went up to read an hour ago. Some days,

she prefers the smaller space and the deeper quiet in the private library. I wasn't fucking around about my plans for the room on the first floor, but I haven't had time for full-scale renovation yet.

Gerard steps into the den as the TV flickers to life. Channel 9.

It's a news channel. And a news broadcast. And a very familiar face. The chyron at the bottom of the screen reads KIDNAPPED CON-STANTINE BRIDE.

"What the fuck."

Rick stands on the sidewalk in front of the Constantine compound, camera lights competing with the dying sun. He has one hand in the pocket of what looks like a brand-new overcoat and a fading black eye from where I punched him. The other hand clutches a piece of paper.

"—engagement announcement was a painful day for the family. In all the confusion, no one thought to stop it from being printed. But Haley had already been taken. I'm here to ask for her safe return." His eyes come up to the camera, and he takes a big nervous breath. I hate this mother-fucker. He's right to be nervous. "I'm so worried. We're obviously—we're offering a reward for her safe return."

"When did you last see her?" one of the reporters calls. A press conference. Caroline planned
this. Every detail. It's not just that she wants him
to kill me. She wants to set it up first.

"I haven't seen her in almost two weeks." This
is the truth, and my stomach sinks. They're going
to run the same play as before. The one that made
Haley cry. *They said things that were close to the
truth.* Rick Joseph Jr. is going to stand on live TV
and tie the truth in knots. "I was attacked, and
she was taken."

Clever. He was attacked, and then I took her
back. Gerard makes a sound off to my side. I can't
see him. My vision is going dark with rage, and if
I'm honest, if I am doing penance and opening
my goddamn heart—

Fear, too.

"Do you know where she's being held?"

"No," Rick lies, and he's almost convincing in
this. "I didn't get a good look at my attacker and I
don't know where Haley is." He swallows hard
and looks directly into the camera. "If anyone
watching this has any information about her
whereabouts, please call the Bishop's Landing
sheriff's office. I—" He holds a gloved fist to his
mouth. "I'm begging you. If you have her, please
return her to us. She needs to be with her family.

Haley is a sweet person who only—who only deserves the best. And if you've seen her, don't wait to call. Every second counts."

A photo of Haley flashes up on the screen. It's her college ID. In the photo, she's wearing a dove gray shirt and grinning like whoever took the photo told her a joke.

"Is there anything else you can tell us about her, Rick?"

He consults the paper in his hand. "She was last seen wearing a white nightgown. She's five foot three, slim, with blonde hair. She has beautiful blonde hair. And she—she always loved to read." Rick chokes out the last few words. The wail he lets out next is the highlight of his performance.

I yank a hardcover off the nearest shelf and throw it at the TV. It splinters the screen, turning Rick's face into shattered glass. Another book. It hurtles through the air. This time, the circuitry shorts. I can't breathe. I can't see. I want my hands around his neck again. I would make the right choice this time. I would end this. I don't know I've thrown another book until it bangs against the windowsill. A framed print that Daphne gave me falls. More glass breaks. I want more broken glass. I want more destruction. I draw back a fist, aiming for the window, and someone catches it.

"Enough. Enough."

"It's not enough," I spit at Gerard, shaking his hand off mine. He doesn't accept this. He locks his arm around mine and pulls me away from the window. My back screams. "You saw. I'm going to kill him."

"We'll figure out a strategy." I try to lunge past him, and he blocks me. "You have bullet-proof windows. Mr. Morelli. Leo. Your hand will break before the windows, and you won't be able to help Haley."

I shove him one more time, but he's right. God, I hate that he's right. The red clears from my vision. My breathing slows. The pain doesn't budge. It won't. It's never going to stop. I'm going to be in hell forever. Penance forever. I cover my face with both hands, intensely aware of Gerard's eyes on me.

I never do this in front of people.

It takes too long to drag them back down.

When I do, Gerard's expression is neutral. The rest of him is not. He's poised to stop me from destroying my own home. From destroying myself. He might not have a choice, in the end, if Caroline won't leave Haley alone.

"I want to call in the second team," I tell him. He pulls out his phone without hesitation. "I want every shift doubled. Nobody is getting in here. Call my legal team and have them on standby. They're going to stand at the door if that piece of shit sends the cops."

"What else can I do?"

Help me. Fucking help me. Find a way out of this.

"Just do your job. Keep them out."

I leave Gerard in the den and go to find Haley. My heart pounds. It's been set with needles and every one of them digs in with every beat. She's curled up with her fantasy book again, Jane Eyre waiting in reserve, and I hate that I'm going to ruin this moment for her.

At the expression on my face, she scrambles up from her chair and comes to me. "What's wrong?"

I do not and will not ever deserve this woman, this angel, who puts her arms around me with infinite care. She does touch my scars now, since the day in the study. It's always the lightest pressure. I'm a selfish bastard, so I let myself hold her for a minute before I answer.

"I got a text from Eva." Haley lifts her head from my chest and looks into my eyes. "Telling

186

me to turn on the TV. Caroline sent Rick to do a press conference."

Her brow furrows. "What does that even mean?"

"She called in a bunch of reporters for him to make a statement about you on the air."

The color disappears from her face. "About the engagement?"

"No." I run my fingers through her hair. It's soft, and beautiful, and I hate that Rick talked about it like it belonged to him. "He announced that you'd been kidnapped and that your family is offering a reward for your return."

Haley slips out of my arms, her hand to her mouth, and paces away. "A reward," she murmurs. "A reward. She's crazy." She stops at the table and brushes her fingertips over the cover of Jane Eyre, then moves to the window. Her shoulders go up and up and up. Haley leans over the windowsill.

She's holding her breath.

This is worse than outright crying. Her shoulders shake, but she presses both hands over her mouth. "I just—" A frustrated inhale. "I just—why?" Her eyes, made brighter by her tears, land on mine. "Why are they doing this?"

I go and sit on the windowsill. Pull her between my legs. Take her face in my hands. Her lips tremble, but she takes another long breath. I know she's tired of crying. It's not a release for her now. Not unless I'm making her do it. "They're trying to get to you."

This is almost the truth. They're trying to get to me. And it's working.

"Should I—" Her hands come up to mine, as if she's afraid I might let go. Fuck letting go. "Should I just go back? Should I just go back home?"

"Absolutely not, darling."

Her breath is coming faster. Ratcheting up into panic. "How does this end, Leo? When? Do I need to call the press? The police?"

"Not yet." Not ever. None of those people will help the situation. No matter what Haley thinks I am, I'm the Beast of Bishop's Landing to the rest of the world. The press will only take Haley's words as evidence that I've brainwashed her, and the police are useless. "I'll figure it out."

Haley doesn't believe me. I can see it in her eyes.

I put a hand around her throat.

There.

Her shoulders relax. So do her hands on mine. The rest of her body goes pliant and waiting, her breathing settling, and this—this is a miracle. That she's like this for me. That she walks the earth and isn't afraid of me. Or that she is, but it's a trustworthy fear. She knows I'll only exploit it to make her hot. To make her wet.

To make her calm.

"I'll figure it out."

Her lips part, and she blinks back tears. The tip of her tongue wets her bottom lip. "Do you promise?"

I kiss her first. Squeeze her neck until she gasps in my mouth. I'll mark this promise on her. I'll keep it. No matter the cost. I'll ask for help, if that's what I have to do. I'll admit weakness. I'll call in reinforcements. Anything. "I promise." The color has come back to her cheeks. I knew it would. She can't help but respond to me. If I didn't know better, I'd think she was sent. A gift. "If I touch you now," I muse, keeping my eyes on hers, "what will I find?"

Her face goes scarlet. "That I'm wet."

I lean in and bite her earlobe. Haley arches in my hand. "Take off all your clothes and bend over the bed. Don't make me wait."

CHAPTER SEVENTEEN

Haley

M Y BIRTHDAY ARRIVES, and Leo wakes me up with a kiss. More than one, in fact. A trail of them down my neck and between my breasts and over my stomach.

And lower.

He keeps my legs spread with his body and licks three orgasms out of me. I can't breathe by the time he looks at me from between my thighs, dark eyes glittering, hair a gorgeous mess. It's work to catch my breath. "Is that all?"

He licks my clit again, a precise movement that sends a tremor through my legs and makes my head fall back on the pillow. "Greedy," he scolds, and then he crawls between my legs and fills me up.

It's a whirlwind day, with more people in and out of the house than I've seen. His front door keeps opening and closing. It gets louder every time, because Leo's security team checks everyone who comes in. I'm forbidden from going into the dining room. I'm required to have lunch brought to me on a silver tray while I read.

In the afternoon he sends Mrs. Page to bring me to the guest suite, where two women in black uniforms wait to give me a makeover.

Daphne's waiting too, her hand at the collar of her shirt. She can't stop biting her lip. "Hi," she says, her smile lighting up and disappearing again under the awkwardness. I haven't seen her since she came into Leo's room. I didn't want to bother her. "Happy birthday."

"Hey, Daphne. Are you here for a makeover too?"

"I can just go," she says quickly. "It's your birthday. You probably don't want me in here, given—"

I grab her hand and tug her toward the door. "Listen. I don't care that you walked in on us."

"Oh my god." She covers her face with both hands. "I'm so sorry. I should have knocked. Leo's usually up late and I wasn't thinking."

"Are you okay, though?" This isn't a conversation I expected to have in front of two stylists. But here we are.

Daphne blows out a breath and lets her hands fall to her sides. "It's complicated." A small smile.

"I had no idea. And I probably have no right to be mad at him for not telling me, I just—I wish I'd known."

"He didn't tell me, either."

"He didn't?"

"No. I walked in on him. If he could have told you, Daph, I'm sure he'd have done it."

She sighs. "It's a lot. Living here is a lot."

"I know. You don't have to get ready with me, if you don't want to. I wouldn't blame you."

Daphne rolls her eyes, and it's so pretty it makes me laugh. "I want to come to your party. I want to get ready with you. That's pretty simple, at least."

"Is it? Because—" My cheeks heat. "Okay, so, I've never gotten ready for a party like this before. My sister always did my hair. Are there any rules I should know about? I don't want to make a fool of myself."

Leo's sister presses her lips together in pure, kind sympathy and pats my shoulder. "No, there are no rules. Just tell them what you want."

They've brought a big mirror and chairs for us, and it turns out I don't have to tell them what I want, because Leo already has. Daphne raises an eyebrow when the stylist tells me that he's already given instructions. "He is such a control freak."

I meet her eyes in the mirror. "I find it pretty hot."

"Gross," Daphne whispers, and then she dissolves into laughter.

It's nice, getting your hair done by someone with skills. It doesn't feel terrible to be touched. Leo's taken that on as his own personal mission. The shower was only the beginning, and it's working.

He's so much more than I thought. So much more than everyone gives him credit for. He would be furious if anyone knew, and I get it. He uses his reputation as a tool to protect his family. To protect me. To protect himself. So I wish things were different, but not too different. It's an impossible task, untangling him from his past. I don't think everything happens for a reason. That pat bullshit people say when they can't think of anything better. But at some point, it all added up into the man he's become.

"What are you thinking about?" Daphne asks. "You're so quiet."

My eyes are closed so the stylist can put on eyeshadow. They wouldn't be here if Leo hadn't approved their presence, and this is his sister, so I feel relatively safe in my honesty. And I'm tired. Tired from having nightmares. Tired from worrying about what Caroline will do next. And from the good things, too. "I was thinking about Leo."

"You are, like…so in love with him."

There's no denying it, and no point in denying it. Daphne wouldn't even be the first person I've told. She wouldn't be the first Morelli. "It's true."

"Are you happy?" I'm so glad, *so* glad, that my eyes are closed. That the sweep of the makeup brushes is keeping them that way. I hope Daphne's not looking. "You sound like it's complicated."

I don't have the words. Just like with Eva, everything I could say about Leo falls short of him. Disastrously short. And if I try to describe to Daphne how I love him, I'll cry and ruin all my makeup. I'm not sure I could force those descriptions past the lump in my throat. How my heart aches every second I'm apart from him, and sometimes more when he's in the room. How the only thing that settles the fear and uncertainty of this moment in my life is his hands on me. How the sound of his voice is the closest thing I'll ever feel to an answered prayer.

"He was sick," I say instead. "After he came home from the hospital. He had this awful fever."

"I know," she answers. "Eva told me. She wouldn't let me come over." Daphne clears her throat. "She said he wouldn't want me to see him like that. Which isn't fair. He's my brother, too. He keeps me at arm's length and then he turns around and makes me live here for safety."

"My brother helped Caroline kidnap me."

"Jesus." Daphne's quiet for a long time. "Leo said you went out to meet him. He didn't say—"

"He didn't say that Cash called me and asked me to come. Caroline's man beat him up first and made him do it. That's why I went outside in the first place." I breathe slow and deep. I'm not going to screw up this makeup. This party. "I don't know what point I'm trying to make. Just that brothers are complicated sometimes."

"So things are not easy with your family."

"No. I talked to Eva about this when Leo was sick, and she said I would have to choose between them and Leo. After everything that's happened, I'm worried we'll never have any peace. I'm worried she might be right."

"She won't be." Daphne sounds confident about this, at least. "Not if Leo has anything to say about it. He always gets his way." She knows it's not true. I know it's not true. But it's a step onto lighter ground, which is where we're supposed to be for a birthday makeover. "My collector has been texting me."

"You can open your eyes," says the stylist, and when I do, I find a completely neutral, friendly expression. I would bet anything that she's deliberately not paying attention to our conversation. It's probably part of her contract.

"Have you texted back?"

"No." Daphne bites her lip. "I don't know what to say. Leo would be pissed if I told him where I am, so I haven't said anything." She groans as her stylist applies a rosy shimmer to her cheeks. "He's not a bad guy. Leo should settle down."

"I don't think that's in his DNA. How long are you going to hide him, though? Do you have a secret name for him in your phone?"

"Collector," says Daphne. "Obviously."

I laugh harder. The stylist quirks her lips and waits for me to stop. "My sister had a boyfriend when she was in high school. She didn't want my dad to know who it was, so she saved him in her phone as a smiley face emoji. It was funny because her face made that same expression every time he texted her."

Daphne grins, her dark eyes lit up. "Did they run away together? Get married?"

"No, they didn't make it past senior year. She married someone that was Constantine approved. An investment banker." Jeremy Rand seems nice enough, in a severe kind of way. He manages the finances for most of the Constantines. Except for my father, of course, who doesn't have enough money to manage. He has strict ideas about what Petra should wear and say and do. "I miss her, but I feel like I don't know her very well anymore."

"Yeah," says Daphne. "Sometimes I feel like I don't know anyone at all."

"You know me. What you see is pretty much what you get."

Her smile crinkles her eyes. "No way. You look like a Constantine—you *are* a Constantine—but you're kind. And you look quiet and soft, but when you're with Leo, he listens to you."

Something about her voice makes me reassure her. "He listens to you, too."

She makes a face. "No, he doesn't. He just tells me what to do. *You have a stalker, Daphne. Move in with us, Daphne. Don't get murdered, Daphne.*"

"Well, the last one seems like good advice," I say, unable to hold back a laugh.

"I'm a grown woman, but he treats me like I'm a child."

"He cares about you. That's why he's so protective."

"Overprotective," Daphne says. "I mean, the whole idea is offensive. Someone likes my paintings, so they must be a crazy stalker?"

"I'm sorry," I say, not because I think Leo is wrong about this collector. More because I can see the hurt in Daphne's eyes. It's painful not to be taken seriously by your family.

"Whatever," she says. "Enough about Leo."

"Enough about him," I agree. "He's not interesting in the least. Besides, I want to hear more about this collector. There's something in your voice when you talk about him."

"He likes my paintings. That's all."

"Maybe," I say, my tone noncommittal. "Maybe he only cares about your paintings, but what about you? Do you only care about him as a customer?"

Her cheeks turn pink. "I don't know. How are you supposed to know?"

The jumble of feelings I have for Leo rises— the love and the hate, the frustration and the fear. He's everything good and hopeful in a dark world, but he would hate to hear me say that. "I think if you don't know how you feel about him, he's already more than a customer."

CHAPTER EIGHTEEN

Haley

DAPHNE LEAVES ME alone to get dressed. The stylist stays to help me. It's a good thing, because it's a fancy gown and I need her help to get it over my head without smudging my makeup. She does the zipper, fluffs the fabric, and turns me to face the mirror.

"Wow." I can't stop looking at myself. "You did a good job."

"You were an easy client," she says with a smile. "Beautiful from the start."

I look like spun gold. He's chosen a gold gown with layers of gossamer fabric that float and shimmer in the light. My hair is in soft curls, perfect and shining. My makeup is darker than the dress. More dramatic. I have to blink with purpose to keep from crying. I've always told myself it wasn't important to have expensive clothes and nice makeup. And it isn't. Not really. But that doesn't mean I didn't want it. My cousins always looked so gorgeous at Constantine parties. They looked like something out of a dream. More than anything, I wanted the dream. I know now that it couldn't have been real. People's lives aren't the way they look at parties.

One night would have been more than enough. And now Leo's going to give it to me.

The stylist helps me into my shoes and sends me out.

Leo waits for me at the top of the stairs. He's looking down as I approach, his head bowed almost as if he's praying. He stands in a dark suit, black on black like always, except tonight he has a gold pocket square. I can tell, even from several feet away, that it's made from a piece of my dress. Black and gold. His eyes brought to life. Everything about him is sharp and beautiful, like a breath of winter deep in the night. The sight of him wakes me up. Trips all my nerves. Pulls them to him. He has my heart tucked in his pocket with that flash of gold. So much beauty to hide so much pain.

My dress makes a soft sound, and he looks up. Sees me. His lips part, and his entire face—

It reminds me of when his painkillers kicked in in the hospital. A change came over him. Only this time he's not slipping into unconsciousness, he's throwing the door to himself open wide. Astonishment flares in his eyes, followed by want, and he shakes his head a little. Disbelief that I'm here. That I'm real.

I feel like a dream.

He stands tall as I come to him and takes my face gently in his hands. "Look at you," he breathes. "You're the prettiest thing I've ever seen."

It takes my breath away, and my voice, and all I can do is smile at him until he leans down and kisses me. He tastes like starlight and fire. I never want to stop, but eventually he laughs. "I won't let you miss your own birthday party. Come on."

There are no nerves like the frantic butterflies I get descending the staircase on his arm. For once in my life, I feel exactly right. Dreamlike. But Leo hasn't said a word about the guest list, if there is a guest list. Having other people at the party besides Daphne is too much to hope for. I don't let myself hope.

Leo leads me past the bodyguards lined up in the foyer. The lights have been dimmed for the evening. My veins don't have enough space for how excited I am. My face is hot before we get to the dining room door.

It's hot before I hear the voices.

Because there is music coming from the dining room, filtering out into the hall, and voices. Someone laughs. It sounds like a party.

We turn the corner into the dining room.

I stop dead in the doorway.

Leo has decorated his dining room for me before. It's a private space, but it's not particularly small. He could have a table for twenty in here, if he wanted. Instead, he's filled the room with the most beautiful party I've ever seen.

White and gold balloons are absolutely everywhere. The ceiling has been draped in gold and white, making it look both taller and more intimate somehow. Tiny lights run along the draping like stars. Those lights spill down behind a three-tiered cake in the corner. It's wrapped in white fondant with gold-dust roses painted across. Nearby is a small stack of gifts, also in gold. And all this beauty, all this love, is just the backdrop for what else he's done.

In the middle of it all, framed by gold and white, are his siblings. Daphne's here, a glass of champagne in her hand, but she's not talking to Eva. She's talking to Elaine. Elaine, who laughs again. Eva stands nearby with Lucian, gesturing at him with her own glass of champagne. He has one hand up and is talking over her wearing a handsome, devilish half-smile that has to be intimidating in the real world. Not to Eva.

Every one of them is dressed for my party in black with gold accents. A gold headband glints in Daphne's hair. A gold necklace shines around Elaine's neck. Eva's hair is held in its elegance by an arrangement of gold hairpins, sprays of flowers and leaves winking in the light.

"I couldn't give you a Constantine birthday."

I look up at Leo and find him watching me, and I know he's been watching me since we arrived at this room. I can feel him waiting for my reaction. I can feel his hope, and underneath that, his worry that this isn't enough.

"I wanted—" He clears his throat. "I would have made it a bigger party, but I couldn't find a safe way. That was the most important thing. I trust the people here."

"You invited your family."

"I know. It's not what you wanted, but—"

I reach up and cover his mouth with my hand. Tears gather at the corners of my eyes but I breathe through them. "You offered me your own family and I—" He takes my hand away and kisses my palm. "You're a prince. And I want all of you. They're a part of you. Even when it's hard." My chin starts to tremble but I stop it through sheer force of will. "I don't need a bigger party. They count for thirty people. Maybe a hundred."

He runs the pad of his thumb over my cheek. "Cry for me later, darling. Not now."

I hold my breath for a count of three. "I'm not crying now. This is perfect."

"Lucian, shut up, she's here," Daphne says, and I was right. There are only a handful of them, but they sound like a full ballroom when they shout happy birthday. Daphne comes to pull me into the room, and it doesn't matter that it's a small party. I'm surrounded by joy. Everyone gathers around to see my reaction to the cake. Eva puts champagne in my hand. "I was promised dinner," Elaine says after she kisses my cheek. There's a table set up at the other side of the room, and I already know it won't be like the first dinner we had together. There's no awkwardness now.

Because.

They were raised to attend parties. To be a credit to their family. But this isn't a show. This is real.

"Presents first or dinner first?" asks Eva. The music is just loud enough for atmosphere, not so loud it drowns her out.

"Dinner," I answer quickly, before anyone else can. They're already doing so much for me. I don't think I can stand here and open gifts without actually starting to cry.

"Then let me get the last guest." Leo presses a kiss to my hair, and then he goes for the door.

Daphne takes my arm. "Do you like it? There are a lot of balloons, and that's partially my fault."

"I love it. It's—" Of course I loved my birthdays with my family, with the box cake Petra would make and the gift Cash would bring me from the corner store. Of course I did. And I won't say a word against them. "I've never had a party like this before."

She grins, and then she looks past me. At that moment Leo arrives behind me and puts his hand on the small of my back. I turn toward his touch, and over his arm, I see who he went to retrieve.

Cash stands a few steps inside the door of the dining room in a suit like Lucian and Leo are wearing, his lips pressed together, hands in his pockets.

I step out of Leo's arm and rush across the room to him, fast as I can go in my heels. Cash tenses as I get close. "Haley—"

"Hi." I throw arms around him, careful not to squeeze. It hasn't been long enough for his ribs to heal. My heart fills. Bursts. I missed him. Cash hesitates another moment, and then he puts his arms around me and pulls me close. "You were almost late for dinner."

"Yeah, there was a surprise dress code," he teases. "They made me change into it before I came inside." He takes a deep breath. "Are you pissed?"

"I'm hungry," I tell him, stepping back to look at Cash. He looks good. Tired, but okay.

"I meant—"

"I know what you meant. We don't have to talk about all that at the party." I squeeze his hand. "I know you wouldn't have done it if you had a choice. Will you sit next to me at dinner?"

Cash does sit next to me at dinner, with Leo on my other side, and Eva works a kind of magic over the table so there's no lull in the conversation. Not a single awkward moment, though Cash stays quiet. They can't quite draw him into the conversation, and he can't quite open up to them. It's no one's fault. They're all trying.

Afterward, they all stand close while Leo lights the candles on top of my cake. Daphne produces a camera from somewhere and takes a million photos of me blowing out the candles with Leo at my side. Cash is the first one to start singing the birthday song, but it turns out all the Morellis can sing. It's the most beautiful, in-tune version I've ever heard.

After that, there's dancing. I'm drunk on champagne, and Leo is a good dancer, and the only reason anyone stops is to talk in pairs or threes. Midway through the night, I meet Cash on the quieter side of the dining room. Leo and Daphne are talking by the gift table. Lucian, Elaine, and Eva stand nearby, the three of them close together.

"Hey, Hales," says my brother.

"I didn't think you'd want to come," I say, a little too loud. Too much champagne, probably. Too much honesty. But it's my birthday.

Cash looks away. "Of course I wanted to come. You're my sister. But Leo..." He shakes his head. "I don't like him. I don't trust him. But if you do..." He pauses, gathering himself. "If you do, then that counts for something."

For the hundredth time tonight, tears well up in my eyes. "Thank you."

"Don't thank me yet. I don't think Caroline is going to give up anytime soon."

We both let several moments go by in silence. What Caroline's doing is going to end up affecting both families in the room, one way or another. She's already done enough damage. I don't want her to ruin the fragile peace we're building.

"I'm glad you're here." I look Cash in the eye. "Really glad. It means a lot to me, Cash."

He nods, glancing down, and I've never seen him so hesitant. So out of his depth. He was the sibling who was best at the Constantine parties. Cash takes a deep breath and narrows his eyes conspiratorially. "Want to dance?"

"Only if you promise not to step on my feet."

Cash takes one big step away and starts dancing. He's slightly stiff. His ribs must be hurting him. It takes weeks for ribs to heal. "I never stepped on you," he says. "But you did elbow me in the face once. Remember that?"

He reaches a hand out and spins me toward him, and we dance.

"That was an accident. I thought there was a bug."

"I barely survived," he says seriously. And then Leo is there, taking me in his arms.

I stay in this golden, glittering dream, hoping it never ends. The cake is so good I could cry. The presents, wrapped in thick gilt paper and glittering bows, contain expensive, luxurious gifts. I unwrap my first-ever Louis Vuitton clutch while

Daphne leans over to see and my face turns hot, then hotter.

There's everything I could have wanted for a birthday party, but even in my wildest dreams, I never could have conjured up Leo Morelli. He watches me with those dark eyes, the ones that scared me at the beginning. They seemed full of violence. Now I know it's true. He promises a million sleepless nights, holding me, hurting me. This birthday is more than a special day. It's a milestone, one where I'm no longer a little girl. I'm a woman now, and I'm not afraid.

CHAPTER NINETEEN

Leo

HALEY IS PINK and pleased after her party, and so exhausted she falls asleep the moment her head touches her pillow.

I, on the other hand, cannot sleep. The pain is too much. It's set off by stress, and I can't relax about it until after the meeting is over.

The next day comes too early all the same.

Cash wasn't the only Constantine I made contact with in the run-up to the party. Haley's brother was the more difficult call. He didn't believe there was going to be a party at all. The only way to convince him to come was to offer him his own personal bodyguard. Fine. Done.

In the car on the way to the city in the morning, I wish the second call hadn't been so easy. It was too fucking simple. Like it was meant to be.

I invited Cash to Haley's party because I had to. If I'm going to make this work for her—if I'm going to make being with me work for her—then

I'm going to have to solve all these problems with her family. Isolation from them would break her heart. So I arranged for Cash to attend. I just need her to see that she doesn't have to choose.

That I'll make whatever she wants a reality.

She was happy last night. Happy with how things had gone with Cash. Which means there's one other Constantine I need to get under control.

I can't deal with Caroline directly for obvious reasons. So, in the way of powerful families since time immemorial, I have set up a meeting with her eldest son. Winston didn't even put up a fight. He just scheduled the damn thing.

It feels very much like penance. Opening my heart to Haley is turning out to demand more pain than I thought possible.

Thomas parks in a structure near Halcyon and accompanies me into the glass building. All of my drivers are also skilled bodyguards, so he should be enough. I hate going to Constantine properties at the best of times. I don't want to be here now. But showing up with a full team is off the table. Not if I want a compromise.

He stays with me outside Winston's office. The bastard makes me wait three minutes past our appointment time, and then his secretary shows me in. Thomas posts himself at the door.

Perry stands near the corner of Winston's desk. He has a black eye and a bruise on his cheek. "Hey, asshole," he says. "I hope you're in a better mood today."

"Perry." Winston doesn't look thrilled to see me. He looks like he always looks. Clean cut. Cocky. And irritated. "I'll talk to you after lunch."

"I can't wait." A sarcastic tone. Perry snaps up a folder from Winston's desk and leaves, walking around me in a wide arc. "Try to keep your hands to yourself," he mutters to me.

Winston watches him go, then crosses his arms over his chest. I take the seat opposite him.

And wait.

After a minute he lets out an annoyed breath. "You wanted to meet with me, prick. Did you come to apologize for beating the shit out of my brothers? And in our own house."

"If you want an apology, you'll have to ask your mother."

"What the hell does that mean?"

"Listen." This is already the most painful thing in my existence, bar none. I cannot go back and forth with Winston right now. "I know we hate each other. I know you're pissed at me for beating up Keaton and Perry. But this shit with

Haley has to stop."

"She was sick. My mother was only trying to help, and you broke into her house like a psychopath. Are you even taking care of her, or do you have her locked in a dungeon?"

"She wasn't sick. Caroline sent one of her bulldogs to take Haley from my house. To kidnap her. She didn't intend to let her go."

Winston scoffs. "Let her go where? She's my cousin. She belongs with us. I don't care what kind of deal you signed with Phillip. No Constantine belongs in a house with you."

"This isn't about the deal with Phillip."

"Then what is it about?" He checks his watch. "I don't have all day to listen to your bullshit complaints, Leo. Are you sad you didn't get to fuck my cousin enough times to make up for some perceived slight? Get over it. You're lucky we haven't pressed charges."

There's no other way to explain it.

I've turned it over in my head a thousand times. There's no other way to explain why Caroline is doing what she's doing without going back to the beginning. Every muscle, every cell, resists taking out my phone. Opening the correct app. Pulling up the videos.

I've had them for eighteen years. I can't stand

to see them. I only look when I have to transfer the files. Fire ripples out from the scars and covers every inch of my skin. My own body trying to warn me. This is too far, too far, too far.

It's also necessary. Winston and the rest of the Constantines invest heavily in reputation management. In building a narrative featuring them as the benevolent rulers of Bishop's Landing and my family as the convenient evil foil.

What Caroline did goes against every story the Constantines tell about themselves. He'll have to see it to believe it.

I turn the phone around and put it in the center of Winston's desk. He stares at me over it, eyes narrowed.

"That's what this is about."

He picks up the phone gingerly and glances at the image on the screen. "What the fuck is this," he says, his voice flat.

I don't answer. I'm not going to describe what he's about to see. I'm not sure I could.

Winston presses play, and his thumb searches for a button to make sure the volume's down. It already is.

Part of my mind shears off and goes somewhere else while Winston watches. I know what's in each of the videos. They were taken from the vantage point of my backpack from school, propped on a chair.

He'll be able to see me and the bed. For the first twenty seconds, that's all there is.

"Leo, tell me what I'm looking at."

At twenty-one seconds, Caroline steps into the frame. Winston's face pales. His teeth lock together. He wants to turn it off. His wrist flicks as if to set the phone down. He keeps watching. By forty seconds, I'm on my back on the bed, Caroline on top. The sex was always that way.

This is the longest ninety-two seconds of my life.

When it's over, Winston looks at me, my phone in his hands.

"Is there more?" His inflection stays steady. Stays flat. He must know by now that there is more. His eyes glint with an emotion I can't name, but his expression remains stoic.

"Swipe and find out."

He does and stabs his thumb into the center to make it play.

Same angle. Same day. Different scene. Caroline with a whip in her hand. Welts appearing on my back. Welts turning to cuts, turning to rivulets of blood. Toward the end of this video, a moment arrives when she thinks she might have killed me.

I've stopped moving. Stopped responding to the blows. Caroline purses her lips. She looks beautiful, even like that. A beautiful coiled snake. And then she draws back her arm and opens another wound.

"How old?" How old am I in the videos, he means. He does not want to ask this question.

"Fourteen."

Winston curses. "How many are there?"

"Three."

"I've seen enough." It's too late for him now. It's been too late since he pressed play on the very first video. If he'd have thrown me out, if he'd refused the meeting, he wouldn't have to know this. "How much to keep this quiet?"

"Keep going."

He glares at me.

I glare back.

The last video is objectively the worst. Winston grits his teeth and presses play.

I've only ever looked at the first few seconds of this video and the last few seconds to make sure it's intact. I'll never watch the rest, except in my memory.

Except when I can't keep it buried.

In the story I tell about that day, if I tell it at all, I leave this part out. That was the story I told

Eva. That Caroline whipped me, and then she sent me out onto the sidewalk to get home or die trying. It's close to the truth. She did whip me. And she did send me away. I left out her name, and I left out one other part.

The video shows what happened after the whipping. And before she let me go.

In one way, the content is substantially similar to the other two. There is the bed. There is me. There is Caroline.

She's even in the same position she was in by the halfway point of that first video. Straddling me with an imperious expression.

The difference is the blood on the sheets from the wounds on my back.

That, and the screaming behind gritted teeth.

Winston makes it fifteen seconds before he drops the phone, stands up, and paces to the window. I stand up too. Put the phone in my pocket.

And wait.

It takes time to process a scene like the one I've just shown to Winston. My whole chest is a minefield. It's going to explode. Watching him watch those videos made them all play again, in full, in my mind. It doesn't matter how hard I've tried to forget. It's like taking a blowtorch to my soul. I never imagined I'd tell someone else, much less a Constantine. But I'd do anything for Haley. Even this.

Winston turns to face me, his hands in his pockets. "You didn't care about that building."

He's talking about a building I bought just to fuck with him. He made up a whole scheme to force me into selling it back, which of course I did. Winston fancies himself the king of New York City real estate. It's a vulnerability that's easy to exploit.

"No. I didn't."

"And you didn't care about Ash."

Ash, his girlfriend. I made a bit of trouble for them via posting a few videos on the Internet. I had them all taken down, wiped completely, after the game was finished. It was a bullshit thing to do, but I didn't care who got hurt. Back then, I hadn't met Haley Constantine. "No."

"That was a fucking message. To her." He means Caroline. "To show her what you could do."

"Yes."

No more waiting. No more delaying. The moment of penance has arrived. I feel it like a rushing wind against my scarred back. I have not come to bring peace. Not to Winston. I have come to lay down my sword.

And so I open my mouth and tell him. All of my organs, out in front of him. What it was like to find myself in over my head at fourteen. The whipping. The revenge games. What it was like to drown in my own blood. What it was like to burn in the fever afterward.

Everything I can bring myself to say.

"She took Haley," I say, my voice hard as a diamond. "Now she's announcing an engagement and sending that asshole to press conferences to accuse me of kidnapping. It's hurting Haley. I need it to be over."

Winston studies me for a long time.

"Is that the price for you to keep your mouth shut? Me, calling off my mother?" He knows as well as I do that videos like the ones I have won't ever go away.

For the first time ever in front of Winston Constantine, I drop the Morelli mask and level him with a look that's entirely me. "It's not a bargaining chip. I'm not threatening to release the videos. Do you think for a second I could live with that?"

"You released videos of me and Ash. We had to live with it."

"You weren't raping her in those videos."

The eldest Constantine son looks away. "If you're not going to release them, then why the fuck did you show me?"

"Would you have taken my word for it?"

"No."

"That's why."

Winston puts a hand to his forehead and releases a heavy sigh. He's a calculating bastard. And now he's having to recalculate his entire life. I don't expect it will change his view of me, and I don't care if it does. All I care about is Haley. All I care about is giving her what she wants, which is a life free of Caroline's bullshit. Even if it means carving into my flesh and bone to do it.

"You want this finished," Winston says finally. "Does that mean you're going to stop, too?"

I give Winston an incredulous look. "I've wanted this to be finished since I was fourteen. I didn't have a choice in the matter."

A long pause. I survive painful heartbeat after painful heartbeat. I survive another trip through my memories. I survive another burst of searing pain across my back.

"Fuck." Winston takes in a deep breath and gives the window one last glance. "I can't make any guarantees. But I'll talk to her. I'll find a way. This has to stop."

"Good."

There's nothing else to say. He doesn't want me here. I don't want to be here. I've made my penance. "Leo," he says as I reach the door. Push it open.

I look back at him.

"I'm sorry." Winston stands by the window, a look of genuine concern on his face. Not for me. It's for his mother, and his family, and their reputation. It might not collapse if I released these videos, but it would be damaged.

"It was a long time ago," I tell him.

He doesn't say anything else.

One more minute, and we're out of Halcyon. Thomas shuts the door to the SUV behind me and jogs around to the driver's seat. He keeps his eyes firmly on the road. I'm the only one to witness how badly my hands are shaking. I can't hold my phone.

Now that the meeting is over, now that we're away from that building, my body has recognized the size of the threat. A delayed response to reliving what Caroline did and to the act of showing another person. I never have before. My lungs constrict and my heart tests the boundaries of my rib cage, looking for a way out. I have a flash fever. Rising fast.

"Pull over."

Thomas doesn't hesitate. He pulls directly to the curb. I have just enough time to get to an alley before I'm sick on the ground.

CHAPTER TWENTY

Haley

LEO'S HOUSE IS quiet the morning after my party, but it's a good quiet. The quiet of a space that was very recently bursting at the seams with joy. Everyone but Daphne left with drivers at the end of the night. I've taken a long, long shower and dressed in soft clothes. I'm sore from the party. I don't know if it's from the heels or the dancing or my nerves.

I go downstairs to look for Leo and find Gerard waiting in the foyer instead. "Good morning, Haley. How was your party?"

"It was amazing." There's a tense set to his posture. Gerard's eyes go back to Leo's large double doors. "Is Leo in the dining room?"

There are usually three places I can find him if he's not in the bedroom when I wake up. His office, the den, or the dining room. Sometimes I find him reading at the table with a cup of coffee at his place. The first day I was here, I found him just that way. His plate in front of him, and his book. He'd abandoned the book in favor of making me take all my clothes off and come all over his fingers. I told myself it was awful, and cruel, and humiliating, but in reality it was over for me. I was never going to be the same after that. I was never going to want anyone else. I just didn't know it yet.

"No. He'll be arriving back at the house in about five minutes."

"Back at the house? Where did he go?" Worry clenches my stomach in a fist. Leo didn't say a word about leaving. The last time he invited me for a walk, he turned out to be very, very sick. "Is everything all right?"

"He had a meeting in the city. Everything is secure. We've had no problems on the grounds."

Secure is not the same thing as *all right.*

I go to the dining room to wait for him.

The space has been transformed back into its usual arrangement. All that's left from my party are the gold hangings on the ceiling. He made that perfect night for me, and then he went to the city without telling me. I don't know whether to be pissed off or afraid or both. The house feels like a cavern without him. It feels like a popped balloon. Someone has put his book back on the table. It's a battered paperback. I recognize it. It's a story about building a cathedral.

Voices in the foyer. Footsteps in the hall. And Leo appears in the doorway.

I've come into the room many times while he's backlit by the window. He has the most cutting profile, the most beautiful profile I've ever seen. The light always catches on the planes of him, casting shadows that take my breath away.

It's a different view from his seat. That first day when I came into this room, I almost stopped breathing at the sunlight on his cheekbones. He would have seen me, lit in a soft glow. He's standing in it now. What I didn't know on that day was how it showed everything. It's the kind of light that makes hiding impossible.

This is his house. He's choosing to let me see him this way. In his pristine black clothes. They were made for him. To highlight his body, yes. To show off the lean muscle on his tall frame and his perfect thighs and strong shoulders. But they were also made to protect him from as much pain as possible.

I don't think it's working.

He's wrung out, his dark eyes haunted. Leo stands up the tallest when his pain is bad. There's another level beyond that, though. There is. He hasn't admitted it to me out loud, but I can tell by looking at him that we're almost there now. A pressure in my chest expands. I want answers. I don't want to ask for them. Not because I'm afraid of the answers, but because I don't want to hurt him. Not any more than this meeting already has.

Leo looks at me for a long, long time. Until I can feel him struggling. Until the silence seems heavier by the second. His eyes go to his book, and then back to me. "Are you ready for breakfast?"

"Are you?"

His hands come up and he covers his face. Runs them right over his eyes and down. It's over in a split second and it's probably nothing. Except it's not a gesture Leo makes. It's not something I've ever seen him do. And not with trembling hands. "I'm not hungry."

"What if we just—" I cross the room and take his hand. Leo squeezes mine and brings it to his mouth. Grazes his teeth over my knuckles. "Sometimes, if I was having a really shitty day, my sister would send me upstairs to start over. So I'd get in bed and take a nap and wake up again, and then it would be better. Or at least bearable."

He lets out a breath. "I'm fucking terrible at

napping."

"Then let's not nap."

Leo pushes me back against the doorframe then. He drops his head and kisses my jawline, kisses my neck, kisses my mouth. He puts both hands on my face, and the shaking disappears. Like I'm the only solid thing in the room. In his life. He feels like the only solid thing in mine. "Upstairs," he says against my skin, and then he picks me up and takes me there himself.

THE DAY PASSES. The night. The next morning. Leo doesn't tell me about his meeting, and I don't ask, but I know he's thinking about it. I keep catching him staring off into nothing. I go to him every time. I can't resist it. He'll tell me when it's time, when he can, but until then—

Until then, I can kiss his cheek. Drag my nails down the back of his neck and make him shiver. Beg him to take me to bed.

It's nightfall, and I've been reading in the den. Daphne sits on the opposite chair, her legs over the arm, staring at the ceiling while she bickers with Leo about her room. "I just want you to have an opinion about it."

"I have no opinion about your mural, Daphne." He's standing at the window, looking out.

"It's going to be on a wall in your house. You could at least say if you want a forest scene or an ocean scene."

"You only paint oceans."

"Maybe I want to paint a forest."

"Then paint a forest."

Daphne gives a dramatic sigh and flings herself off the chair. She goes over and gets up on tiptoe to brush a kiss to Leo's cheek, then flounces away. "We're not done with this discussion," she warns with a glare. He rolls his eyes.

"Go to bed."

"You go to bed," Daphne says, and then she's gone.

I'm about to make a joke that's not really a joke about going to bed when Leo pulls his phone out of his pocket. He takes one look at the screen, and then all the quiet of the evening is shattered. Leo's phone hits the floor, forgotten. He strides across the room to the fireplace and throws open a panel in the wall above it to reveal a TV that's brand-new and surrounded by fresh paint.

"I didn't know you had—" The rest of the sentence never makes it to the air.

Because my dad is on the news. On TV.

My blanket pools on the floor, slipping off

legs gone numb. The TV is partially blocked by Leo's shoulder until I'm up next to him. So close. Too close. I reach to touch the screen before I know what I'm doing.

"He looks—" He looks so old. He looks so afraid. So tired. My dad is washed out in the bright lights from the cameras, his face pale, sweat gathering at his hairline. The podium in front of him is too tall. "Oh, Jesus." He's not alone. Caroline stands next to him, her arm looped through his. It's meant to look like she's steadying him, but I bet she's not, I bet she's keeping him there. Making him do this.

Leo pushes another button on the bottom of the TV, and I can hear him.

I can hear my dad.

"—her fiancé has already spoken to you, but it's not enough. It hasn't been enough. I'm asking you—asking as a father." His voice is unstable. Trembling. He raises his sleeve to dab at his forehead. "Please return my daughter to her family. We are all worried sick. We need Haley in our lives. Our Haley. She's about to graduate college next semester. Her whole life is ahead of her. All she ever wanted—"

He puts a hand to his chest, his fingers curled into a fist. I can feel it on my own chest, like a brand, burning through my heart. Goose bumps fly down my shoulders to my fingernails. I dream of Leo dying almost every time I fall asleep. This is a waking nightmare. It was one thing for Rick to work with Caroline, to agree to give a press conference, to lie. It's another for her to scare my dad like this. I thought Cash would tell him I was okay after the party. And maybe he did. But Caroline obviously told him something else.

She's been nodding along with everything my dad says. Caroline nods again. But she's nodding at silence. I can't take my eyes off my dad. He's wincing.

"All she ever wanted—" He clears his throat.

"Dad," I say, and I know it's foolish, I know he can't hear me. I know. The fist at his chest spreads out and a matching horror takes wing across my heart. "Something's happening. Leo. Something's happening to my dad." I grab for his arm and hold tight.

"Haley," my dad says. His face contorts. I think he might sob, or beg, but he doesn't.

He collapses over the podium, his hand clutching his heart.

It's chaos on the screen. Someone runs in from the side, and Caroline's bending over him. I launch myself at the TV and get both hands over him before the picture cuts out, replaced by the news studio.

"Oh my god." I let go of Leo and scramble for the couch. For my phone. "Oh my god. I think he just died on TV. I think he just died. I think he just had a heart attack and died on TV." My face is numb. My heart is numb, or it hurts so much I can't feel it. I don't know who to call. The phone screen swims in front of me. "Oh, help. Help." I go back over to Leo. "Please. I don't know who to call."

"It was for nothing."

"What?" I try to push my phone into his hands. "What are you talking about?"

He turns, and all the worry, all the uncertainty of the past few days, is gone from his expression. He looks like the man I met in the street a lifetime ago. The mean, devastating man who took pleasure in my fear. The beast.

Leo glances down at me like I'm a stranger. He takes in my face. My clothes. My tears. And then he shakes his head, like I've overstayed my welcome at one of his business meetings. "This is over."

My mouth falls open. I can't close it. "Just—I just need to know who to call."

"You can call anyone you want from the car,

but you're leaving. It's over."

"Leo, what—" He's killing me. His eyes are so blank, so devoid of warmth, that they could freeze me in a blink. "What car?"

He walks away from me. Turns on his heel, and goes away. Picks up his phone from the floor. He dials a number and puts it to his ear. "Haley's coat and a car out front," he says into it. "Now."

"No."

"Time to go," he says.

I turn and run. He's not doing this. He's sick, or he's upset, or he's in pain. He's not actually doing this. I'll barricade myself in the first room I find. I'll make him understand.

Or I'll run headfirst into Gerard, who stalls me long enough for Leo to catch me.

I fight him.

I fight him with everything I have. With fists and feet and all my weight.

I fight him, and I lose. Leo takes me to the front doors like a doll or a discarded piece of furniture. He holds out one of my arms so Gerard can put my coat on. The pink coat he bought me. I pull my arm back, fighting, fighting, fighting.

"It's freezing," Leo snaps.

"Then don't send me out. Leo. Stop." He gets the coat around behind me, and no matter how hard I pull, I can't stop him. It's over both arms. "I want to stay with you."

"You don't belong here." Gerard opens the door, his eyes unbearably sad, and stands by while Leo takes me out into the cold. To the waiting car.

The driver opens the door. Leo tries to put me in the back seat, but I fling both arms out and grip the frame with both hands. "Stop," I scream at him. "What are you doing?"

"I'm sending you home, where you belong." There's no blank look in his eyes now. It's fire and rage, heat and hurt. "I don't want you here with me. You're a complication. A liability."

"You need me here. And I need you. I'm choosing you. I can just stay here with you. I only wanted to call and find out if he's alive."

"You're going to do better than that, darling. You're going to go see him. They'll be taking him to a hospital. Gerard will find out which one, and Thomas will have that information before you reach the highway."

I take one hand off the car and get my fist into his shirt. "I'm coming back to you. I don't care what you say. I want you. I choose you. I love you, Leo. Please don't do this."

His eyes linger on my lips and hope tears

through the air, through my lungs.

Leo brushes my hand away from his shirt and pushes me into the SUV. He traps my face with his hands. "You're a Constantine." He practically spits the name. It sounds so ugly when he says it like that. "And you're sweet. You were fun to toy with, like the rest of them, but you're not worth my life."

"You don't mean this. You don't." It's half sob, half scream, like getting louder can get through to him. I grab for his wrist. His hand. My heart won't beat. It hangs in pieces. "Please. Don't do this. Please, let me stay."

He pats my cheek, sarcastic and mean. "We're finished now, Haley. Done. Don't come back."

CHAPTER TWENTY-ONE

Haley

THE PUBLIC HOSPITAL at the outskirts of Bishop's Landing is a threadbare place. It's not like the gleaming hospital wing where Leo went when he was shot. Where I went. This place is all fluorescent lights and yellowing tile and the sharp smell of disinfectant. I look ridiculous in my pink coat. I feel worse than ridiculous. I feel like there's a giant bloody hole in my chest that everyone can see and no one can fix.

"This way," says the nurse who's taking me to see my dad. "He's in room number nine. We're going to be monitoring him very closely through the night. The surgery will be first thing in the morning."

"He's—" I hate this. I hate this. "He's awake? He's talking?"

The nurse puts a compassionate hand on my arm. "He's shaken up, but he's talking. The man just survived a heart attack. You'll have to take things slow."

I don't know what that means, but I don't get a chance to ask, because we're here.

My dad is tucked into a narrow hospital bed, the rails up on one side and a lamp burning behind him. He doesn't look any better than he did on TV. His face is colorless and clammy and he looks so small. So helpless. His eyes go to me the second I step in the room. "Haley," he says. "Sweetheart."

He lifts his arms to me. I drop down on his bed and hug him back like he's made of glass. He's so much older now than he used to be. There's so much more gray in his hair. I didn't pay much attention before. The change was gradual, and we were busy, and he was happily consumed in his work. We weren't rich. We were never that kind of Constantine. But life was simple. "Hi, Daddy."

His sigh sounds off. "I'm so sorry, honey. I'm sorry you had to see that." A tired laugh. "I didn't mean to have a heart attack in the middle of my speech."

"Daddy—" I let myself listen to his heart for a few more beats, and then I sit up so I can see him. "Why were you doing that? Did you really think I'd been taken? I told you it was all right."

The corners of his mouth tremble. "I didn't think you'd been taken. I heard what you said. And Cash said you were doing fine."

"Then why?"

"Caroline came over." His eyes cloud. "You know my mind is always on my work. It's hard to stop it from wandering. There's so much to do, and now that you kids are grown up, I don't have to worry. Not quite so much, anyway. But she said so many things, Haley. She had so much to say about you, and about Leo, and about my work. She said—" His brow furrows. "She said if I made this one speech, I could have you back. My work would be protected. There were more cameras than I expected. I didn't feel well."

I touch his cheek, and my dad closes his eyes.

"Caroline made it impossible to refuse that speech. But everything I said was real. Even if she forced me to say it. I want you to come home. I want you to be safe and happy. I want—" He closes his eyes again. "I just want you where I can see you. I know you'll be out in the world soon enough, but it doesn't have to—" His eyebrows lift like he's trying to stay awake, but he doesn't look at me. "Not quite yet. Not yet."

My dad's breathing evens out.

I ease myself off the bed and fold myself into a

hard plastic chair nearby.

"Miss Constantine?"

"Yeah?" I watch my dad's chest rise and fall under the hospital gown and scratchy sheet.

"Could we speak in the hall?"

"Of course." I leave my coat on the chair and follow her out. This is a different nurse from before. One with green scrubs and a clipboard. She has dark hair and kind eyes.

"I wanted to talk with you about your father's situation. The doctor can go over things with you in more detail in an hour or two, but I like people to have their bearings."

I'm not going to have my bearings for a long time. Maybe forever. I feel perpetually off-balance, like my head is swinging heavily toward the walls, a different direction every time I move my eyes. My heart keeps searching for Leo. He's not here, and he's not going to be. I can't go back.

And I can't think about that now.

"Thank you," I tell the nurse.

"You're welcome." She pats my elbow, then flips over the page on her notebook. "Your father has suffered a major heart attack involving at least two arteries. The surgeon can tell you more about the procedure in the morning, but for tonight we're focused on keeping him stable. The event sapped a lot of his strength, so after the surgery, he'll require a lot of assistance to recover. First steps, we stabilize his condition for the surgery. We have all the signatures we need to go forward with that, but we can't help you with funding for in-home care."

"Signatures?" My brain hangs up on that word. My dad is one person.

She flips another page and scans down it. "Your father is currently in a gap in his insurance coverage. There's a chance you can apply for reimbursement after the fact, but hospital admin won't let us proceed with the surgery without a funding agreement. It's so lucky that his sister was here when he arrived."

"That was my aunt. She's his sister-in-law."

"She's a good one." The nurse shakes her head, her eyes going wide and sympathetic. "It takes a little finessing with the paperwork, and we have to check for her approval at several points along the way, but your father's surgery and care here will be paid for." She leans in and studies my face. "Are you all right, Miss Constantine?"

"I'm—" Dying. I'm dying. "I should call my siblings. Is there anything else I need to know?"

"Not for now. Go make your calls."

Another plastic chair waits outside the door to

my father's hospital room. I lean in to check on him before I dial Petra.

He's asleep, but it's a restless sleep. His hand is up on his chest. Every so often, it flutters up and comes back down again. I can't watch for very long, or else I'll cry, and I have to hold it together.

I sink down onto the rigid plastic and dial Petra's number with my hand over my eyes. She answers on the first ring. "Hey, Hales. What's up?"

"Hey, listen."

That's all I manage before the sobs get the better of me. The more I try to keep them quiet, the worse they sound. Petra makes a bunch of soothing noises over the phone, but I can tell she's freaked out. I would be, too. I feel like I'm swallowing broken glass but I do it until I can speak.

"So." I wipe my whole sleeve over my eyes. "Dad had a heart attack."

Petra drops her phone. It thunks against her kitchen counter and there's a static sound as she grabs it back up. "Is he okay?"

"No, he had a heart attack. He's not dead, but he's in the hospital. I'm here with him."

"I'm on my way."

"Petra, no. No—don't come over here. It's late at night, and there's nowhere to sit. He's asleep anyway."

"What did the doctors say?"

"I haven't talked to them yet. But the nurse said it was a bad heart attack. There's going to be a surgery in the morning. I think he's going to be here for a while, and then—then someone's going to have to be home with him. To help him. He's really weak."

"I should be the one to do that."

"You're married. You have a life. And Cash has school. I'm the only one with the time. I can—I can defer the last semester of college and graduate next winter instead."

"Wait, wait, wait." I can see her pacing around her kitchen. Petra used to do the same thing when we were younger. Pace around any available space. "What are you saying? I thought you were staying with Leo Morelli. You said you wanted to be there."

"I do want to be there." I want to not cry in this hallway anymore. I want for this terrible night to unwind itself until I'm back in the den with Leo. I want for my father to say no to Caroline, and for her not to be so awful.

"So I'll come and take over," Petra says briskly. "I'm the oldest, and I'm most prepared to—"

"I'm already here." My sister lapses into silence. "And things are over with Leo. I don't have anywhere else to go."

"Hales...are you sure? You don't sound—I don't know. Maybe I don't know what the hell I'm talking about. Are you sure it wasn't some kind of misunderstanding?"

You were fun to toy with, like the rest of them, but you're not worth my life.

"I'm sure."

"And there's no chance you could talk it out with him?"

"Petra. You're really trying to convince me to make up with Leo Morelli?"

"Yeah." Her voice has a helpless shrug written all over it. "You've never sounded so sad. And you don't say things you don't mean. So I have to think you meant it when you told me you wanted to be with him."

"I'm sad because Dad had a heart attack."

The truth. Just not the full truth.

"Was it him or you?" Petra asks.

I want you. I choose you. I love you.

"Him."

"Then you didn't want to leave."

"It doesn't matter what I want." I straighten

up in my seat. "What matters is that someone has to be here for Dad. I have to be here for Dad. I'll keep you and Cash updated, obviously, but it's best for everybody if it's just one of us."

"Haley—"

"I have to go. The doctor is coming to meet me. I'll text you after, okay?"

"Okay, but—"

I hang up on her. It doesn't feel great, but it feels better than listening to my older sister talk about this. She gave up the man she loved to obey Caroline Constantine. She wouldn't understand my dilemma. I tip my head back against the hospital's concrete wall. It's painted a drab sandy color that makes me vaguely sick. A white stripe runs along the middle of the wall. This place is in desperate need of a person like Daphne. I'd rather look at the ocean. I'd rather let the waves swallow me whole.

CHAPTER TWENTY-TWO

Leo

I LOST HER.

I lost her.

I lost her.

It's the only thought that circles my mind as clouds cover the stars and the moon sets. As the weak winter sun rises over fresh snow. As I tell Daphne that Haley is gone and won't be back. As I take in her shocked expression with detached recognition. Why is she surprised? This is how it has to be. The sun peaks and falls below the horizon.

I lost her.

It's irritating for its inaccuracy. I didn't lose Haley. I sent her away. With my own two hands. She fought. Screamed. Cried. I put her in the SUV anyway and sent her to her father. I did it because I had to. We were at the end of the line. She touched her father's face on the TV screen and I knew, I *knew*, that was it. That's all I could ever offer her. Winston wasn't convinced, or he couldn't convince Caroline. Either way. Haley can't live like that. I'll never be a replacement for her family. She loves them. They love her. People like Haley belong with their families.

End of the line. Now I'm past it.

Mrs. Page comes into my office on the second day with a sandwich.

She tries again on the third day with a bowl of my favorite soup.

On the fourth day, she's desperate. The teacup trembles in her hands. "It has milk and sugar," she says. "You need to have something if you're not eating, Mr. Morelli."

"I'm not sleeping, either. Is there anything else you wanted to know?"

She leaves the tea on my desk. It goes cold, and after a few hours, it disappears again.

I don't stop eating to spite Mrs. Page. It just no longer seems worthwhile. Sleeping would be an escape, but it's not available to me. I've never stayed so long at the peak of my pain. It started when I watched Haley lose her shit over her dad having a heart attack and it hasn't let up. It makes no distinction between my back and the rest of my body. My head throbs and burns. My bones are broken shards. My nerves are piano wire cutting through flesh.

For these four days, I sit through meetings like a fucking corpse. I don't hear a thing anyone says. I send emails I don't remember sending. My business runs on autopilot. Daphne pokes her head into my office every afternoon and talks to me with worried eyes. She's painting a wall in her suite. She's painting the ocean. She's painting an underwater forest. Are you okay? I'm fine. I'm busy. I'm working. Go back to your painting, Daphne.

I am not fine.

I'm a pillar of flame. A torched cathedral. Ash burns to ash. It hurts too much to bear. The pain tears out my mind and throws it on the pyre of my soul. Dante would have jumped into boiling glass to escape the heat of purgatory. But he was promised paradise. There's no such promise for me. I had her in my hands, and I let her go.

On the fourth night I attend a last, desperate Mass at St. Thomas's. I spend the entire thing on my feet, gripping the back of a pew. Sitting is beyond me. Kneeling is beyond me. When I approach the altar for Communion, Father Simon asks if he should call an ambulance.

Of course not, of course not. What would they do? Bring her back to me?

It's past one when I return and climb the stairs. I've been avoiding my bedroom, and my private library, because Haley's books are there. I thought it would spare me more pain, but the opposite has happened. As of this morning I've started to hallucinate her.

I don't go to the library. I go to the medicine cabinet in my bathroom. If my mind is already short-circuiting, which it is, I might as well lean into it.

There is a bottle in the medicine cabinet. Every six months, it gets taken out and replaced with a new one. I suspect Gerard, or Mrs. Page. I suspect they are in league with Eva. In eighteen years, I've never opened one of the bottles.

Father Simon told me once that refusing painkillers isn't a penance that's required of me, but that's not why I do it. Or—penance is the least of those reasons. When Eva brought me home from the hospital all those years ago, seven pills came with me in my bag. Taking the first one was enough to know it wouldn't be an option. Not for me. Not if I wanted to be alert enough to protect my siblings from my father, and to protect my secret from my siblings. The amount it takes to touch the pain is enough to render me unconscious. I told myself that one day

I would be in a position to take them.

It's never been true. The years have added more responsibilities. More threats. And a reputation that makes it more necessary than ever not to offer that kind of weakness to my enemies. I would never forgive myself if I missed something. If I let danger through because I couldn't handle the pain.

I woke up from that first and only pill in a cold sweat. It had made me defenseless, made my siblings defenseless, and stole my ability to know when our father was arriving home. The clutching fear set off a new round of pain.

It's been a long eighteen years.

I take the bottle out of the cabinet and shake it. It's full. A month's worth of pills at least.

Enough.

In my office, a bottle of whiskey waits for me in my desk drawer. I don't particularly like whiskey. Lucian gave it to me as a joke. It burns going down, but my brother was right. It is a joke. A fucking joke. It goes to my head but it doesn't touch the pain. I can see Haley out of the corner of my eye. Not all of her, just a flash of blonde hair and the glimmer of sunlight in her blue eyes. If I look directly at her, she disappears. I make a game of it. Drink. Look for her outline. Drink some more. Consider the glass paperweight on my desk. Drink. The paperweight is shaped like a rose. Daphne gave it to me when she was twelve. She was so proud of it. The whiskey loses its burn and its taste.

I'll never see Haley again. She'll stay with her father, and she'll help him recover from his heart attack, and she won't be able to leave. She won't want to leave. She'll realize that's where she is supposed to be. A good daughter. A good sister. Not mine. Never mine. God. Fuck. It hurts. Does it make me a coward to open the pills and take one out? Does it make me a coward to take one? What about two? Three?

I abandon both bottles and take out my phone. I have a question for a person I talked to once. Does it make me a coward that I couldn't ask him before? I'm quite drunk now. Drunk enough that it's difficult to search my call log for the number. Consciousness starts to play hide-and-seek between rings.

"I don't have anything you want, Leo. You got your book. Did she like it?" The coldest voice I've ever heard spears through my drunkenness. Colder than Lucian's voice. Colder than snow. Colder than the void of my life without Haley.

"She wept to see it."

A silence. I hate Hades' silences. What a prick. "You've been drinking."

"I've been dying."

"In what sense?"

"All of them. And me with no one to say the last rites."

"If it's a priest you're looking for—"

"No. No. I wanted an answer." Ah—there she is. Getting clearer all the time. Hallucination or dream? I'll take either one.

"I'll require the question first." In the background, a door closes. Is he in his office too? Or somewhere with his wife? I don't have a wife. I don't have Haley.

"You're so fucking demanding."

"This from the man who's called me in the middle of the night. Ask."

"You said you were acquainted with pain." Haley disappears again. "What kind is it?"

"It's nerve pain related to a genetic sensitivity to light. My past history worsened the condition."

"You get headaches or something?"

"I have seizures. Preceded by pain I would describe as excruciating. It's the feedback loop of the pain that causes the episodes. This isn't what you want to know. Ask the question."

"You can't be a ruthless terror if you have—"

A hiccup interrupts me. "If you have seizures. That would make you weak."

Hades laughs, the sound icy and dark, the tone a vivid illustration of *fuck around and find out.* "Perhaps. Though it has had little to no effect on my reputation."

"How?"

"No one in the outside world knows. As far as they're concerned, I am—how did you put it? A prick with strange eyes."

"*I* know. You just told me."

"You're drunk. And you sound like you've taken pills."

"Just a few. But I can't take them normally. Only on special occasions."

"What's the occasion tonight?"

"I lost Haley. I sent her out of my house to save her. I won't see her again. And even if a miracle happened, even if she came back to me, I have nothing to give her." I stifle a bitter, unhinged laugh. "I'll die like this. Either I'll die from the pain, or I'll be a coward and die from a hit while I'm incapacitated by painkillers. I have too many enemies to risk them." The dark is closing in. Haley brushes her fingertips over my cheek. "Did you find a way to live with it? Did you find some secret? Or do you just wait to die?

That's what I want to know."

"A secret for a secret. What happened to you eighteen years ago?"

God help me. I tell him. I just tell him, slipping into a nightmare. He's a voice on the phone. A windswept mountain. A prick with strange eyes. A confessor. He remembered what I told him in our last conversation. And he keeps his word. When I'm done talking a lifetime later, he tells me a story like a fever dream. About a farm and a mountain. A white building in the city and the sea. And a wide green field with red poppies.

I fold my arms on my desk and put my head down. Bless me, for I have sinned. I don't receive absolution before I fall into a black, eternal night.

A door opens.

A gasp.

"Leo."

I've been here a long time. I don't want to wake up. Don't want to come back. Can't move.

"Oh, shit. Oh my god. Oh my god." Glass scrapes on wood. Shut up. Shut up. I'm not here. A muffled sob. "No, Leo, No. Oh, shit, what do I do? What do I—Leo. Please? Leo—"

A hand meets my shoulder blade and pain erupts over my skin. It takes me off the desk with a roar. I sweep one hand out to get them away.

"Don't touch me. Don't *touch* me." Jesus, it hurts. Fuck. Fuck. Fuck. I stand up to get out from under it and brace two fists on the desk.

"I thought you were dead." Daphne stares, her face pale, eyes shining with tears and terror. "You weren't moving, Leo. Have you been in here all night? Did you drink all of that?" She points a shaking finger at the bottle on my desk.

"Get out." I glare at her, and she shrinks back. "Get the fuck out."

"No. I can't leave you in here. I thought you were dead. Did you try to kill yourself? You're— you're scary like this." I sit down hard in the chair, the fight going out of me. The pain stays. It's Daphne. My sister. It's just Daphne.

"I didn't try to kill myself. I'm fine."

"You're lying." She swallows. Clears her throat. "You're so pale. And you were so still. I know you're not fine. I can see you." She approaches the desk, and I hate this. I hate what I've become. "I think I should call Eva. She would know what to do."

"She has her own heartbreak to deal with. Her own life."

Daphne tugs on the collar of her shirt. "Why don't you go to her? Why don't you go to Haley?"

I rub my hands over my face and try not to

resist the pain. Resistance only makes it worse. "Because I love her."

"That doesn't make any sense." Daphne's crying now, and I see how badly I scared her. "If you love her, you should be with her. And you do. I know you do."

"My love for her is more than that. It's strong enough to let her go." I take a breath I don't want to take. A breath that hurts like a bitch. "She has a family. Those are her people. I was always fooling myself that she could be mine."

CHAPTER TWENTY-THREE

Haley

LEO WAS A dream, and I'm awake now. Awake in a hospital room next to my dad's bed. Awake with a book in my hands, wearing old clothes from my closet.

Back in my old life.

Though in my old life, I could fall into a book and let it take the hours away. Now the words make no impression. I keep having to start the page over. My dad sleeps in his bed, oblivious to everything. He's improving now that we're a few days past his surgery. Sleeping better.

I've read five paragraphs without taking in a thing. Maybe I shouldn't have submitted my deferment this morning. Maybe schoolwork would be easier to concentrate on. There are grades to think about, at least.

I swallow a snort. Grades. I don't think I could bring myself to care about grades. They used to matter to me. They used to be everything to me. Grades and books and my family. They'll be everything to me again. Hopefully by spring semester.

It would be a good idea to get a notebook and a pen and make a plan for the next few months. First thing on my list is to get my dad back to good health. He's the only parent I have left, and I love him. I need him and his disorganized presence in my life. Second is to figure out how I'm going to get back to school after a semester-long delay. And third is to hope against all hope that I'll stop feeling like a clawed animal has reached inside my chest and torn it apart for sport.

"Hi, Haley." The evening nurse bustles in, keeping her voice low. She's efficient with her checks. "I wanted to let you know, hon, that we'll have to reauthorize the hospital stay within the next twenty-four hours."

"Okay." My heart rate spikes. Reauthorizing the stay means coming to a new payment agreement with Caroline. If Caroline won't pay, the hospital will discharge my dad. They can do it as long as he's in stable condition. Which he is. I'd just have to keep him that way at home. "Will you let me know if you need anything from us?"

"Of course I will." She takes some notes on

her clipboard. "Back in a while. Use the *Call* button if you need anything. If I'm not here another nurse will help you."

There's no dedicated team just for my dad here. The difference between his hospital stay and Leo's breaks my heart. Everything breaks my heart. I'm going to be walking around with a useless muscle in the center of my chest forever. If only it would ease up on the aching hurt. I'd settle for being numb.

Soft footsteps come in through the door. The nurse must have forgotten something from her list. Good. I can ask her what medicine is in the IV. I open my mouth to do it.

And shut it again.

It's not the nurse moving into the room as if she owns it.

It's Caroline.

She's in her beautiful Prada coat. A brilliant white against the tired walls. Her hair is in a shining, complicated knot. Bright eyes. Pink cheeks. I could be standing at a Constantine party like we went to as kids. Me in threadbare clothes, trying not to do anything embarrassing in front of perfect Caroline. My skin crawls. Her perfection is a lie. Below the glamorous clothes and the gorgeous face is a corrupt nightmare.

A genteel tilt of her head as she peers at my dad. "He hasn't breathed his last?"

My book snaps closed in my hands. How dare she? Prickling indignation makes my muscles ache. I can't react to her. I can only respond. We need her now, so I have to be polite. I can't risk my dad's care. "He's in stable condition after the surgery. They had to go back in yesterday for a minor fix, but he's resting a lot more comfortably now. His doctors don't want him released for another few days so they can be sure he's ready for the next step."

"Mm-hmm. Your father is going to have a long recovery."

"I'll be by his side. I'm not leaving."

Caroline's eyes meet mine for the first time since she came into the room. Cold. The blue in her eyes is so cold, and edged in satisfaction. "Good. You've spent too long as a Morelli whore as it is."

My breath catches in my throat. Her words should be meaningless. They shouldn't sting at all. But they're side by side with the truth. I was a whore for Leo Morelli. I couldn't get enough of him. I wanted all of him, forever, and Caroline destroyed everything we had.

I blink at her, lifting my eyebrows a fraction

of an inch. A hint of shock. I've seen Caroline deploy this expression at parties to keep the people around her in line.

She narrows her eyes, and I lose my nerve. Shame runs hot over my cheeks. I'm ashamed of everything. Of turning back into quiet Haley Constantine, the girl with her book, and not standing up for my dad. For myself. I'm ashamed that I let her comment sail past. I'm ashamed I didn't fight hard enough to stay with Leo.

"We need to get you settled," Caroline pronounces. "It will be the best thing for everyone, including your father."

"What does that mean?"

It could mean anything. She's kept my dad under house arrest before. She could keep me in our house, too.

"It means you'll marry Rick on the second of February. The venue has been booked, and invitations will go out in three weeks. Traditionally, the bride's family covers most of the costs. I know your father isn't in any position to do so, but you're a lucky girl. You have a loving extended family."

Horror is a hard plastic chair in a too-small room. It's endless beeping from machines that monitor whether your dad is going to live or die.

It's a woman who's done unthinkable things laying out your entire future in a reasonable tone.

"No."

Caroline purses her lips like I'm a child who's refusing to sit down for dinner. "You'll do as I say."

"You can't make me take any vows. You can't make me say *I do*."

Her cool gaze flicks to my father and holds. The threat digs into my gut. Into my heart. "Actually, darling, I think I can."

"I'll never marry him." I want to sound strong. Defiant. Unafraid. But my voice trembles. It gives me away. All my doubt. All my fear. That little shake is enough of an admission.

The corner of Caroline's mouth turns up. She looks me up and down one more time. "Enjoy your book." She moves to the door, graceful as ever, then stops. "Oh—I thought I would stop by the billing department on my way out. I believe there was something to reauthorize. A form or two." She laughs a little. "There's always so much paperwork when it comes to hospital stays. I suppose I could make it easier on myself if I bowed out and left things to you."

This is how it happens. Caroline stands here in her white coat and her beautiful makeup and pretends the choice she's giving me is a real one and not the cruelest possible joke. My eyes sting with tears that I am not, *not*, going to let fall in front of her. Caroline already knows how far I'll go for my family. She knows I was with Leo. She'll know why I was with Leo. The difference between them is that Caroline pretends to be a queen when she's a monster. Leo pretends to be a monster when he's a prince.

He *is* a prince.

Isn't he?

The things he said when he sent me away can't have been things he meant. Things he felt. They had to be a cover for something else. That's how Leo is. He shows people what they expect to see so that he can keep his true self hidden. So that he can keep himself safe.

Unless it's the beast who's real.

In the end, it doesn't matter, does it? In the end, he's not coming to save me. I've spent every day here in this hospital room, wishing he would come for me. Wishing he would fold me in his arms and take my chin in his hand and kiss me until it hurt. But he's not. He's allowing Caroline to be here instead.

She lets go of her sleeve and tucks her hands into the pockets of her coat. "What do you think,

Haley? Should I tell them I'm all finished funding your father's care?"

Yes. I'll figure it out. I'll get a job. I'll work nights so I can be with him whenever he's awake. I'll take the risk with his health to prove a point to you.

My mouth is bone-dry. "You know you can stop paying for him any time, Aunt Caroline." I could cry. I could scream. "I wish you wouldn't. Please help him."

A smile that cuts. A smile that slices me open. A smile that demands what's left of my heart in ribbons. "All right. But only because you asked so nicely. After all, I'm always here to help my family. Just like you want to help me. Don't you?"

What will she demand? I already know the answer. Everything. My fake engagement to Rick will become a reality. And more. My whole life will belong to her. I swallow around the knot in my throat. It means saying goodbye to Leo. *No.* I can't. My father looks so pale in the hospital bed. He needs me. His life is on the line. "Yes," I whisper.

CHAPTER TWENTY-FOUR

Leo

DINNER IS A travesty.

Daphne sits across from me at the dining table, wired with tension. She holds her fork too tight and eats her salad with a vengeance. As if it's the salad that scared her and not her snarling beast of an older brother.

"You're not eating anything, Leo."

"I've eaten." It's all tasteless. Pointless. The texture of everything serves only to remind me that I have the most painful hangover in history.

"Okay, but you know you have to eat more than that. You're going to starve to death. Plus, it's good salad."

"I hate salad."

Daphne drops her fork and puts her hands over her face. "Why are we having salad, then?"

"Penance."

She's in the middle of rolling her eyes when shouting starts. Daphne's head snaps up. "What is that?"

"Go up to your room." I get up from my seat. Something's happening in the foyer. "Put on some music and don't come down until the album's over."

Daphne runs to my side. "You'll have to carry me there yourself."

"Might be a little short on time." I can see Gerard from the hall. He's huddled with the security team. Two of them are shouting. He's talking over them. Gerard sees me coming and holds out a hand.

"Go back," he says. "Go up."

I don't. I keep walking toward him like a fool, so Daphne and I have just stepped into the foyer when the police breach the front doors. I understand now why an argument had broken out among my security staff. Situations with police often get ugly, then uglier. Everything will be heightened by the fact that my house is full of hired firepower.

Which is why they've sent so many of them. They pour in the front door two by two, guns drawn. Gerard glues himself to my side and stands in front of Daphne. And I go to the middle of the foyer and put myself in the way.

Ten. Twenty. Thirty. They're running

through my house like an army, and part of me is furious. Part of me is dead, and has been since Haley left my office. More detectives. And then the captain, who is brandishing a piece of paper.

"You're supposed to show me the warrant before you invade my house," I tell him.

He advances on me, glaring, sneering. "Mr. Morelli, we have a warrant to search your property for evidence of the kidnapping and captivity of Haley Constantine. We had reason to believe there would be interference with the collection of evidence, necessitating a no-knock entrance."

"Her toothbrush is upstairs in the master bath, if you'd like to start there."

"My god. You have the right to remain silent, you sick fuck. Everything you say can and will be used against you in a court of law. You have the right to an attorney. If you can't afford an attorney, one will be provided for you. Do you understand the rights I've just read to you?"

"You didn't read them. Let's strive for accuracy."

"Do you understand your rights?"

"Yes, Captain, I do. Everyone's body cameras on? Let's make this simple. I kidnapped Haley Constantine."

"Leo, stop. Let me go." Daphne wrestles away from Gerard and rushes over to me. "Stop. Don't say that." Her face is white. "You can't say this."

"Haley Constantine was my captive." They're getting quieter, probably so that my full confession is clear in the video. "I held her here, and I didn't let her leave."

"Leo." Gerard comes to my other side. "That's not what happened."

"I forced her to sign a contract with me in exchange for releasing her father from a business deal. I coerced her. Exploited her."

It's all close to the truth. They'll accept it as the truth.

Gerard curses under his breath and takes out his phone. Cops are crawling everywhere, down all the halls, all through the foyer. There's nothing for them to find there. I think there's nothing to find until one of them pulls out a coat. Haley never wore it. There was never an occasion for her to wear a black coat. But it is her size. There's a tag on the hanger with her initials on it. It goes into an evidence bag.

"Eva," Gerard says. "There's a situation at the house."

Let him call her. I don't care. There's nothing she can do. The police are already here, and I'm not going to do anything to stop them. Set the machine in motion. Let it destroy me. What's the worst they can do?

Daphne pulls hard on my elbow. "Don't lie to them, Leo."

"I'm telling the truth. God as my witness. I held Haley Constantine hostage."

"You didn't." Daphne sounds horrified. "You didn't hold her hostage. She wanted to be here. What are you talking about?"

"I held her hostage. She wasn't free to leave. Or would you prefer if I called her a prisoner?" I'm talking to Daphne. I'm talking to all of them.

"It's not true." Silent tears streak down Daphne's cheeks. "Stop lying. Stop, stop, stop."

"Sorry, sister mine. I'm not the man you think I am. I'm as bad as your collector. Worse. Dry your tears. They're not worth crying for me."

Daphne sucks in a breath and holds it. She swipes at her face with the back of her hand, and through the pain, through the hangover, through the despair, I hate myself. I hate that here, in my house, she has to put on that mask. It's not what I meant. I just meant that it's worthless to cry for a sinner. A ruined man. A hell-bound soul.

"Anything else you'd like to confess?" The police captain is having the best day of his life.

His people are coming down my stairs with boxes of evidence. They've turned the house upside down in ten minutes flat. I have no doubt it's because someone is guiding their search. Caroline's only been in this house once. She'll never see a blueprint. There are no public records of the inside of my home. But she'll have planted ideas in their heads about where Haley might have spent her time. It's too large a space to search it all this quickly.

They appear to have enough.

"They're already in the house," Gerard is saying. "I couldn't get him to stop talking. He confessed everything. No. No. The lawyer isn't here. There was nobody except the security detail."

"Leave her alone, Gerard," I tell him.

He ignores me. Keeps hovering around. Barking orders at the security team to stay back by the walls. It's so loud in here. My home has never been invaded like this. I can't summon the will to be shocked. Caroline will do anything to fuck with me. Anything. It doesn't matter that she has Haley back.

I laugh out loud, and the police captain's lip curls. "Is this funny to you?"

"I'm entertained. Of course I am. You and

thirty of your buddies are in my house, rifling through my things because you're so convinced I kidnapped a woman. Fine. I agree. I kidnapped her. It doesn't matter that she came here by herself, does it? Or that she's home with her family as we speak."

They're filing out the door. Boxes and boxes. I don't know what they could have taken that would be proof Haley was here. Her clothes, probably. That's most of what she left behind. All the clothes I bought for her. The clothes I wanted to see her in. I want to see her every day of my life. And if I can't see her, then I don't want a life.

Not that I'm going to mention that on the record. They have what they need.

The police leave, several of them taking the time to jostle me on the way out. Daphne lets her hands fall to her sides and stares up at the police captain, who wants to savor every moment on the job. He waits until all of his men have gone. Then he straightens his tie. The motherfucker didn't lift a finger throughout this little raid, but now he's putting himself back together.

"Charges are pending investigation, Mr. Morelli." He makes a show of looking around the foyer. "I bet you'll miss this place when we put you away."

I let a grin creep over my face. Show him my teeth. I watch the realization dawn that he's standing in my foyer alone, with none of his men around him.

DAPHNE MOVES TO stand in front of me, brave in the face of uniforms and guns and search warrants. "Stop trying to scare us. You've done your job."

The policeman gives her an interested look, a very male look, and I growl low in my throat. "Get the hell out of here."

He leaves, and then it's only me. And my sister.

"Why did you say that?" she says, turning on me, her eyes alight with frustration. "Why did you say that you kidnapped Haley when you didn't? They're going to use that against you."

"Because it's true." I am exhausted. I have had enough. "So close to the truth, it might as well be true. I forced her to be with me. Did you think your brother was kind and noble? No, sister mine. I made her trade her body to save her father."

I deserve the shock in her eyes. The condemnation. And I deserve for her to walk away, to run up the stairs and leave me standing here, alone.

❖   ❖   ❖

I'M ENTIRELY UNSURPRISED when Gerard comes into my office an hour later with his phone in his hand and his jaw set. "The Constantines aren't done yet."

"Who are they sending now?"

"Rick Joseph Jr. is looking for you. He's on his way over."

The last time Caroline sent someone to my house, I made Gerard and the rest of the staff leave. Haley was the only one in the house when Ronan shot me. "Fine."

"I can stop him at the gates."

"No. Let him come. I've waited too long to kill that motherfucker." I let Haley live with the knowledge of him in the world for too long.

"Don't, Leo. Don't do it tonight. You're not thinking clearly."

I raise my eyebrows at him. "If you don't want to be a witness, you can leave."

"I'm not leaving."

"Guard Daphne's door, then. Show that bastard in and make sure my sister doesn't come out until it's over."

It used to be me telling Daphne to stay in her room until a nightmare had passed her by. Gerard will have to do it now, though he'd rather play his old part. He'd rather put a bullet through Rick's head before he could step into my foyer. It's what my father would have ordered him to do without a second thought. He's fielded similar orders many times, I'm sure.

It's different now. Both of us know it's not Rick he'll be protecting Daphne from. It's me. It's the sight of me keeping a promise to Rick on a knife's edge.

He makes up his mind. Stands up tall. "You don't need more blood on your hands."

"And if I want it?"

"Let me do my job."

"Your job is to stand in front of my sister's door and guarantee her safety. We can make it an order, Gerard. I don't care. I want everyone off the first floor and on the second, with you. Anyone who wants to leave can go. When is Rick arriving?"

Gerard sighs. "He'll be here within the hour."

I send him away, though not out of the house, and return to the master bedroom. My favorite knife waits for me in the weapons safe in the corner of my closet. A pistol. I bring both back to my office.

All the lights should stay on for this, but in addition to the clawing pain in my back, I have a splitting headache. I don't get headaches. Having one now gives the sweet release of death an added appeal. The drilling in my skull tugs at a memory I can't reach. Something nonsensical about someone else's headaches.

I don't know. I don't care. This is why I don't drink, except when I need to be seen drinking for a social event.

It's possible Rick will kill me tonight. I don't intend to let him have an easy victory, however. He'll have to do it with his eyes open.

He's left me some time to set up my office.

He's left me some time to sit in my chair by the fire.

He's left me some time to pray.

I wasted it, the day Ronan came. I was too consumed with getting all the staff out of the house. Too consumed with the Constantine girl I'd sent away. By the time I started, by the time he was standing in my office, my thoughts were too disorganized to do anything but ask for a swift end to the pain. The pain in my back, yes. But more than that, the pain of tearing the new green shoot of what I had with Haley out of the ground and throwing it into the fire.

I wanted more time with her. I knew I'd never get it. *Bless me, Father, for I have sinned. Make it fast, make it fast, make it fast.* Ronan wouldn't shut up. He was squeamish about shooting me mid-prayer. I dragged it out to spite him. And I dragged it out because my mind's eye had caught on Haley like the image of the cross. It was her I asked for forgiveness. Her I asked for absolution. It was no act of contrition. It was not perfect. But in the end, all I could think of was her name. *Haley, Haley, Haley.*

God has a sick sense of humor. He answered my prayer. I got more time with Haley. Enough time to scare her. To scar her.

Forgive me.

A tap on the window interrupts my final request.

A little bird perches at the sill. Tap, tap, tap. I go over and put my finger to the glass. "It's the middle of the night," I tell it. "Go back to your nest."

It taps again.

"It's not going to be pretty," I warn. I don't know what it's doing here. It's dark, with blustering snow in the courtyard. The bird ruffles its wings and settles into the corner.

A loud voice echoes across the foyer. Gerard, letting Rick in. His footsteps move past the door. The firelight doesn't reach him.

Another shape is framed by the doorway a

moment later. Shoulders rising and falling. He's breathing hard.

"If you wanted a meeting with me, all you had to do was call."

"I don't want a meeting with you." Rick steps into the flickering orange light. "I want a life."

"You have a life, pathetic as it is."

"Not after tonight."

I trace my knife, flat on my desk, with a fingertip. "I understand she promised you Haley."

His eyes flare. "Not just Haley. A big, Constantine wedding. I'll finally have a place in the family. I'll finally belong somewhere." Rick catches himself. Pulls back. He's not accustomed to terse expressions. The scowl he puts on would be laughable if it weren't so sad. He sees the Constantines as a shining city on a hill, but he'll never find safety there. Never find peace. "All I have to do is kill you. All I have to do is make sure you never hurt her again."

"Then let's not waste any more time."

Rick hesitates for a single heartbeat, and then he rushes me.

The man isn't a fighter. He wasn't born for it, wasn't bred for it, but he's desperate for this reward Caroline's dangled in front of him. He's desperate to be the hero. Giving in to his desperation is his biggest mistake.

He could have shot me from the door, but a shooting in cold blood doesn't fit the narrative. A fistfight does.

I might as well give it to him.

Rick tackles me with the zeal of a convert. The only thing I didn't account for was how bad the pain had gotten. How much the headache had affected my balance. I find it too late, after we're already on the floor. I get the first punch in. Rick lands one on my ribs. Levering him off the floor takes more energy than I would have thought. The chair by the fire goes over.

Everything hurts.

Not because of Rick, though the wild hits he manages to land don't help. It's possible this is additional penance for when I kill him.

A glass vase on a corner table tips off and shatters. I've lost a minute. I don't remember getting to this corner of the room. But the sound of that breaking glass snaps me out of this purgatory. I promised I'd kill him if he touched Haley, and he did. There will be no more mercy now. I want him to feel the knife break his skin. I want him to feel it spilling his blood. It's not far to my desk. I'll take him there. God help me.

Fear flashes into Rick's eyes. Then he's out of time.

CHAPTER TWENTY-FIVE

Haley

THE HEATER IN my brother's car is broken. It blows winter air into my face. I've never cared less that this car can't protect me from the snow. All I care about is that it gets me back to Leo.

I'm nothing but heartbeat and panic. No skin, no bones. Just a thundering muscle howling his name.

Thank God for this car. Thank God for my brother, who brought it to the hospital so I'd have a way to get home. I'll never be the kind of Constantine who has a new car and a uniformed driver. I will never, ever be that kind of Constantine. But the life I had was enough. It got me to Leo, and it'll get me to him again.

Please. Let me get to him in time.

I didn't expect to see Eva's name on my caller ID. I didn't expect her to sound breathless with fear when I answered the phone. She's the capable older sister, like Petra. She's the one who knows what to do.

"I'm trying to get there." Her voice shook so badly it was hard to understand her. "I'm not going to get there in time. You have to stop him."

I left my dad sleeping in his hospital bed and went into the hall. "Eva, who? Where?"

"Leo." The story tumbled out of her in a frantic rush I only half understood. The police. Constantines pressing charges. A raid on his house. "Caroline sent Rick to his house. He's going to kill him."

I dug Cash's keys from my purse and ran for the car. No coat. Just the jangling keys and Eva's voice in my ear. "I'll talk Rick out of it. He'll listen to me."

"No. No. Leo will murder Rick. He's already made up his mind, and I can't get there. You're the only one. Haley, you have to stop him."

My hands are freezing. Teeth chattering. There's no heat. But I wouldn't warm up even with it on full blast.

I know why Eva's so afraid. I know what it means if Leo takes the bait and kills Rick. It means prison, and more than that, it's proof the rumors about him are true. Caroline will get to hide behind her flawless image forever, and Leo will go down in history as a monster. It won't matter that Caroline kidnapped me, or that she ordered Rick to rape me, or that she tried to force me into a marriage I never wanted.

It doesn't matter that Leo sent me away. It doesn't matter that he said we were finished. I love him too much to let this happen to him.

I just have to get there in time.

The car door sticks when I arrive at Leo's gate and I have to force it open to punch the code in. He hasn't changed it. The big gates slide open. No guards wait on the other side. My stomach sinks. Please, let this not mean I'm too late.

I take the rest of the driveway too fast and stop at the bottom of the wide steps leading up to his door. Leo's castle rises into the night, the windows glowing softly, like everyone is about to go to sleep. A gust of wind cuts through my clothes and my hair as I wrench the front door open. It swings shut behind me and I hold my breath, my lungs screaming. I need to hear if he's dying. I need to hear if he's alive.

Empty foyer. Empty hallway. And the sound of a fist connecting with flesh.

I don't know whose fist it is. I don't know whose flesh is being beaten.

Are all nightmares like this? Do they all repeat

over and over until you can hardly see anything else? I've been here before. Hurrying to get to Leo. Not knowing if he was alive or dead. History repeating itself, only it hasn't been long enough to become history. I don't want this to be my life. I don't want this to be Leo's life. We can make a new one. I'll make it apart from him, if that's what he needs, but not this. Not this.

The lights in his office are off. A fire burns in the grate, casting everything in orange and gold.

Casting Leo in orange and gold. All the dark lines of him. All the hard planes. All his terrible beauty.

He drags Rick up off the floor, but Rick is fighting him. Rick came here with a purpose, and I see now what it is. He came here to fight Leo and kill him.

He came to kill Leo and he found the beast.

There's no shimmer in the air, only the sharp tang of violence. *He's a dead man.* If there's one thing I know about Leo, it's that he keeps his word.

Rick shoves at him, and Leo laughs.

He *laughs*.

And I know.

I know how much it hurt him to send me away. I know how dead he feels inside, how agonized.

I know that in a few moments at most, it will be too late.

Leo gets both hands around Rick's throat, and I take a deep breath. I feel that shimmer. That sense that his moment carries weight. Only it's settled on my shoulders. I'm supposed to be here. I'm meant to be here. And it's because of Leo.

I had foolish, childish ideas of what sacrifice means. I thought it was a transaction. My body for my family's freedom, and nothing else. I thought I could trade that to Leo without coming to know him. Without letting it change me. But I was wrong.

It's not a real sacrifice if it doesn't involve your soul.

Leo has given up so much of his for the people he loves.

Neither man turns as I enter the room. They're too busy fighting. Rick is railing against Leo's hands, throwing his body around, putting them both off-balance. He doesn't see that Leo is only waiting for the perfect moment to kill him. He doesn't see how much stronger Leo is. How much harder. How much he's already lost.

Leo backs Rick up against the desk and punches him in the face. "Fuck you," spits Rick.

"Fuck you. I'm going to kill you."

"I'm getting impatient." Leo's hand goes down to the desk in a simple, graceful movement, and firelight flashes in the blade of a knife.

"No." I run the last few steps, run right into this moment, and reach for him. "Leo. Stop."

He takes in a breath. I don't let go. Now that I'm touching him, I can feel the fury singing under his skin. I can feel his bloodlust. Determination draws his muscles tight. He's decided to do this. He's given himself over to it. It must feel peaceful, in a way, giving in to his need. Leo's held himself back for so long. In so many ways. He sacrificed the person he is to be the person who could keep his family safe. He gave up any hope of being understood. Of being loved. And he's done. I know he's done.

Leo has one hand so tight around Rick's throat that he's beginning to crush his windpipe. Rick tries to pull his hand away, but Leo is too focused. He's always been so focused. He's always seen everything about me, even the things I refused to see myself. The whites of Rick's eyes are huge. Terrified. A part of me wants to let Leo kill him for what he tried to do to me, but I can't. It would only cause Leo more pain. It would teach Caroline nothing. It would be for nothing.

The knife is an inch from Rick's throat.

"I can't," Leo says, his voice rough with agony. "I can't stop. He hurt you."

"Yes, he did. He scared me. He made me feel dirty and helpless and afraid. And he would have done more, if you hadn't saved me. But killing him won't fix anything."

"If I end him now, he'll never touch you again."

I thought a heart could only break so many times, but mine does it again. It comes apart like rose petals in a storm.

Leo is trying to give me what he could never give himself.

He could never bring himself to kill Caroline, because it meant putting his family in danger. He's willing to give up his own life, his own freedom, for me. So that I won't have to suffer the way he did. The way he still does.

"He means nothing to me." Leo's arm tenses under my hands. "You made me feel clean again, Leo. You made me feel safe. And if you kill him, I'll never have that again. I'll never have you. And I need you."

Rick wheezes. He's past the power of speech.

I run my hand over Leo's. Over the one gripping the knife. I use the softest possible touch. I do it the way I would touch his scars. The way I would touch any part of him that had been hurt. "I need you," I tell him again. "Come back."

"I can't. It's so hard. I want—I want—" His grip tightens around Rick's throat.

"I want you. All I want is you. All I've ever wanted is you. This man is nothing. Don't leave me for nothing. Please."

The knife grazes Rick's neck.

"I know it's hard, Leo. I know it's the hardest thing you've ever done."

"Weak," he forces through gritted teeth. "I should have done this a long time ago."

"You didn't do it because you are so strong. You're the strongest, bravest man I've ever known. And you're mine. You can come back. It's okay. Put down the knife." I reach up and stroke his cheek. "Let go."

"Fuck, darling," Leo whispers. The knife drops. In one movement, Leo shoves Rick away and takes me in his arms. His arms are tight around my body, tighter than they've ever been, and he breathes me in like I'm all the air he'll ever need. "You're so soft," he says. "You're the softest thing."

Soft. The best thing I could be for him. He's had to claw scraps of softness from the world so he could tolerate living. I can be that for him. I am that for him.

I take his hand. "Let's go." I don't have a plan for where we'll go, I just know we need to get out of here. Out of this room.

"Wait," Leo says, but I'm already turning. Already creating space between the two of us.

Rick is a white streak in the corner of my vision, a hand coming up high. Coming back down. He's aiming for Leo. Whatever he's doing, he's aiming for Leo with a wild, half-crushed growl.

Both of us move at the last second. I don't know who's pushing, who's pulling. No more. Don't touch him.

An impact at the side of my head rattles my teeth. The floor wheels up and something hits my head again. Something sharp, like the corner of a desk. It pushes through my skull, through the spot that's already aching, oh, that hurts so much. Too much. I can't see the firelight anymore. I land in someone's arms, softly, softly.

"Oh, fuck." Rick. "Oh, shit. Oh—"

His voice cuts out. There's only silence left. And then there's nothing at all.

CHAPTER TWENTY-SIX

Leo

HALEY IS SO soft in my arms. So small. So still.

Rick stunned her with the paperweight. A glass flower in his hand, hurtling toward my skull. And then, somehow, Haley's. For that split second he looked like a Morelli. Men like Rick Joseph Jr. don't know violence. They only know the idea of it. The illusion. The reality is always different. In this reality Haley didn't drop straight down. She lost her balance and her head hit the corner of my desk. Two blows to one delicate temple.

I fell to my knees. Caught her before she could hit the floor. It was too late by then.

I pull her close, as close as I can get her. Cradle her body in one of my arms, stroke her hair back from her face. She did this for me once. She tried so hard not to hurt me, even though I'd hurt her. Even though I deserved to be left on the hard floor to bleed out alone. I would give anything to hear her voice. Anything for her to open her eyes. Every second that passes forces more fear down my throat. Haley's unconscious, and I never knew how awful this was, I never knew how deep the terror went. The day Ronan came to kill me, I heard her scream as the world faded away. I understand that scream now. It's happening in my own mind.

She was screaming for help.

I know better than that.

"That's not what I meant." Rick's voice quavers, and if I had anything left, I would hate him. But all I have is pain. It's impossible to separate the pain in my body from the pain in my soul and the all-encompassing pain of loving her. Desperately. Furiously. Against every rule I've ever made for myself. In spite of the threat of me. I love her.

Rick drops the paperweight. The glass spiders and cracks next to my knee. The structure of the petals separates, each one of them catching reflections of the fire. Those petals used to refract the light from my window. "Oh, fuck," he says again, that coward. "I didn't mean to hit her. Caroline sent me after you, not her. Fuck."

I can't hear if she's breathing. I don't think she is. Rick babbles more excuses. More apologies.

He's a stain on this room. On this moment. He deserves to die for what he's done to Haley, but I would have to put her down to kill him. I will never let her out of my arms again.

"Get the fuck out of my office. Get out. Get *out.*"

He runs. Trips over the fallen chair and scrambles away. His footsteps are replaced by quiet. Not silence. The fire crackles softly in the grate. Snowflakes graze the window pane on a night breeze. Air moves in a harsh saw in and out of my own lungs. I have to be calm for her. I have to be steady. I don't know if I can do it.

Because she's not breathing.

I press a hand to her chest and pray for it to rise.

"Please. Darling. Wake up." Her chin in my hand feels unbearably fragile. "Please, take another breath. It's all right. It's okay. You're going to be okay. One breath. Wake up."

Nothing.

"Haley. Darling. You have to keep breathing." I press down on her chest, trying to coax the air out of her. Into her. It shouldn't have stopped her breathing. Hitting her head shouldn't have stopped her lungs from working. But then Caroline shouldn't have been able to cause permanent damage to me. If it were simple, it would be easy to fix, it would be easy to get her to start again. Haley was strong enough to survive me, to survive the darkest parts of my rage and pain. She weathered me like a storm. Cried for the storm. Loved it, too. I want her to be too strong for this. I push harder, feeling the echo of her hands against my chest. In her nightmares, she's trying to keep my heart beating. I'm trying to keep hers beating now, though I don't know if I'm feeling her pulse or mine. "Please."

Nothing.

I kiss her, put my mouth on hers to feel the sweet movement of her breath. When I kiss Haley her whole body responds to me. Now there's nothing. I make the sign of the cross over her with a shaking hand. She's innocent. She's perfect. God's mercy is supposed to be never ending. He could offer her a scrap, even if He offers me nothing. Any grace should go to her, not me, not me. I have never been able to accept endless mercy. Always wrestled with it, no matter how many times Father Simon claims to know the truth.

And maybe this is my failing. I knew violence to be a limited resource. The more violence I accepted from my father, the less he would have for my siblings. Why wouldn't the mercy of God be the same? The more he gives to one sinner, the less he has for another.

An endless capacity for anything is a danger. Endless mercy can lead to endless violence. Endless sacrifice can lead to endless pain.

All of this falls away. What does it matter now? I don't need endless mercy. I only need one act of grace. Please, for Haley. I confess my love for her. I confess it's everything, all I feel. I'm sorry, I'm so sorry, my entire heart does not belong to God, so much of it belongs to Haley, and if that means I'll burn forever, then so be it.

She's not breathing.

Panic winds itself around my pain and screws itself into my flesh. My heart. Raw terror threatens to separate each piece of me from the whole. It's pulling out ribs and organs. One by one. "God, please. Darling, please." A little shake to her face. "Not this way. You have to survive this. You have to survive me. I'll let you go if I have to. I'll let you go. Anywhere you want to go, just don't leave." Don't leave the world. Exist in the world. It will be enough if she exists. "Forgive me. Stay with me."

Nothing.

"Anything." I feel a presence here. I feel witnessed. I don't allow myself to be seen like this, I don't, but I can't stop it, and nothing matters but Haley. The air grows heavy. Harder to work in and out of my lungs but I am painfully awake, painfully alive. "I'll do anything. I'm so sorry, darling. With all my heart. I chose the wrong things. I've done terrible things. I've sinned, Jesus, so many times and I would do it all again, I would suffer it all over again if you'll wake up. Let me take your place. Let me take her place."

I look down into Haley's peaceful expression and my soul tears apart. A raindrop falls to her cheek. Another one. It's too cold for rain but angels could weep for her, Jesus, please. "I'll sin again. I have to do it. But don't take her from me, please, please. I'll do anything. Let her live. She's so soft. She's so sweet. Let her live." Her head is heavy in the crook of my arm, her eyelashes a gentle shadow on her skin. I put my hand to her face, to her perfect face, and run my thumb over her cheek. "You're—" Another raindrop. "You're dreaming, darling. Wake up. I love you."

Haley stirs, the movement so subtle I think it might be me. I hold my breath. Try to stop moving. A stretch in her legs, like she's wiggling her toes. I don't dare look down toward her feet.

The fingers on her hand curl in. I gather her

arm closer. Take her hand. Squeeze at her fingertips. "Please, darling. Please."

Her chest hitches, almost like a sigh.

It rises.

It falls.

I put my hand over her heart. Hope is excruciating. It hurts so fucking much. But over that pain, I feel her breath. It's light. Soft. Like she is.

Firelight caresses her face. I put my hand there too. Give me this one mercy. I know I don't deserve it. Take her under the shadow of your wings. Protect her, protect her.

Haley's eyelashes flutter. Another raindrop falls onto my hand. And then I'm looking into the clear, warm blue of her eyes. They move over my face, her lips parting in soft surprise. Her eyes open wider. A bolt of fear threatens—what if she doesn't know me?—but the presence in the room holds it at bay. Like vast wings over us. A temporary shelter.

A frown tugs at the corner of Haley's mouth. She reaches up for me. Her fingertips brush against my cheekbone. "Oh, Leo, you're crying."

At the sound of her voice, at the sound of my name, my balance deserts me. I rock back until I'm sitting heavily on the rug, my back to the fire. My shadow covers Haley's body but there's enough light surrounding us to see her eyes. Haley loops her arms around my neck and lets me hold her. I kiss her forehead. Her cheeks. Her chin. I turn her face in my hand and breathe a silent prayer to the bruise darkening her skin. Never again. They'll never hurt her here again. No one will ever hurt her again. A light hand, light as air, rests on the top of my head for a fraction of a breath.

Small hands on my face bring me back to her eyes. I never thought I would see this shade of blue again, except in my dreams. "Darling. You came back."

She smiles, a little sheepish, wholly perfect. "I'll always come back. You can't scare me away."

"I love you." The words are so small. My love for her so great. I want to make her understand that these words are like grains of sand in comparison to the size of the universe. I'll take a lifetime to do it, if she'll give it to me. "I should have told you before."

Haley breathes a laugh. "You did. I don't think you knew you were saying it. We were—" So many things we've done together, so many things I've done to her, and she blushes for me. "The night you brought me home." I was rough with her that night, and Haley begged me for it.

She wasn't afraid. "But I knew. I always knew."
She puts my hand over her heart again. The beat
is strong and steady under my palm. "I could feel
it here."

"But I was—I've been—"

"I love you," she says. "You showed yourself
to me, over and over again, even when it hurt."
Haley runs her fingers through my hair and over
the contours of my face. "For a beast, you really
wear your heart on your sleeve."

"My heart has been in your pocket from the
moment we met. Stay with me." I bring her hand
to my lips and kiss her knuckles. "Forever. I don't
care where we go. I don't care if we have to live
with your family or go to the ends of the earth. I
need you."

Haley shakes her head. "My home is here,
with you. In your house." Her nose wrinkles, and
it's so adorable I could die. Or live. "You have a
castle, Leo. I don't know why you won't admit
you're a prince."

CHAPTER TWENTY-SEVEN

Haley

D APHNE THOUGHT LEO was a control freak about the makeup for my birthday party, and maybe she was right. But it's nothing compared to how he is after I hit my head. After Rick hit my head.

He summons Dr. Carina Jain to examine me, along with a full team including a neurotrauma specialist and a neurologist and three other people with intimidating titles. They recommend ice, rest, and ibuprofen for the pain. It's Leo who insists on keeping me in his bed for those days. It's Leo who wakes me up in the night so he can look at my pupils for signs of concussion and ask me questions to look for signs of confusion.

"It's just a headache," I tell him in the middle of the third night as he stares into my eyes. "Do you ever sleep? How can you sleep if you wake me up all night?"

"I wake you up once every night. Do you

remember where you are?"

His hands are so warm, so gentle on my face. I'm so tired. My eyes burn. "Your house."

"Where's my house?"

"A castle."

Leo frowns.

"A castle outside New York City. It's not in Bishop's Landing."

"And who am I?"

He asks me this question every time, his tone almost teasing. "Leo Morelli. Beast of Bishop's Landing. A man with a terrible temper and an even worse reputation."

"And?"

"And the love of my life." Leo leans in and kisses me. His teeth sink into my bottom lip. His hand wraps around the back of my neck. But before he can put any real pressure on my body, he's gone. Turning out the low light in the bathroom. He puts his arm around my waist and ushers me back to the bed. Puts me in. Pulls the covers up tight. I let out a frustrated groan, fighting uselessly against the blanket. "I wish you would just—"

"Fuck you?" Leo says from the other side of the bed. "Is that what you were going to ask for? You still blush when you want sex. But I think not, darling. Not until you can take it."

"I can take it now," I say, pouting.

"Can you?" His fingers in my hair. His voice in my ear. "You're already falling asleep."

"I'm not," I say, but it's a lie. My eyes drift closed against my will. The last thing I see is Leo's face blurring into light and shadows as dreams overtake me.

On the fourth day, in a quiet moment between making plans and consulting with lawyers, Leo tells me about the videos.

"I'll show them to you if you need to see," he says, voice tight. "But I'd rather you not have those things in your memory, too."

On the fifth day, the doctors clear me for light physical activity. Leo says that doesn't include fucking. I tell him he's never been so mean.

On the sixth day, I wake up with a pit in my stomach and jittery hands. Early, because we're going into the city for the meeting. I wanted to go sooner. Leo didn't. I pretend not to be nervous when he takes me into his enormous shower, with its wide shelf and its wide bench.

When Leo has the temperature the way he wants it, he pulls me underneath the stream and kisses me. Hard. Harder. So hard my body responds, coming alive again after days and days of missing him, of wanting him, of having a headache. It's better today. It's a lot better. The bruise isn't. He backs me up to the stone bench and pushes me onto it under the force of his kiss.

And then he starts kissing down my body. He takes each of my nipples between his teeth, one by one, and by the time he's on his knees between my legs I'm a hot, panting mess braced against the wall. Leo wraps his arms around my thighs and spreads them open for more access, and Jesus, it's good. It's good. It's so good. I'm not used to it, my muscles straining, but the first lick of his tongue chases that feeling away.

He's careful, but he's not gentle.

Oh, thank god.

I can't breathe for what he's doing. Tongue and teeth and relentless pressure. His fingertips dig into my legs the way they always have, hard, hard, hard, and the pain makes me feel less like a delicate creature made of glass and more like myself. The woman who loves Leo Morelli. The woman who wants him every second. Pleasure spikes from my center and wraps around my hips, which buck against it, fight against it. It's like the time he did this on his dining room table. My whole body fights him. My whole body wants him to win.

And I'm going to explode, I'm going to fly apart from this indescribable thing he's doing with his tongue on my clit, when he slows.

Leo's body shifts back and I reach for any part of him I can touch. His hair. His shoulders. "No. Don't stop. No. Please."

He's looking at me from between my thighs, his big hands holding me still, dark eyes on my face.

"Why?" Frustrated tears gather in the corners of my eyes. My body is still sore and exhausted, but I need this intimacy with him. "Why did you stop? I'm fine, Leo, I'm okay, please…"

"You're the prettiest thing I've ever seen," he says.

I arch toward him again. He's so close. His mouth is so close. I feel his warm breath on the inside of my thighs. "I'll do anything, Leo. I'll—I'll beg, if that's what you want. Just—"

"Marry me."

I feel the heat of his words against the heat of me, and now I am crying, now the tears are set free. I'm still trying to get his mouth back on me. His tongue. His teeth. Please. I get my hands on his face, and oh, how dare he. How dare he. "Now? Now's when you're going to ask? Today?"

"I'm not asking." Counterpressure on my

thighs, holding me down. Oh, I love this. I love this. "I need you. I need this." He strokes his tongue through my slickness, a dark grin in his eyes. "And you. I can't breathe without you. I don't want to breathe without you. Marry me."

"Yes. Yes. Yes. Please."

He leans down to taste me then. Takes his time. There's no part of me he doesn't touch. Doesn't mark. "Your pussy loved that," he says, and then he closes his mouth over my clit and I'm lost. "Your pussy wants to marry me. It loves the feel of my tongue, doesn't it?"

Leo's first act as my fiancé is to make me come so hard my thighs ache and my vision darkens, shutting out everything but the pleasure he's giving me. The pain. Everything but him.

Leo

HALEY DRESSES FOR the meeting in the city in black. I bring in her favorite stylist to do her hair and her makeup. My fiancée glows the entire time, which eases the tight knot at the center of my chest. Haley has been insisting on the meeting since I got her up to my bedroom after that asshole Rick fled the scene. Insisting. On meeting with Caroline.

She wanted to go alone—to meet with her Constantine to Constantine—but there's no way in hell. So we're both attending the meeting.

I've given her everything I could think of as armor. Access to my lawyers. A custom Armani dress. Delicate earrings and a necklace that puts a glint of gold at the hollow of her throat. I asked her if she wanted any other color but black for her clothes, but she shook her head. "I don't want to look like a Constantine. I want to be yours."

And now there's a string around her finger, a length of thread taken from one of my shirts. "This is a placeholder," I said as I slipped it on, and Haley nodded, her eyes shining. The last shield between her and this day, except for me.

Thomas pulls up to the curb outside one of New York City's many glassed-in high-rises, and I take Haley's hand in mine. "We can send the lawyers without us. You don't have to meet with her. All this can be resolved another way."

She lifts her chin, her blue eyes filled with determination. "I want it like this," she says.

I will give her anything she wants. Always.

We are first to the meeting room on the ninth floor, a detail I demanded in negotiations. Haley has time to get her bearings with the lawyer and her associate, and I'm standing at her side when

Caroline comes in with hers. Four lawyers means four witnesses.

Caroline, all in white, takes her seat with an air of impatience, tucks her purse into her lap, and looks me in the eye. "I'm not sure why you asked me here, Leo. What the prosecutor does is out of my hands. The police have your confession to them on the record."

"His confession?" Haley tilts her head to the side, so graceful and queenlike I could fuck her right here on this table. "We didn't come to discuss the charges against Leo."

Haley's aunt directs a fake, sad smile across the table. "Sweetheart, it's best if you stay out of these negotiations. You've been through so much. The family will protect you, if you would only let us. He's twisted your mind so much you think he's helping you."

My darling returns that fake, sad smile to her with such accuracy I get goose bumps. In this moment I can see the Constantine in her—the ferocity. "I'm so glad to hear that, Aunt Caroline. I'm going to need your help with the case."

"Case?"

"The case against Rick Joseph Jr.." The corners of Haley's mouth turn down. "Now that I'm able to sit for interviews, I'm pressing charges for assault."

Caroline's eyes narrow. "He didn't assault you, darling. The two of you had a perfectly lovely dinner date. Your outburst near the end was completely understandable, given what Leo has put you through. You were distraught."

"The dinner date," Haley muses. "The dinner date was lovely, up until he touched me without my consent." I breathe through a sharp spike of rage. Keep it in check. Haley wears a symbol of my love for her on her finger, and she's sitting on my side of the table, and she's mine. "All the way up my inner thigh. Almost to my—"

"Haley," Caroline scolds, and the hairs on the back of my neck stand up. This is the same bullshit tone she tried to use with me the night I whipped her. The same false calm, as if she's in control of the situation instead of spiraling out of control.

"It was odd," my darling continues. "Because he leaned over me and reached for his belt, and then he said—" Her gaze flicks toward the ceiling. "He said *this is what we're supposed to do.*" A heartbeat, and Haley shrugs. "I'm not sure who told him that he was supposed to rape me, but—" She waves this away. "That's not the assault I'm talking about."

"He didn't assault you." Caroline laughs, incredulous, icy.

"Yes," Haley says. "He did." And then she turns her head so Caroline can see the enormous bruise covering her temple. "He hit me with a paperweight."

Caroline can't stop staring. "I had nothing to do with that. I'm sorry to see that happened to you, but I've tried to warn you about Leo Morelli. His violence is renowned."

Haley's brows draw together. The picture of innocent confusion. "But, Aunt Caroline, Rick called you. He called you so many times. Twenty minutes after he attacked me. He didn't tell you? Sarah, can you show her the phone records?"

"Absolutely." My lawyer slides a folio across the table to Caroline, who opens it with her fingertips. There are Rick's call logs. There is her number, highlighted in yellow.

"There's also the recording," I add, and Caroline's eyes dart to mine. "He mentioned your name."

Caroline's lawyers tense. This was not part of the original discussion. And it's not close to the truth. It *is* the truth. I don't have cameras in my home, detest the thought of them, but I did set up a voice recorder the night Caroline sent Rick to kill me. Insurance purposes, mainly. Less likely for anyone to believe I killed myself.

"And there are others." Haley takes a deep breath and reaches for the clutch in her lap. "Other recordings, I mean. These ones are a bit different. A bit older. You're in them," she says lightly. Her hand is at the lip of the table. "I've learned a lot about the laws in New York, Aunt Caroline." Jesus, I'm so proud of her. "About how there's no time limit on crimes that—"

"Enough." Caroline has one hand flat on the table. No more color in her face. Her lawyers lean in now, faces blank. "How dare you turn on your own family? That's enough."

"Is it?" I ask, and Caroline hates it. She hates to look at me. I wonder if her back hurts as much as mine. "Too painful to relive the past?"

She gives a tight smile. "It would be best for our families if we didn't. Families such as your sisters, Leo. And your brother and sister, Haley. I'm sure we can come to an understanding."

"Like…" Haley bites her lip. "Maybe if you left us the fuck alone?"

Caroline jerks back like Haley slapped her, her hand going into a fist, but she recovers. "There's no need to be vulgar. No need for all these lawyers. A misunderstanding among family."

"And you'd obviously place a call to the prosecutor as soon as we step out," Haley says. "I would find it very *vulgar* to be dragged through a court proceeding against my will."

A swift nod. Caroline stands, and Haley does, too. I'm right beside her. I won't leave her alone in Caroline's presence, even in a public setting.

"I have some calls to make, if that's all—"

"Apologize," Haley says, and I've never heard such frigid resolve in her sweet voice. She looks as hard and as furious as any Morelli. She's shaking with rage, and I know that if I wasn't holding her hand she would hurl herself at the woman. I felt her sick fury when I told her about the videos. She hasn't seen them but she knows they exist. I can't forget them, but she doesn't have to have the images burned into her mind. "For what you did."

Caroline draws herself up to her full height. She looks down on Haley with bitter imperiousness. "I'm sorry, sweetheart, if you felt hurt by something I did."

"To Leo."

Her fist clenches around her purse. "That boy—" She can't believe this. "That boy doesn't deserve the slightest—"

"That *man* is my fiancé." Haley leans into me

and traces the thread around her finger with a fingertip. "He'll be my family soon. And I feel so strongly about doing what's right for my family." She rests her hand on her clutch, her grasp inches from her phone. "I'm sure you understand loyalty to family."

Caroline glares at Haley for three solid heartbeats before she turns her head to me. Her crystal blue eyes blaze with impotent anger and resentment. "I apologize."

"Do you mean it?" Haley demands.

"It doesn't matter," I murmur, pulling her close. "She means nothing to me. It's sweet of you to demand an apology, but the truth is she doesn't have power over me anymore." I face Caroline, the woman who was my lover and my abuser. She figured into so many nightmares. But what I told Haley is true. Now she's just a woman. A sad, desperate woman clinging to threads of power. It's not the marks on her back that helped me move on. It's the woman standing beside me. "You're done here," I say to Caroline, my voice soft. "I don't even wish you to hell. You mean nothing to me. You *are* nothing." It's the ultimate insult to a woman as attention hungry as her. She wants to be adored or hated. Apathy is unbearable, but I can't summon any feeling for her—other than wishing her gone from the room.

Emotions flash across Caroline's face. Outrage. Regret. A deep-seated loneliness. And then she turns and leaves the room, taking her coldness with her.

Haley watches her leave. After the lawyers disappear from view, she lets out a breath. "I know she didn't mean it," she says softly, her eyes meeting mine. "But that felt good."

I pull her close. "Better than this morning?"

Haley blushes. "No way."

"There's more waiting in the car, if you think you can handle it."

She loops her arm through mine, tugging hard for the door. "Let's go," Haley says, her voice so light, so free, the darkness of Caroline Constantine, the pain of the past left behind in the room. "Hurry, hurry, hurry."

CHAPTER TWENTY-EIGHT

Haley

THE KNOCK AT Leo's front doors comes an hour before my engagement party.

It's a clear, dark night, and Leo's house glows with candles and sprays of light. Eva has been staying over to plan it with Daphne, and the two of them have taken the castle and transformed it into another dream.

Guests will follow a lighted path through to the ballroom in the far wing of the house. Eva and Daphne haven't let me in yet. They want the full impact of the decorations to be a surprise. I can't wait to see it. I can't wait to be at the party with Leo.

But first I step into my spot by the double doors and wait for Gerard to open them.

My dad and Cash hesitate on the threshold. Cash, because he's looking into the foyer with trepidation, though he's been here before. My dad, because he's looking at me. My gown for the evening is such a pale pink it's almost white, and it glimmers in the candlelight. His hand comes up to cover his mouth, and when he takes it down again his eyes are shining. "You look—" The same hand goes to his chest. "You look just like your mother."

I come out onto the border of the cold and take their hands. "Come in. Come inside." Cash allows himself to be pulled inside. Gerard closes out the night and steps away while I kiss their cheeks. "Thank you, Daddy. I'm so glad you're here. Both of you."

They're in suits and overcoats, dressed for the party, but my dad stops. "If you want us to leave, Haley—"

"I don't."

"I'm sorry." His heartbreak shines in his voice, but he doesn't waver. "I'm sorry for so many things, Haley, but I shouldn't have agreed to help Caroline, no matter what she did to me. I shouldn't have tried to get you to stay home. I don't blame you if you can't forgive me."

"I'm sorry too, Hales." Cash's cheeks are an ashamed red, and I can't stand it.

I pull them both into my arms, as much as I can. "No more apologies. Okay? You're my family. You'll always be my family. I want you in my life, and I want you at my engagement party and at everything else. All of that's in the past."

My dad tilts my face up so he can see my eyes. "You're happy here? You love him?"

He's never judged me. Not once. And there's no judgment in his voice now. "I love him so much." I let him see me smile. Let him see my happiness. "He's the only man I'll ever want."

He grins. "Then you've made the perfect choice. I'm so happy for you, sweetheart."

"Me too." Cash sticks his hands in his pockets. "I mean it." He leans in to hug me. Then clears his throat. "Is everything settled, then? With Caroline? With the cops?"

"Yes. It's all okay now."

Another knock at the door, and Gerard reappears to open it.

My sister comes in alone, her eyes huge, looking over everything in the foyer. Her face lights up when she sees me. "Hey, Haley. Am I late?"

"You're early. I wanted you all here early. Where's Jeremy?"

She shakes her head. "I came alone. He didn't want to come." Petra shakes her head. "I'm sorry, but nevermind about him. You look gorgeous."

My heart squeezes. It's a big deal for Petra to come against the wishes of her husband. He won't approve, but she came anyway. For me. For family. "Thank you," I say, my voice hushed.

"Of course. This is a beautiful house." A shy smile. "I'd love to see it, if we have time."

We do have time. It feels good to show my family around my home. It feels better to have Petra *ooh* and *aah* over the decorations and have my dad appreciate the den and have Cash joke about the size of the kitchen.

I have a moment of nervousness when we arrive back at the foyer and find Leo waiting there with Eva and Daphne. Leo's shaking his head, breathtaking in all his gorgeous black. Daphne's laughing at him. They've made peace, for now, about her stalker. About the collector.

Eva could be a glamorous runway model, also in black.

Leo sees me first. I'll never get used to the way his face changes when I walk into a room. Sometimes his expression sharpens with want, and sometimes it softens with relief, but his eyes always, always burn with love. My nervousness feels ridiculous now. I lead my family to him and pull him to my side, where I want him. Where I always want him. "Leo, you've met my dad and Cash before, but I thought we could start over. This is my dad, Phillip. My brother, Cash. And my sister, Petra. Family, this is my Leo."

He shakes their hands like the prince that he is.

"Leo, we have to talk," my dad says. "Have your lawyers looked over the paperwork yet? My inventions are languishing. I always knew you could see the vision."

"Dad," I say, scandalized. "I can't believe you."

Leo laughs. "He's right, Haley. We'll talk after the party, him and I."

I shake my head, but I won't stand in their way. The truth is that Leo does have the money. And the vision. And my father's inventions could change the world. It's not lost on me that my dad saw Leo for what he was even before I did. Focused, he said. It was the truth.

Leo introduces Eva and Daphne to my family, and then Lucian barges in with Elaine and they're the first of the many, many guests who arrive to celebrate our engagement.

I've never seen so many people in his house before. Leo and I stand at the door, greeting person after person in beautiful clothes and smiles that seem real enough to trust, at least for tonight. The rest of his siblings arrive.

His parents arrive.

There's one frosty moment when they step in the door, but Leo's presence overwhelms it. He shakes his father's hand. He kisses his mother's cheek. He introduces me to them as his fiancée, and then he sends them to the party. I only realize afterward that he's kept me slightly behind him the entire time.

More people are coming, but Leo puts his hand on the small of my back and pulls me in close. "We're supposed to make an entrance now," he murmurs into my ear.

"We could run away instead. We could hide in the bedroom."

He laughs. "My sisters would never stand for it." Leo catches my hand in his and kisses the loop of thread he put there after he asked me to marry him. "Come, darling. Let's go to the party."

Gerard waits at the entrance to the ballroom. The sound of the party flows out into the hall and over us. Old nerves make me squeeze Leo's hand harder.

He clears his throat. "It's not too fancy, understand? Not like the Constantine parties."

The doors open to let us in. I'm not planning to cry, not at all, but the tears spill over immediately, ruining the makeup I spent so long on. "It's perfect."

It's not like the Constantine parties. It's better. Leo is warm and solid at my side, and the ballroom is breathtaking. Eva and Daphne have themed it in black and white and pink and gold and everything is delicate and strong under a candlelit, starlit glow.

And the windows—

The giant picture windows look out over a courtyard that is illuminated with falling stars. Small lights over Leo's bench and his tree and everywhere. The middle panes of the window, which were covered when he brought me here before, are on display. It's a larger version of the stained-glass door leading to his courtyard. A brilliant rose, set against the night and glowing with the light from our party. It's a vision, and it serves as the backdrop for another vision, which is a ballroom full of beautiful people in dark tuxedos and jewel-toned gowns who burst into applause and cheers at our presence.

The music that had been quietly running underneath all the conversation gets louder, and Leo takes my hand. "About the dancing," he says.

I freeze. "We are not dancing in front of all these people."

"It was Eva's idea, and everyone's looking at us." There's laughter in his eyes, and I can't believe it. I can't believe he would agree to this like an easygoing person.

"And you're just going to go along with it?"

Leo shrugs. "I want to dance with you. I don't care who sees."

He doesn't give me any more time to argue. Like always, Leo takes charge. And it doesn't matter that I've never had dancing lessons like my Constantine cousins. He makes a frame with his body and I briefly float out of mine to see him move me around the ballroom in front of glimmering stained glass.

He's stunning. He's mine. And together we're the center of this party. When he spins me off to the side of the ballroom, the volume of the party crests. But we don't disappear into it. Leo introduces me to person after person. Everyone wants to see us. To see me. It's a good feeling, but it's not the best one. The best one is looking at him. I don't know why I wished so hard to be the center of attention at a party when what I want more than anything is to be able to stare at him. Maybe that makes me lovesick.

I'm okay with it.

Someone calls his name a while into the party. Leo leaves me by a standing table near the stained-glass window with a kiss on the temple and a promise to be back before I know it.

Eva's had the window backlit for the occasion. The colors fall over the white tablecloth and I trace them with a fingertip while I sip champagne. It's the first chance I've had to really look at the party.

It brings tears to my eyes. There's my dad, talking animatedly with Eva. Leo's parents hold court in one corner of the room. They don't look thrilled, exactly, but both of them wear small, party-appropriate smiles. Cash stands with one of the Constantine cousins, who frankly looks shocked that the party is so nice. Petra has found two other women to talk to. Her face is pink, the corners of her lips lifting in a smile I know means she's genuinely pleased.

"You're all alone." Daphne abandons her empty champagne glass on the table, and it's instantly whisked away by a server. "You don't feel nervous, do you? Because of all the Morellis?"

"No, they'll be my family soon. I'm people-watching."

She makes a humming sound and turns to face the crowd, her dark gaze going over the guests in their finery, the smiles, the glittering jewels and glasses of champagne.

"It's the best part of any party, don't you

think?"

She laughs, turning to get another champagne flute from a tray flashing by in a uniformed waiter's hands. "Winston Constantine is here."

"What? Where?"

Daphne points him out with a nod. I can't place him here. Can't believe he's here. Leo told me about his meeting when he told me about the videos, but I didn't expect Winston to support us this way. He puts a card into a basket set up in a floral arrangement near the door. The floral arrangement is accompanied by a framed photo of Leo and me. Daphne took it at my birthday party. We're both in the glow of the candles from my cake, and I look beside myself with happiness, cheeks pink, hands clasped at my collarbone, leaning into Leo. I'm beaming at the cake with stars in my eyes. Leo's looking at me. My joy reflects in his face, in his eyes, in his grin.

Winston looks at the photo for a long moment, then continues into the ballroom, his shoulders relaxed. He nods at Cash. Turns. Leo's there, crossing nearby, and I stop breathing.

A confrontation between the two of them would be a disaster.

But neither man moves to attack the other. They size each other up for the longest heartbeat of my life. And then Winston speaks. His hands come up in front of him, a quick gesture that says *I tried.* Leo nods once. Twice. I'm not sure which one of them offers his hand to shake first. But they do, Winston leaning in to say one more thing. Leo replies, and then they both continue on like they haven't just sidestepped a disaster.

"Okay," says Daphne. "That's not how I thought it would go."

I finally exhale. Things will never be fully resolved between the Morellis and the Constantines. There's too much pain in the past. But tonight, at least, for my engagement party, no one has killed each other. No one has even thrown a punch. And Winston and Leo shaking hands?

A tenuous, unprecedented peace.

I lose myself in the glow of the party. The shine of fairy lights on Eva's dress. Leo's parents' faces in candlelight. They all have his dad's dark hair, but there's more of his mother in their features than I imagined. The delicate fall of white and gold fabric. The way white is nothing without the contrast of black. The way gold shines best when there's night behind it.

"Whoa." Daphne's eyes go wide. "Which Constantine cousin is *that?*"

I follow her eyes to the opposite side of the

ballroom, and it's obvious who she's talking about. The man stands inside the doorway, dressed in impeccable black and very tall. He's blond and beautiful the way a knife is beautiful. Sharp enough to cut. There's something familiar about his features, but something's off. Something is wrong.

And then there's the dog.

A gorgeous black dog, huge and lean, waits at his side with a stillness that makes me think it's a service dog of some kind. Meticulously trained at least. People are starting to notice the man. People are starting to notice the dog. A shiver drags a fingernail down my spine.

"He's not a Constantine," I tell Daphne.

"He looks like one. Blonde. Tall." She grins. "Handsome."

"Believe me. I've been to Constantine parties since I was a baby. He's a stranger."

He's definitely not a Constantine, but he's interesting nonetheless. There's something arresting about him. A magnetic pull that everyone in the room feels. Leo has noticed him, too. He approaches the man and his dog with an expression of bemused surprise. A flicker of uncertainty. A flicker of worry. Then they speak to each other, and Leo's shoulders relax.

"This night is so weird," Daphne says. "But it's good, don't you think?"

"It's the best night." Someone calls to Daphne. It's one of the women Petra was talking to. All three women approach the table in a flutter of gowns and laughter.

When I resurface from the conversation, Leo's gone.

CHAPTER TWENTY-NINE
Haley

I WAIT TWENTY minutes before I go looking for Leo. It's harder to extract myself from the party than I thought it would be. When it's your own engagement party, it turns out, absolutely everyone wants to talk to you. It's warm in the ballroom. Crowded.

It can be slightly overwhelming, being so happy. And so loved.

Getting into the hallway is a sweet relief. The lights are lower here, the temperature cooler. I follow the decorations down the hall and around the corner.

Leo's in his office. Light angles out the door. More than firelight, less than the big recessed ceiling fixture that Leo rarely turns on. His door was closed earlier for the party. Eva and Daphne made several spaces for guests to go if they needed a break from the ballroom—five or six different rooms, each re-staged for the occasion. Leo swore he didn't care who saw his furniture. Eva ignored him. "I don't like to give out more information than I have to," she told me.

I move toward the half-open door. My heart runs ahead. It's not like Leo to leave me, so if he has, it must be for something important.

At his office door, I shift my position to see in.

That breathless, shimmering sensation sweeps down over me, stronger than I've ever felt it. Goose bumps rush from my fingertips to the tops of my shoulders. I'm simultaneously desperate to understand what's happening and secure in the knowledge that it's okay. That I'll know soon enough.

Leo leans against his desk, one foot crossed over the other. Arms folded below his chest. Head bowed. One small lamp burns in the corner of the room, but otherwise only firelight illuminates him. He was standing just this way when I came back to him the first time. I didn't know what he was doing until he made the sign of the cross. I didn't understand. Maybe I still don't. Maybe understanding is overrated. Maybe there's something to be said for faith.

No Ronan now, tapping his gun against his jeans and waiting to shoot. The man from the party sits in one of the chairs by the fire, facing Leo. He's turned on an angle to the door. I can't quite see his face, only glimpses of his profile. He strokes the dog's head absently. Affectionately. I've never seen another person so at ease in Leo's office.

I'm not looking in on an uncomfortable silence. I'm looking in on a sanctuary.

Leo makes the sign of the cross, lets out a breath, and opens his eyes.

"Catholic?" the man says. His voice is not like Leo's. It reminds me of ice under a dark sky.

"What gave it away?" Leo says.

The man laughs, and a chill works over my spine. "I visited a Catholic church with my brothers not long ago. It seemed to me that all the ceremony and ritual had become part of the stone."

"I can't imagine you sitting through Mass."

"We did not. We were looking for a woman's grave."

"Did you find it?"

"Yes."

A silence falls, broken by a quiet tapping at the window. Leo glances toward the bird. "Go away, busybody." Then he turns back to the fire, to the man. "How long now?"

"Fifteen minutes. We should wait another five to be sure."

A hand on my elbow very nearly startles me into screaming, but I don't. It's Gerard who's come looking. He escorts me away from Leo's office. "You're missed at the party."

"I'll go back," I say quickly. "But what—who—"

"A friend of Leo's. Powerful in another part of the country."

"Perhaps I should go in. Leo might need me."

"He'll be all right," Gerard says, and I believe him. Enough to go back to the party. People miss Leo, too, but we're reaching the point of the night when everyone is delighted and slightly tipsy, and no one questions my excuses. I keep an eye on his office window. The light coming through the pane. I can see the round, feathered shape of the bird in the corner. I lose myself in conversation, in congratulations, for as long as I can stand.

It's not very long.

This time, I slip away without drawing much attention to myself. I'm almost at Leo's office when I see him in the foyer—the man with his dog. Gerard hands him a black overcoat that reminds me of Leo's. His dog sits at his feet as he puts it on. Gerard speaks to him. He answers.

And then he looks at me over Gerard's head.

Even from this distance, I know what's different about him. It's his eyes.

He inclines his head to me, his smile like a cut diamond, and then he steps away into the shadows.

Leo's office seems even larger now. I go in and close the door behind me.

He sits in a chair by the fire, staring into the flames, and I don't know what it is, but something's wrong. Something is very wrong. Leo looks as shaken as he did when I put myself between him and Ronan's gun. Rattled to the core. And something more. I don't know what. And I have to know. I never should have hovered outside the door. Never should have allowed myself to go back to the party.

I go to him and sink down into a cloud of expensive fabric at his feet, between his knees. Pressing close. Goose bumps run riot up my arms, all the way to the back of my neck. Leo takes my face in his hands, using the pads of both his thumbs to memorize me there. He looks into my eyes and his own are so dark, the gold so bright, my heart splinters. "What happened? Who was that man? Leo, please, tell me."

He swallows. "I have a confession."

"Tell me. Please. I love you."

He explains that he was the man from the library—the one with the strange eyes. The one whose wife was like a little moon. That man, a man named Hades, tried to buy Jane Eyre for her, and that's how they know each other. Leo tells me how, in their one phone conversation, that man heard the pain in his voice and asked him about it. He's talking about the pain in his back, the chronic, neverending pain.

"No one else," Leo says. "No one else has noticed it before."

"So you invited him to our engagement party?"

"No. I found out—" He shakes his head. There's a color to his cheeks that's not usually there, and my heart beats in the hollow of my throat. I don't know what it means. "I found out he owns a diamond mine. His master jeweler is the best one in the country. I wanted a ring for you."

"I love what I have." It may not be worth a bunch of money, but it means commitment. It means love. And I would cherish it even if Leo Morelli didn't own a castle.

He gives me a gentle smile. "This is better."

A velvet box appears in my hands, and I open

the lid carefully. And gasp. A large diamond sparkles in the center, but it's not white. Or yellow. Or pink. Or any of the other colors I've seen my Constantine cousins wear. Instead it's a brilliant black. "How?" I manage to say, my voice shaking. "This is... too much. It's beautiful. I can't."

He seems to understand my babbling. "It's naturally that color. Magnolia cut. Five carats."

It's an intricate shape with curling edges, surrounded by a row of plush diamonds, as if it's cradled in a cloud. I tilt the box, moving the ring in and out of the light. In the shadows it looks almost opaque. Only in the light can you see the millions of perfect facets. It reminds me of Leo Morelli himself. "It's perfect, Leo. How did you know?"

"I wanted something unique for you." Leo doesn't quite meet my eyes as he pulls the velvet box from my shaking hands. He takes the ring from the satin and twists it gently. "There's an inscription. There was too much I wanted to say. Not enough space."

I take the ring from him, needing to read it. The gold band has incredibly fine engraving on top, something that looks both antique and timeless. On the inside it's mostly smooth except for a script that reads *I am no bird, no net ensnares me.* Tears heat my eyes. "It's a quote from Jane Eyre," I manage to say, feeling breathless, faint. "My favorite quote."

His dark eyes swim before me like black diamond. Through watery eyes I watch him slide the ring onto my finger. "I want you to be free. Not trapped here, Haley. Not because of a contract or anything else. I want you to choose this."

"I do." And I prove it by throwing my arms around his neck. As always, I'm careful. Even when I'm full of emotion, full of passion, I'm careful that I don't touch too low on his neck. That's where his scars begin. Where his pain begins, and I don't want any pain in this moment.

Leo pulls back and gives me an unreadable look.

"Something's wrong," I say, sensing his uncertainty. "Whatever it is, you can tell me. The ring. Is it too much? Oh, of course it's too much. I don't need something that expensive."

"It's not that. No, darling. It's—" He shakes his head. "Hades. He knows about pain. He's the only one I've ever met who knows anything about the way—" He takes a deep breath. "He has a different kind of painkiller. One that's only made for him, for pain like this."

Leo described it to me once. An unsolvable tangle of nerves and scars. Anything can hurt him. Touch. Stress. Anything. He seems so angry to other people because he is constantly in pain. He uses his rage to distract from the truth.

"How is it different?"

His eyes widen, the expression over so quickly I could have blinked and missed it. "There are no side effects. It doesn't render a person like him unconscious. A person like me."

I don't know whether to hope or despair. I'm caught between the two, and I don't know what the emotion in Leo's eyes means. "He came here to tell you about it?"

"He came here to deliver a ring for you. Along with what he called a wedding gift."

"The wedding isn't until next month."

"That's what I said. He just laughed." Seriousness comes over Leo's features, and it takes my breath away again. It's a miracle I can keep breathing at all when I look at him. "He brought some of those painkillers for me. Enough for a long time. And the nosy bastard sat here watching to make sure they didn't kill me."

"You thought it might *kill* you?"

"No. I didn't. But the pain was killing me. I haven't—" A breath with the hint of a shudder. "I was honest with him. When I bought that book for you. I told him I didn't think I could survive it. It's been so long." He brushes a kiss to my lips. "I couldn't let it take me away from you. So when he offered me a chance tonight, I took it."

"Leo—"

"Forgive me, darling, if the risk scares you. I had to try."

My heart is going to burst if he doesn't tell me now. It feels like I'm standing at the edge of a cliff, my toes curling over. "There's nothing to forgive. But, Leo—did it work?"

"It hurt so fucking much," he says, his voice breaking.

"Did it work?" I hate to press him. I just want this for him. More than anything. He's awake and clear-eyed, the way he needs to be to survive. "Does it hurt now?"

"No." He takes a breath verging on a gasp. "Nothing hurts at all." Leo covers his face with both hands, a sob tearing free under his palms, and lets himself fall back into his chair.

For the first time in years, he lets himself rest.

CHAPTER THIRTY

Leo

H ALEY CLIMBS INTO my lap, into my arms, and it forces out a hot wave of tears to hold her this way. Without also holding myself up and away from the furniture. She asked me for this once. I gave her twenty minutes of her head on my chest, curled against my side, and paid for it with a sleepless night in agony.

I would do it again for her.

But I don't have to.

Now she's the one holding herself up, hesitancy in every muscle. I lean harder into the chair. Pull her in closer. She puts her head on my shoulder, giving me her weight.

I had forgotten what it was like.

For so long, the only place I could touch the memory of living in a body not dogged by pain was in my dreams. Even then it never lasted. It was never complete. I could feel the cuts on my back in the distance. In the last few years it's been worse in increments, like slowly boiling alive.

So when Hades—who looks like a Constantine, how's that for irony—handed me the second black box, I didn't let myself imagine an outcome that didn't involve living in hell.

I remember now, because there is no more pain. No more pressure across the scars on my back, digging into the nerves. No more radiating gashes circling around to the front of my ribs and slicing between. No more nails in the back of my neck. It's just gone. Banished.

It won't be gone forever. These tiny, pill-shaped miracles don't last indefinitely. But if Hades is to be trusted—and I have no choice but to trust him—it will not start at the peak. I'll have time. I'll have a life.

I'll have Haley, her sweetness curled into me, letting me hold her the way I always should have been able to.

Fuck, I was so close. So close to sinking into inescapable darkness. Haley would have stopped it, for a while. I love her too much not to put up a fight. But it would've happened, except for that prick with the strange eyes blocking my path.

That pain was a cage. A physical cage, yes. One that held me away from the physical world. And an emotional one. I don't know what to do with it, all that feeling.

Eventually the floodgates close. The grief eases.

"Are you sad?" Haley brushes an errant tear from my cheek.

"No." I kiss her, and I feel nothing but the softness of her lips against mine. Nothing but the way she takes a quick little breath. Nothing but her. "I'm free."

We go back to the party, and Haley can't stop staring at me. Studying my face. I want to tell her it's the same as it always was, but it's not. I know from the way her eyes shine.

I want to fuck her without having to ignore impending torment. It hurts less when I'm inside her, when I'm touching her, of course it does. Of course it did. But this is different. Being in that much pain was like being numb, in a way. It didn't give me full access to any other sensation.

When the bedroom door is locked behind us, I unwrap her like an engagement gift and lay waste to her panties and bra. I open her like a blooming flower on the bed and bury my face between her legs. She tastes even sweeter for how little it hurts to do this. I can sling her legs over my shoulders and make her come like that. I can let her dig her heels into me while her orgasm shakes through her. I can do anything.

She's tired from the party, so tired, but she gives me all of her. Haley whimpers and cries when I punish her pussy for the crime of being so perfect and cries some more when I fuck her throat.

Her tears are drying when I take her to the pillows, spread her open wide, and make her take me all at once. I love the sight of her body when she works for it, all blonde hair and pulsing muscles. I love the struggle. I love to bite her, and hurt her, and make her pussy tighten in that sweet, filthy rhythm as she comes all over me.

Haley interrupts her own series of moans with my name. "Leo. Leo—"

I bite her again, and she makes a sound of pleasure-pain that I would like to hear every day until I'm dead. "Say it some more, darling."

"Leo," she says, and the excitement in her voice makes my chest ache. "Do you think I could be on top?"

I freeze, my cock buried in her to the hilt, and in the space of this one moment I've been shoved out of the bed. Out of my body. She's been on top before, but never the way she's asking for now. No one has.

Except for Caroline.

I push up and away from her. Need room to breathe. It's awful, it's fucking awful, because I want to keep fucking her. But this innocent question from the most innocent Constantine there ever was has nicked an invisible wire in my brain, or my soul. Somewhere hidden. Way down deep.

And it's now, it's right now, that I understand the final piece of my penance. I understand that there is something separate from the experience of physical pain. It's always been easier to let the torment of fucked-up nerves take up my attention, because something else did equal damage. It played an equal role in turning me into the beast I became.

"Leo." Haley's voice is so soft. She's been saying my name for a while now, I realize. "Come back. Leo."

I bend my head down to her collarbone and lick the bite mark I left. Concentrate on how warm she is around me. How tight, how soft. Let that feeling tamp down the urge to run. Not away from Haley. Never away from her. Away from the sickening memories.

"I've never done that before," I confess to her, and then amend my confession. "I haven't done that since Caroline. Not in—not in a bed."

"Oh," she says. "Oh, Leo."

I don't hear pity in her words, and that, I think, is what compels me to tell her the rest.

I have never told anyone the way it was with Caroline. The way she insisted on being with me. I was too young to see it for what it was. Not a real preference, except a preference for power. She wanted to be the one on top, literally and figuratively, so that's how it was. It might not have left so many scars if it hadn't been for that very last day.

The day I took the videos. I'd been suspicious of her by then, suspicious and increasingly sick to my stomach at how it felt to be with her, and I thought the camera itself would act as a kind of talisman against more of her psychotic behavior. Surely she would assume I had one and call it off. Or come to the meeting as Caroline Constantine, de facto queen of Bishop's Landing.

She did neither. She did worse. And I have paid for it with every kind of pain every day since then.

"My back was nothing but an open wound," I tell Haley, and she does not tense underneath me. She doesn't flinch. She just keeps running her hands over my shoulders, over and over. "The sheets felt like sharp rocks. Like fire. And the pressure of her body—"

"It's okay," she says. She means *keep going*.

"There was no one before her." Haley glides her fingers through my hair. "And I never thought this would be possible afterward. I didn't even fantasize about it."

I confess that the memory has not lost its nauseating quality. I confess that I don't know what will happen if we do this. I confess that I am afraid, I am so afraid, that Caroline has taken it from me permanently. That even with my pain conquered, I'll still be wounded. Broken.

"I was powerless," I tell her. There is no greater sin for a Morelli than to be powerless. Admitting it is probably the greatest risk I've ever taken.

Haley presses a kiss to my shoulder. "Not anymore."

I lift myself up so I can see her face. She's watching me with such love in her eyes. More than I'll ever deserve. She lets me look into that perfect blue until my breathing settles.

And then she arches underneath me, stretching her body, resetting us.

She takes one of my hands away from where I'm stroking her hair.

Haley puts it around her throat. She locks

both hands around my wrist and pulls my arm down toward her until I'm the one controlling the pressure. Until I'm rock hard inside her. Until she's squirming on my cock. Beginning to fight the grip on her throat a little. Beginning to need more air.

"Like this," she manages.

Fresh, animal desire explodes over me. The need to fuck her takes over every muscle, including my throbbing, unsteady heart. I feel huge above her. Solid. Strong against her softness.

I roll over onto my back, taking Haley with me.

I brace for pain before I can override the old habit, but none comes. Not physical pain. Not nerve pain. I land on soft sheets. On a firm mattress.

No pain, but my lungs get smaller, not drawing in enough air. My heart races. My vision sharpens. My body prepares to get me out of this situation. Get me away from the torture I know is coming. The shame.

Except it's Haley.

For all my body knows this is dangerous, this is wrong, it also knows she is right. She's the prettiest thing I've ever seen. More beautiful for the way she lets me choke her while she rides my cock. I was afraid her body in this position would force me into an old memory but I shouldn't have been. I should have trusted that I know her. I've felt her. I want her.

I need her. Like this. Now.

My heart tries to take flight again, but I focus on her. On the squeeze of her muscles around me. On her big blue eyes, staying on mine because she knows how much I love it. She knows how much I love to see her cry. I pinch one of her nipples until she does cry, then the other, her pussy clenching over and over.

The ghost of that powerlessness comes again.

But there's Haley, panting in my grip, her body given over to mine. Sacrificed to mine.

It whispers in my ear.

Haley moans, her hands rising to hold my wrist, but she can't stop me. She does not want to stop me. From causing her pain. And pleasure. She puts herself wholly in my hands.

That sick, terrified feeling shrinks down into a shell of itself. It's no match for her sweet cunt around my cock. It's no match for the silvery tears that streak down her cheeks. It's no match for me, as long as I have her. We're stronger together.

It is less and less and less and then, between one thrust and the next, between one whimpered moan and the next, I let it go.

It's gone.

I angle her closer in so she has to work for it. So she has to brace her fingertips against my chest and pray for control. I bring her all the way down so I can sink my teeth into her earlobe. "You're going to fuck me with that sweet cunt until you're dripping with my cum, darling. I won't touch your clit until I feel it on your thighs. You don't get to come before then."

"No," she moans. "Please. Touch me now."

"You can have my hand on your throat. Try harder than that. Don't make me wait."

I keep my hand on her windpipe, her pulse moving through my fingertips, as Haley struggles. Against my hand. Against her body. It's hard for her to find the rhythm, and once she does, I make it harder. I make her force herself down on me every time. I take a little air away every time she falters.

It feels so fucking good. Gravity is on her side, and for once, it's on my side, too. I can give myself over completely to the sensation of her cunt without worrying about holding myself away from anything.

The harder she works, the wetter she gets. Her slickness only increases the longer I hold her throat in my hand. She's fucking me hard—she's fucking magnificent—when she starts to cry harder.

"I'm going to come," she sobs. "Please let me."

"Fuck, darling. If you come now, you know what I'll have to do."

"Punish," she says. That's all she can get out.

"Yes."

Haley locks eyes with me. I have one hand on her throat, my fingertips in her hair, I have her so close to me. I have all I need.

She comes like I've coaxed it from her clit myself, her cunt clenching hard, and it is sheer, aching pleasure. Her body won't accept anything less from me than it's giving, and it winds up my orgasm and drags it out of me. Haley's thighs are sticky with me by the time I'm done filling her.

My darling falls forward with shaking hands that she runs over my face, my lips, my jaw. "Mine," I tell her. "You're fucking mine. Say it."

Her smile is a lopsided, adorable thing. "Yours," she breathes.

There's nothing to stop me. Not now. Not ever. I roll us over, spread her wide, and start again.

CHAPTER THIRTY-ONE

Daphne

M Y BROTHER'S GETTING married today. My favorite brother. And I know, I know. I've watched it happen. I've lived in his house while the wedding planning went on. He and Haley are perfect for one another. I thought she was maybe too sweet and too shy before, but what do I know?

Not that much. For instance, I didn't know that Leo still went to church. Not only that, but he basically owns one. And that's where he's getting married today. St. Thomas's.

"Does he just like people named Thomas?" I ask Haley as she stands in her dress, glowing in front of the full-length mirror in the bridal suite. It's busy in here, but she is quiet and pink-cheeked and gorgeous. Her sister is here, and my sisters are here. Even my parents came, though my father's half-drunk and my mother sits on the opposite end of the pew from him. "Leo's favorite

344

driver is named Thomas. And then there's this church."

Haley laughs. I'm doing up the laces on her wedding gown. It took both me and Eva to get it over her head without disturbing her makeup. "I honestly think it's just a coincidence," she says. "Though people do tend to go for what's familiar."

"Are you excited?"

Her cheeks get redder. "I've never been more excited for anything. But—" Haley peeks around behind her, at the room full of women who are here to help her. "I wish my mom was here."

"I'm sorry. How long ago did she pass away?"

"I was turning twelve, so I remember a lot about her. The color of her hair. The way she would hug me. But there aren't many photos of her. She was always the one taking photos. My father could never remember to do it, so there aren't many of them."

"I'm sure she's here... in spirit," I say. "She wouldn't miss this."

She gives me a watery smile. "Thank you."

My phone lights up on the table nearby.

I ignore it. I'm here for Haley, not to exchange text messages with my collector away from Leo's prying eyes. He would kill me if he knew we were still messaging. No, that's not true. He would kill my collector.

Fine—he wouldn't kill him. But he would scare him, and then what would I have?

No one would leave me white orchids any-more.

We fuss over Haley until it's time for her bridal portraits, and then we fuss over her some more while they're taken. I leave my phone downstairs in the bridal suite so I can stand up in Leo's wedding. On Haley's side, with her sister and my sisters. I don't think anyone ever expected this out of our families. It's nice. That's the word for it. Good, even.

It hurts a little to watch Haley's dad walk her down the aisle, absolutely beaming. It hurts a little more to watch her with Leo at the altar. Haley joined the church for this even though Leo told her she didn't have to. Jesus, she loves him so much. And he belongs to her.

I'm not some creep who expects her brother to belong to her, even if he is my favorite. Is mild jealousy an appropriate emotion for a wedding? Probably not. So I concentrate on being happy for them. I already *am* happy for Leo. Something changed with him after their engagement party. He's not *that* different. I still wouldn't want to meet him when he's angry. But it's like his mind is clear. That's the best way I can think to describe it. His eyes don't look so stormy all the time.

They say their vows in front of Father Simon, who could not be more different from the priest we had at our old church. My father liked that priest. He doesn't like Father Simon. But that's not up to him now. He's been pushed out of the business, almost pushed out of the family. His position as the head of the Morellis is mostly for show these days.

I'm concentrating so hard on being happy for them, on watching the joy in my brother's face, that I miss the part where Father Simon says he's allowed to kiss Haley. The cheers snap me out of it. Leo whispers something to Haley when he can bring himself to stop kissing her. She laughs, and I've never seen anyone laugh like that for my brother. Their love seems so secret, so self-contained, a private room even in front of all these people. Like I shouldn't be looking.

I clap around my bouquet as he takes her down the aisle. Leo keeps Haley close to his side. He never wants her out of reach. He only scowls at me about half the time I tease him about it, which is a new low for him.

The bridal party gathers in the narthex of the

church. It's basically every available sibling. Haley's brother stood up on Leo's side and did his best not to look wildly uncomfortable the whole time. Guests file out around us. The man from Leo's engagement party is here with a beautiful, petite woman with bronze curls tumbling down her back. He's very tall and has to bend his head slightly to hear what she says. His expression is utterly focused, like whatever she's saying is the most important thing in the world.

His hand goes to the small of her back as they pass by. "Your cheeks are pink, summer queen. I should bring you to weddings more often."

His voice makes the air seem colder, more dangerous, but she just laughs. "I won't go. Not if you're going to pass me notes like that."

"It was vows," he says, his tone mildly wounded.

"We're in a church," she whispers.

Then they're gone, and I'm not jealous at all.

There are photos in the church, in front of a window with gorgeous mid afternoon light. When everyone is laughing from the photos and the anticipation of the reception—to be held in Leo's ballroom, which is more beautiful than it's ever been, thanks to Eva—I run back downstairs to get my purse and my phone. Everybody else grabs their things and heads out.

I follow them.

Slowly.

Because I have a new message from my collector.

Come with me.

Oh, I want to. My heart picks up, racing and racing at even the thought of it. He's not dangerous, no matter what Leo says. But it's my brother's wedding day. I don't actually want to miss the reception. I love parties. Everything is beautiful, and you can smooth over all the complicated things with champagne and pretty clothes.

I can't. I'm not in the city!!

That's where my studio apartment is. And where I'll live again, once Leo is convinced that my security team can handle the collector. I'm moving back after the wedding whether Leo allows it or not. I'll go crazy if I have to live in my brother's house another day longer.

I know where you are, little painter.

Goose bumps pull up on the back of my neck at the name.

And that he claims to know where I am.

You're in the basement of St. Thomas's church

as we speak. Come to the sacristy.

I can hear his tone in his text.

It's not supposed to make me hot.

It does.

I bite my lip. Everyone is leaving the narthex and heading for the cars. I can only delay a minute.

I'm running up the stairs to the main floor of the church before I can change my mind.

I cut across the sanctuary to get to the small room he's talking about. Ornate dressers line the wall. They'll be full of robes and candles and whatever else the church needs for services. A large cherry wood table sits in the middle, its surface charred and dull from use. I imagine a thousand communion wafers counted here, a hundred gallons of sacramental wine poured into a goblet.

Sitting in the middle of the table is a single white orchid.

It could have fallen from a flower arrangement for mass, but I know better. It's from him. The collector. The petals are smooth between my thumb and forefinger.

It's a message. He wants me to know that he's watching.

He was here.

I shiver in my satin bridesmaid's dress. I should be afraid of him. And I am—but I'm also curious. No one's ever wanted my art this badly.

No one's ever wanted me like an obsession.

Thank you for reading Leo and Haley's breathtaking trilogy!

Want to know more about Daphne's stalker? Read DARK REIGN now for a brand new story from bestselling author Amelia Wilde from Dangerous Press...

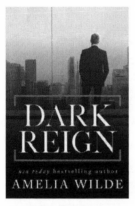

Wealthy. Reclusive. Dangerous. Emerson LeBlanc doesn't enter society much. He only ventures out in pursuit of new art for his collection. It starts with a haunting painting. Then he meets the artist. Innocent Daphne Morelli is more exquisite than anything he's ever seen. He becomes obsessed with her. It doesn't matter that she's a living, breathing person with her own hopes and dreams. She'll be the perfect addition to his collection.

Find Dark Reign at Amazon.com, Barnes & Noble, Apple Books, and more online retailers.

Look at what people are saying about DARK REIGN...

"Dark Reign is sinful, deliciously complex and naughty, with an anti-hero who's hauntingly addicting."

– Marni Mann, USA Today bestselling author

"An exquisite portrait of obsession that grabs you by the throat and doesn't let go."

– #1 NYT bestselling author Laurelin Paige

"Dark Reign is a one-sitting, unputdown-able read. It's obsessive, sinful and dark!"

– Charlotte Byrd, USA Today bestselling author

"Emerson Leblanc is an ocean I happily drowned in, and I can't wait to do it again."

– USA Today bestselling author Stella Gray

"Dark Reign is filled with everything I love in an Amelia Wilde book—pain, power, and pleasure—but it's also over-whelmingly beautiful … this is my new favorite dark romance."

– USA Today bestselling author
Kayti McGee

"Vivid, seductive, highly-addictive. This steamy thrill ride is a masterpiece. Amelia Wilde's words are hypnotic and I'm dying to devour more of them!"

– K Webster, USA Today bestselling author

Have you met Winston Constantine yet? Yes, the one Leo confronted in this book! Find out what happens when he meets Ash, the young woman who cleans his office...

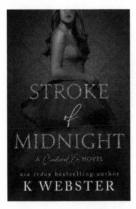

Money can buy anything. And anyone. As the head of the Constantine family, I'm used to people bowing to my will. Cruel, rigid, unyielding—I'm all those things. When I discover the one woman who doesn't wither under my gaze, but instead smiles right back at me, I'm intrigued.

Ash Elliott needs cash, and I make her trade in crudeness and degradation for it. I crave her tears, her moans. I pay for each one. And every time, she comes back for more. When she challenges me with an offer of her own, I have to decide if I'm willing to give her far more than cold hard cash.

But love can have deadly consequences when it comes from a Constantine. At the stroke of midnight, that choice may be lost for both of us.

Find Stroke of Midnight at Amazon.com, Barnes & Noble, Apple Books, and more online retailers.

Do you love reading about the villains? Then you'll want to read Ronan Byrne's story. He's the one who shot Leo Morelli under the orders of Caroline Constantine.

Outside a glittering party, I saw a man in the dark. I didn't know then that he was an assassin. A hit man. A mercenary. Ronan radiated danger and beauty. Mercy and mystery.

I wanted him, but I was already promised to another man. Ronan might be the one who murdered him. But two warring families want my blood. I don't know where to turn.

In a mad world of luxury and secrets, he's the only one I can trust.

Find Ruined at Amazon.com, Barnes & Noble, Apple Books, and more online retailers.

"M. O'Keefe brings her A-game in this sexy, complicated romance where you're left questioning if everything you thought was true while dying to get your hands on the next book!"

— New York Times bestselling author
K. Bromberg

"Powerful, sexy, and written like a dream, RUINED is the kind of book you wish you could read forever and ever. Ronan Byrne is my new romance addiction, and I'm already pining for more blue eyes and dirty deeds in the dark."

— USA Today Bestselling Author
Sierra Simone

The warring Morelli and Constantine families have enough bad blood to fill an ocean, and there are told by your favorite dangerous romance authors. See what books are available now and sign up to get notified about new releases here…
www.dangerouspress.com

ABOUT DANGEROUS PRESS

The warring Morelli and Constantine families have enough bad blood to fill an ocean, and their breathtaking stories will be told by your favorite dangerous romance authors.

If you love forbidden romance, you'll adore LESSONS IN SIN, a scorching hot standalone from Dangerous Press featuring Tinsley, the youngest Constantine.

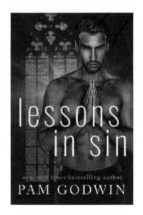

There's no absolution for the things I've done. But I found a way to control my impulses.

I became a priest.

As Father Magnus Falke, I suppress my cravings. As the headteacher of a Catholic boarding school, I'm never tempted by a student.

Until Tinsley Constantine.

"Taboo romance at its best! LESSONS IN

SIN is another dark masterpiece by Pam Godwin!"

If you want more Morellis, you can read DAN-GEROUS TEMPTATION…

He arrives all dressed in black. Diamond cufflinks. A watch on his tanned wrist that cost more than we would ever see in a lifetime of work. He carries a single red rose…

It turns out he is my new guardian.

"Dark, decadent and provocative, Dangerous Temptation is one of my absolute favorite reads in 2021. Tiernan and Bianca set my Kindle on fire! Giana has weaved an exquisite story, I can't wait for the next. READ THIS!!!"

Get intimate with the Morellis in the darkest story yet...

In a single moment, she becomes my obsession...

Elaine Constantine will be mine.

And her destruction is only my beginning.

I've known all my life that the Constantines deserved to be wiped from the face of the earth, only a smoking crater left where their mansion once stood. That's my plan until I see her, the woman in gold with the sinful curves and the blonde curls. My will to dominate her runs as deep as the hate I have for her last name.

SIGN UP FOR THE NEWSLETTER
www.dangerouspress.com

JOIN THE FACEBOOK GROUP HERE
www.dangerouspress.com/facebook

FOLLOW US ON INSTAGRAM
www.instagram.com/dangerouspress

About the Author

Amelia Wilde is a *USA TODAY* bestselling author of steamy contemporary romance and loves it a little *too* much. She lives in Michigan with her husband and daughters. She spends most of her time typing furiously on an iPad and appreciating the natural splendor of her home state from where she likes it best: inside.

Want to read more about the owner of the diamond mine? He's the man who gives up the priceless copy of Jane Eyre for Leo Morelli. And appears at the engagement party...

The king of the underworld...
Luther Hades rules the mountain with a cruel fist. He has no mercy for the young, innocent woman thrown before him. The contract is binding.

The sheltered daughter of his enemy...
Persephone wants freedom from her mother's home. Instead she trades one prison for another. There's only one way to save the man she loves—by sacrificing her body.

He's determined to own her.

She's destined to hate him.

Their battle will bring the mountain to its knees.

Find King of Shadows at Amazon.com, Barnes & Noble, Apple Books, and more online retailers.

For more books by Amelia Wilde, visit her online at https://awilderomance.com.

Copyright

Made in the USA
Monee, IL
09 June 2022

97732080R00213